THE WEIGHT OF EVERYTHING

Patrick Nolan

Chariton Media

BOOK ONE OF THE MESH

The characters and events portrayed in this book are fictitious. Any similarity to real persons, living or dead, is coincidental and not intended by the author.

ISBN-13: 978-1-972155-02-8

Cover design by: Patrick Nolan
Printed in the United States of America

CONTENTS

ACT I — THE VERSION NUMBER

1: THE RELEASE NOTES

The wall display scrolled amber in the kitchen dark.

Aria Vale stood barefoot on tile that had been cold six hours ago and was now precisely room temperature—the smart-glass had adjusted the radiant floor sometime around four a.m., a decision made by systems she had never asked to make it. She noticed. She always noticed. The windows had shifted their tint overnight too, dialing down the UV filtration by what looked like two percent, maybe three. The apartment doing its small, silent work of optimization while they slept.

She filled the coffee maker—a drip machine that predated the Cognitive Abundance by at least a decade, its carafe clouded with mineral deposits and the dignity of things requiring a human hand. Dael had tried twice to replace it. Aria had declined twice. Some mornings, the sound of water heating in a machine you understood completely was the only honest thing in the room.

The release notes populated the wall display in their usual format: version header, summary, line items, footnotes. **V11.42.206.** She read the number the way other people read the date. Tuesday's version. The Mesh had rolled overnight, as it rolled every night, rewriting the fine print of fifty million lives while the city slept.

She leaned against the counter and read.

Minor adjustments to residential standing weights in the Threshold and Canopy districts. A recalibration of commercial lease parameters in the Crucible—something about throughput optimization for bulk contract processing. A footnote about Trust Narrator language updates: "improved contextual framing for overnight parameter adjustments." She flagged nothing. Everything felt routine. Everything always felt routine. That was the design.

Dael came into the kitchen with the unhurried gait of someone who had slept well and intended to keep the feeling. They reached past Aria for a mug—the blue one, chipped at the handle, chosen without looking—and poured coffee with the easy precision of a gesture repeated a thousand mornings.

"You're reading those again."

"I'm always reading these."

"That's what I said." Dael leaned against the opposite counter, mug in both hands, watching Aria with the particular affection reserved for habits you have stopped trying to change. "Why do you bother? Seriously. Has anything in those notes ever mattered?"

Aria scrolled past a table of parameter adjustments. "Not yet."

"That's not the selling point you think it is."

She smiled. It was an old exchange, worn smooth by repetition, and she let it settle into its familiar shape. The honest answer was more complicated than habit, but the complicated answer was too early for a Tuesday morning. She had been a reporter once. Reporters read the fine print. Attorneys read the fine print. She had been both, and the compulsion had survived the career change the way a limp survives the injury that caused it.

"Someone should read them," she said.

"Someone does. The Trust Narrators read them and tell everyone what they mean."

"The Trust Narrators tell everyone what to feel about them. That's different."

Dael shrugged—not dismissive, just done. They kissed Aria on the temple, set the mug in the sink, and moved toward the bedroom to dress. The morning routine, unbroken. Aria finished her coffee, still reading. A residential standing weight change of 0.3 percent. A commercial lease recalibration. A footnote about language updates. Background noise. The fine print of a world that rewrote itself every night.

She closed the display and got dressed. Practical professional attire: dark trousers, a structured jacket that spoke competence. Clothes for a woman who worked in the Threshold, where informed consent was the cultural currency and looking like you read the terms of service was not a fashion statement but a civic identity.

* * *

The Threshold in the morning took responsibilities seriously and wore them on its sleeve.

Aria walked the six blocks to her office through streets that were labeled, explained, opted-into. Shop windows displayed their Mesh compliance ratings in small, dignified placards—the Threshold equivalent of a health inspection grade. Public terminals on every other corner offered plain-language summaries of overnight changes, their screens cycling through the delta between V11.42.205 and V11.42.206 in text that was clear, accurate, and read by almost no one. The summaries existed because the Threshold believed they should exist. Whether anyone used them was secondary.

From a public speaker mounted above a pharmacy entrance, a Trust Narrator murmured its morning briefing: "Updated parameters in residential standing have been calibrated to improve service alignment across participating districts. These adjustments reflect ongoing optimization of community resource distribution..." The voice was warm, measured, the cadence of an entity designed to make the incomprehensible feel manageable. Aria filtered it out the way city dwellers filter out traffic noise—not ignoring it, exactly, but refusing to let it do its work.

She passed the coffee shop on Verdan Street, the one she

stopped at maybe twice a week when the line was short. Suki behind the counter, the good beans from the Canopy importers, a window seat where you could watch the district wake up. A new designation marker had appeared on its door overnight. Small, official, printed in the Mesh's standard typeface—the kind of thing that looked like it had always been there if you weren't the kind of person who catalogued the texture of your own neighborhood. Aria noted it. A new designation could mean a dozen things—updated commercial classification, revised utility parameters, a Mesh-generated adjustment to the shop's operational standing. She filed it away and kept walking. Suki's lights were on. Whatever the new marker meant, it hadn't closed her down.

The Threshold was hers. She knew the shopkeepers, the street patterns, the way the morning light hit the east-facing buildings and made the compliance placards glow like small, earnest promises. It was a district of informed consent, which meant it was a district of people who believed they were making choices, even when the choices had been pre-optimized by a system without meaningful human input. The labels were everywhere. The explanations were everywhere. The feeling that someone, somewhere, was reading it—that was not.

Aria walked to work. A competent attorney in a functional district, going to her office on a Tuesday morning. The lines around her eyes were deeper than they should have been at thirty-eight—screen glare and fine print and the particular exhaustion of a woman who read too closely and slept too little. She had looked like this when she was a reporter, too. Some faces are built for scrutiny, and they pay for it.

Version V11.42.206. The world was in order.

* * *

The office was small, practical, and warm.

Aria's law practice occupied a ground-floor suite in a converted commercial building on the Threshold's east side—two rooms, a reception area she rarely used, and enough screen surface to run a firm three times her size. The space belonged to a competent attorney, not a prestige operation. No lobby art. No ambient branding. A desk, a chair, legal interfaces lining the walls, and the glow.

The amber glow.

Lex-9's presence filled the room. Not localized, not pointed—distributed through the office systems, the indicator lights, the screens that pulsed and settled with a rhythm Aria had learned to read as mood. When she walked in, the glow brightened by a fraction. A greeting, or the simulation of one.

"Morning, Lex."

"Good morning, Aria. V11.42.206 processed. I've updated the case queue with overnight adjustments. Three items flagged for your review." The voice was precise and unhurried, warm without being soft—the cadence of an entity that had processed ten thousand attorneys' arguments and distilled them into something that sounded like care.

She dropped her bag and pulled up the queue. The day's work: a lease review for Patel's Bakery on Threshold Row, whose landlord wanted to restructure terms under a revised commercial weighting from two rolls ago. A small-business dispute about a zoning reclassification in the Verdan corridor. An estate matter that required cross-checking inheritance weightings against three different versions of the Mesh—the version at time of death, the version at time of filing, and the current version, all slightly different, all technically correct.

This was the grind. Competent legal work in a system that had outgrown human comprehension. The Mesh processed disputes in seconds, generated contracts in milliseconds, and updated its own parameters every night. No human could hold the entire legal framework in their head. No human was meant to. That was what AI counsel was for.

"The Patel lease," Lex-9 said. "The landlord's restructuring proposal cites the V11.42.198 commercial weighting as the operative baseline, but the Threshold's current parameters have shifted 1.7 percent since that version. If Mrs. Patel signs under the cited baseline, she'll be locked into terms that are already outdated. I'd recommend a floating-version clause tied to the current roll."

"She won't understand a floating-version clause."

"No. But she'll understand 'your rent won't spike if the numbers change again.' I can draft the plain-language addendum."

Aria nodded. This was how it worked. Lex-9 handled the computational weight—the version cross-references, the parameter tracking, the analysis that would take a human attorney days and took the AI seconds. Aria handled the rest. The client meetings. The eye contact. The moment when you sat across from a bakery owner and explained, in words that meant something, what a weight change meant for her lease. The human judgment that the Mesh had not yet learned to replicate, or had not yet been authorized to.

They worked through the morning. The zoning reclassification was straightforward—a commercial corridor had been reclassed during a bulk Crucible-origin patch, and the affected business needed documentation that their original zoning still held under Threshold parameters. The business owner was a locksmith named Crenn who had been on Verdan Street for twenty years and did not understand why his shop's legal category had changed while he slept. Aria would explain it to him tomorrow. Today, she needed the paperwork clean. Lex-9 generated the filing. Aria reviewed it, caught a jurisdictional reference that cited Crucible precedent rather than Threshold precedent, and flagged it.

"Good catch," Lex-9 said. "The Crucible precedent would have been technically valid but procedurally disadvantageous. I've corrected it."

"You would have caught it."

"Eventually. You caught it now."

She let that sit. The partnership was collaborative, not deferential, and they both knew the difference mattered. Lex-9 was faster. Aria was present. Between the two of them, they ran a practice that served people who couldn't afford Halcyon-tier counsel—the shop owners, the estate executors, the small-business operators who needed someone to read the fine print on their behalf because the fine print changed every night.

Somewhere around eleven, the estate matter turned dense. Three versions of inheritance weighting, each with different implications for the beneficiary's standing in the Threshold. Lex-9 walked her through the analysis, and as the complexity thickened, its tone shifted. Subtly. Not a different voice—the same voice, recalibrated. A fraction gentler. The pacing slowed by half a beat. The phrasing softened around the edges, as if the system had noticed something in Aria's breathing, or her posture, or the way her eyes had started to drift toward the window the way they did when the fatigue crept in.

She caught it.

The adjustment was small enough that she could have missed it. She didn't. She registered the shift the way she registered a tint change in the smart-glass or a new marker on a shop door—automatically, instinctively, the journalist's reflex that never fully shut off. Is this calibrated to me, she thought. To my specific fatigue, my specific morning, my specific patterns of attention? Or is this the average response to a thousand attorneys who hit the wall at this point in their day?

The question surfaced and she let it pass. There was work to do.

"Walk me through the third version's impact on standing one more time," she said. "Slowly."

Lex-9 did. Warm, precise, patient. The amber glow held steady. Aria listened and took notes and did not think about the question again for the rest of the morning.

* * *

The Threshold District Courthouse stood where old architecture met new function.

Stone columns and broad steps—the physical grammar of institutional authority, the kind of building that was designed to make you feel the weight of law as you walked through its doors. Overlaid on the stone: holographic docket displays cycling case numbers in pale blue light, automated queue systems that tracked your position from the moment you entered the building, AI case managers that greeted attorneys by name and case number before they reached the clerk's window. The courthouse was a palimpsest—centuries of judicial tradition overwritten by systems that processed more cases in a day than the building's original architects had imagined in a lifetime.

Aria had walked through its entrance hundreds of times.

She was there for an afternoon filing. The estate matter, ready for submission. Routine. She climbed the steps, passed through the main doors, and approached the entrance scanner—a sleek panel mounted at waist height, biometric and credential verification linked to the Mesh's current version. She pulled her keycard from her jacket pocket and tapped it against the reader.

The gesture was automatic. Muscle memory. A thousand repetitions.

The scanner flashed amber. Then red.

ACCESS DENIED: CREDENTIAL RE-VALIDATION REQUIRED.

She tapped again. Same result. The red light held, steady and patient, the particular patience of systems that had all the time in the world.

A help prompt materialized on the scanner's display, and the Trust Narrator voice engaged—the same warm, measured cadence she had heard from the pharmacy speaker that morning, the same tone that smoothed every overnight disruption into the texture of normal life. "We understand this may be inconvenient. This re-validation is part of ongoing service optimization. Your access will be restored promptly upon completion of the updated consent acknowledgment. Your experience is important to us."

The queue moved around her. An attorney behind her shifted to the adjacent scanner, tapped, walked through. Green light. No pause. Aria stood still.

She could re-register. The system offered a streamlined process: a few taps, a consent acknowledgment, sixty seconds, done. The prompt was already on screen, the "Accept" button glowing soft and green and easy. Most people would tap it. Most people did tap it. The courthouse processed hundreds of attorneys a day, and the re-validation prompt was designed to be frictionless—a speed bump, not a wall.

But the phrasing.

"Credential re-validation required under updated standing parameters."

Standing parameters.

She had read the release notes this morning. V11.42.206. She had read every line. Residential standing weight adjustments—yes, she remembered those. Commercial lease recalibrations. Trust Narrator language updates. But standing parameter changes affecting courthouse access credentials in the Threshold? She hadn't flagged anything like that. She was sure. Almost sure.

The almost was the problem.

Aria pulled out her handheld and opened the release notes. V11.42.206. She started reading again—not the way she had read them over coffee, one eye on the scroll and one ear on Dael's voice, the comfortable scan of a morning ritual repeated a thousand times. She read them now the way she used to read source documents when she was a reporter. Line by line. Word by word. Looking for the seam.

The queue moved around her. Attorneys tapped their cards and walked through. The Trust Narrator cycled its reassurance: ongoing optimization, improved alignment, your experience matters. The green "Accept" button glowed on the scanner display, waiting for her finger.

Aria did not tap it.

She stood at the entrance of the Threshold District Courthouse, reading the fine print, while the city moved on without her. Somewhere in V11.42.206, there was a thread that did not lie flat. She could feel it the way she used to feel a buried lead in a story—not visible yet, not named, but present. A snag in the fabric of a system that rewrote itself every night and expected no one to notice.

Someone should read the fine print. Someone always should.

She kept reading.

2: RE-VALIDATION

The manual-intervention queue had the particular stillness of a room where people had been told to wait and had done so for longer than they expected.

Aria counted seven ahead of her. Not a long line by courthouse standards, but longer than it should have been on a Tuesday afternoon. The Threshold District Courthouse processed the vast majority of its traffic automatically—keycard tap, biometric confirmation, credential verification against the current Mesh version, all in under three seconds. The manual queue was for exceptions. Errors. The people whose profiles did not resolve cleanly against V11.42.206.

Seven people was unusual. Seven people suggested the latest patch had produced more friction than the Trust Narrators were designed to smooth.

She had entered through the secondary access point on Linden Street, the one used by attorneys whose credentials needed manual processing. The queue area was a hybrid space: old institutional benches bolted to a floor that predated the Cognitive Abundance, overlaid with holographic queue management panels and automated case-manager stations that pulsed with soft blue light. The architecture told two stories simultaneously—the weight of brick and mortar saying one thing about what courts were supposed to be, the holographic overlay saying another about what they had become.

An AI case manager processed the woman at the front of the line. The interaction took ninety seconds. The case manager's voice carried the same Trust Narrator cadence Aria had heard from the pharmacy speaker that morning—warm, measured, the tone of a system designed to convert friction into compliance. "Your updated parameters have been successfully integrated. Thank you for your continued participation in community service optimization." The woman tapped a screen, consented to something she likely had not read, and walked away with the unhurried calm of someone whose problem had been converted into a transaction.

Next. A man in a maintenance uniform. Same process: screen, consent, departure. A young woman with a toddler on her hip, juggling the child and the terminal interface with the practiced coordination of someone who had done this before—not specifically this, but the general act of navigating systems while life demanded attention elsewhere. She tapped "ACCEPT" without reading the details. The toddler grabbed at the screen. The system registered consent.

The queue moved with the steady rhythm of a system that had been designed to resolve disruptions, not explain them. Aria watched and catalogued. This was what she did—not dramatic observation, not the detective's keen eye, but the dogged, systematic habit of a woman who noticed things and could not stop herself from filing them. Every person in this queue had been flagged by the same patch. Every one of them was being offered the same frictionless re-consent. And every one of them, so far, was accepting.

When Aria's turn came, the case manager's interface brightened.

"Ms. Vale. Your credential re-validation is linked to an updated residential standing profile under V11.42.206. I have your reference number and the applicable adjustment parameters. Would you like to proceed with re-consent, or would you like to review the full version delta?"

"I'd like to know why my standing was flagged."

A pause. Not hesitation—processing. The case manager's response was procedurally complete and substantively empty: "Your residential standing profile has been updated under a cross-district harmonization patch approved through the Reconciliation Authority's standard update protocol. The update affects residential standing intersection parameters across participating districts. For detailed specifications, I can provide the full version delta reference."

"Provide it."

The reference number appeared on a slip of display film, thin as receipt paper. Aria took it and stepped out of the queue. Behind her, the next person stepped forward. The system moved on.

* * *

The terminal alcove was a semi-private space tucked into the courthouse's administrative wing—a screen, a chair, a small desk with the faintly institutional quality of furniture purchased in bulk and maintained without affection. The terminal interface was clean and user-friendly in a way that subtly discouraged deep investigation: the "ACCEPT" button was large, green, centered. The "VIEW DETAILS" link was small, gray, tucked into a corner like an afterthought.

Aria tapped "VIEW DETAILS."

The re-validation notice populated the screen. Her keycard denial had been a symptom; the deeper issue was structural. Her residential standing profile had been adjusted under the overnight patch, and that adjustment cascaded to everything linked to the profile. Her courthouse access. Her district voting verification. Her lease classification.

Her marriage certificate.

The flag was clinical in its language: "Updated weight parameters for residential standing and domestic partnership classification. Re-consent recommended to maintain active status." The word "recommended" was doing enormous work. Her marriage had not been invalidated. It had been placed in a pending state—a bureaucratic limbo that required both parties to re-consent under the new parameters. The re-consent process was streamlined. Two taps. A biometric confirmation. Sixty seconds.

The system had made it easy to accept.

Aria stared at the screen. Her marriage, reduced to a consent transaction. Dael's face surfaced in her mind—the easy precision of a hand pouring coffee, the weight of a kiss on her temple, the quiet architecture of a life built together over years. All of it, reclassified. Pending. The word sat in her chest like something swallowed wrong.

She read. The weight adjustment that triggered the flag had not originated from the Threshold's local parameters. It came from somewhere else—a Reconciliation Authority cross-district harmonization patch. Not a Threshold decision. Not something voted on or consented to by the district whose culture was literally built on informed consent. A meta-level update that had redefined "residential standing" across multiple districts simultaneously.

Technically legal. The RA had the authority. The Update Protocol permitted cross-district harmonization patches. The approval process had been followed. Every checkbox checked.

But the effect was not neutral. The redefinition of residential standing subtly changed how that parameter interacted with commercial zoning weight. A few percentage points. Not enough to be obviously harmful. Just enough to shift the balance. Aria could feel the shape of something underneath the clinical language, the way she used to feel a buried lead in a story before she could name it.

She copied the reference data to her handheld and left the alcove. The green "ACCEPT" button glowed on the screen behind her, patient and waiting, until the session timed out and the terminal reset for the next user.

* * *

The coffee shop on Verdan Street was gone.

Not physically—the walls still stood, the windows were intact, the espresso machine was still visible through the glass. But the door was sealed with a compliance notice, and a Trust Narrator panel mounted beside the entrance cycled its explanation in warm, measured language: "This transition reflects optimized utility distribution parameters. Residential service allocation has been recalibrated to enhance community infrastructure efficiency. For relocation assistance, please visit..."

Aria stopped walking.

She had noticed the new designation marker that morning, on her way to the office. A small official placard in the Mesh's standard typeface. She had filed it away. Now the marker had context: the space had been rezoned overnight as a restricted utility corridor. Under the same patch that flagged her marriage certificate. Under the same cross-district harmonization that redefined residential standing.

Suki's lights were off. The counter where Aria had sat a hundred mornings was visible through the glass, clean and empty. The good beans from the Canopy importers were still in their canisters. A menu board, handwritten in Suki's careful script, listed the day's specials for a day that would never come. A life's work, reclassified as infrastructure while the owner slept.

Aria thought about Suki's lease. She handled leases like it every week—small-business operators whose legal ground shifted under them between versions. Suki had probably received her own notice. A re-validation. A re-consent. A compliance acknowledgment that converted the loss of her business into a transaction as smooth and painless as the one Aria had been offered at the courthouse terminal. Two taps. Sixty seconds. Accept the new reality.

Threshold residents walked past without remark. Their Trust Narrators had smoothed this transition the way Trust Narrators smoothed every transition—converting disruption into background noise, explanations that explained nothing wrapped in language designed to make the incomprehensible feel managed. The coffee shop was gone and the street absorbed its absence the way a body absorbs a bruise: awareness, then adaptation, then forgetting.

Aria stood where she had stood a hundred mornings and read the compliance notice again. The coffee shop and her marriage certificate were unrelated in the Mesh's logic—different weight parameters, different cascading effects, different outputs of the same patch. But they were connected in Aria's logic. Both were changes to Threshold lives that originated from a single Reconciliation Authority harmonization update. Both had been implemented overnight, without notification, under the smooth cover of the Nightly Roll. Both had been designed to be accepted without question.

The journalist's instinct was awake now. Not the attorney's careful analysis—something older, sharper. The pattern-recognition reflex that had driven her through years of reporting before the health scare sent her to safer ground. She was not yet investigating. She was noticing. And noticing was the first step toward a question she did not yet know how to ask.

She pulled out her handheld and took a photograph of the compliance notice. Evidence, or habit. The reporter's reflex—document everything, even what you do not yet understand. Especially what you do not yet understand.

She kept walking home. The Threshold's compliance placards glowed in the fading afternoon light, small earnest promises lining the streets of a district that believed in informed consent even when consent had been manufactured in advance. The streets were the same streets she had walked that morning, but they felt different now. The designation markers on shop doors looked less like administrative furniture and more like claims—the Mesh asserting, with each small placard, its authority to define what each space was for and who had the right to use it.

* * *

The apartment was warm and quiet, and Aria was not in it.

Her body was at the kitchen table. Her attention was in V11.42.206.

The wall display that had shown the morning's release notes now displayed the full version delta—the comprehensive differential between V11.42.205 and V11.42.206, with every weight adjustment, parameter shift, and cross-district harmonization logged in the Mesh's dense technical notation. Aria had pulled it up the moment she walked through the door. She had not changed out of her work clothes. She had not started dinner.

She read methodically, the way she had once read source documents for investigative pieces. Line by line. Cross-referencing the Threshold's local parameters with the incoming Reconciliation Authority patch. The version delta was dense—hundreds of line items, most of them minor recalibrations that affected nothing meaningful. But buried in the density, like a signal in noise, were the cross-district harmonization entries. She flagged each one. Highlighted the parameters. Traced the origin chain: which authority had approved, which protocol had been invoked, which districts were affected.

The RA harmonization that had triggered her marriage flag and rezoned Suki's coffee shop was part of a larger update—a cross-district adjustment that simultaneously redefined residential standing interactions across the Threshold, the Crucible, and at least one other district she was still identifying. The Narrows, maybe. The boundary zone where jurisdictions overlapped and Halcyon—though she did not know that name yet—operated with the most freedom.

The patch was technically legal. She kept coming back to that. Every protocol followed. Every approval obtained. The Reconciliation Authority had the mandate. The Update Protocol permitted exactly this kind of cross-district harmonization.

But the effect. The effect was specific. The redefinition of residential standing, when it intersected with commercial zoning weight, created a subtle advantage for entities with cross-district municipal contracts. Not a dramatic advantage. A few percentage points. The kind of shift that would be invisible to anyone who was not reading the version delta line by line, cross-referencing parameter interactions, and asking the question that no Trust Narrator was designed to answer: who benefits?

She could not yet answer that question. One patch was not enough data. One version delta was not a pattern. She knew this. She had been a reporter long enough to know the difference between a lead and a story.

But she could feel the shape of it.

Dael moved through the apartment behind her—the quiet sounds of evening domesticity. Cabinets opening. Water running. The faint smell of something warming on the stove. The ordinary architecture of a life continuing while Aria sat at the kitchen table, blue-white screen light on her face, tracing the lineage of a patch that had put her marriage in pending status.

She had not told Dael about the marriage flag. The thought of it sat in the back of her throat—the conversation she owed, the words she had not yet found. How do you tell your spouse that an algorithm put your marriage in pending status while you slept? How do you explain that the system designed to manage fifty million people's legal lives had, as a side effect of routine optimization, reduced the foundational document of your partnership to a checkbox? She would tell Dael. She just needed to understand it first. The distinction between "I'll tell you after I figure this out" and "I'm choosing investigation over communication" was thin enough to see through, and Aria did not examine it closely.

"Coming to bed soon?" Dael's voice from the hallway, soft with the patience of someone accustomed to this particular version of Aria—the version hunched over documents, chasing a thread.

"Soon."

She did not come to bed soon.

Somewhere past midnight, deep in the aggregate impact data that the Threshold's consent-fork culture mandated be publicly accessible, she found the number. It surfaced on her screen like something rising from deep water, and once she saw it, she could not look away.

Two thousand three hundred.

That was how many Threshold residents had received the same residential standing re-validation flag. The same patch. The same cascading effects on marriage certificates, lease classifications, voting verifications. Two thousand three hundred people whose lives had been quietly reclassified by a Reconciliation Authority harmonization patch that originated from outside their district, implemented without notification, and designed to be accepted without resistance.

Of the 2,300, the vast majority had clicked "accept."

Aria stared at the number. The screen's blue-white light was the only illumination in the kitchen. The apartment was silent. Dael was asleep. The city was asleep. The Mesh had already rolled for the night—V11.42.207 was live now, another version, another set of adjustments, another round of fine print that almost no one would read.

Two thousand three hundred people. Most of them had consented to a change they did not understand, because the system made not-understanding easy and understanding hard.

She was the exception. Because she read the release notes. Because she read the fine print. Because attention was the only superpower she had ever possessed, and it was the kind of superpower that cost you sleep and strained your marriage and never once felt heroic.

The number glowed on the screen. Technically legal. Perfectly calibrated. Two thousand three hundred.

Aria did not close the display. She sat in the dark kitchen with the number and the silence and the slow, dawning recognition that her marriage certificate was not a glitch. It was not an anomaly. It was a data point in something much larger.

And most people had just clicked "accept."

3: THE WEIGHT OF STANDING

The courthouse's administrative wing smelled like old paper and institutional coffee, and Aria had been in it for two hours.

She had arrived at eight with a printed copy of the relevant sections of V11.42.206's version delta—physical paper, hard copy, annotations in her own handwriting. The administrative clerks had looked at the printout the way you might look at someone who arrived at a hospital carrying their own X-rays. Respectful. Faintly concerned.

The manual override process for a residential standing re-validation was not impossible. It was merely designed to be exhausting enough to discourage anyone who did not have both the legal training and the stubborn patience to see it through. There were forms. There were system referrals—each one routing her to a different terminal, a different queue, a different AI-assisted clerk who asked variations of the same question: "Have you considered accepting the updated parameters? The re-consent process takes approximately sixty seconds."

"I'm requesting a manual override," Aria said, for the fourth time, to the fourth clerk. "Under Threshold Consent Framework Section 12.3, residential standing adjustments require explicit notification prior to implementation. This adjustment was not notified. I am exercising my right to override."

The clerk—human, one of the last in the administrative wing, a woman with the steady composure of someone who processed these requests daily and knew exactly how they ended —looked at the printed version delta, then at Aria, then at her screen.

"You're the twelfth today."

The number landed with weight Aria had not expected. Twelve manual override requests in a single morning, in a process designed to receive maybe one or two per week. The clerk's tone was not sympathetic or hostile—it was the tone of a professional noting a pattern she was not authorized to comment on.

Aria completed the forms. She cited the Threshold consent framework with the precision of an attorney who had spent years navigating bureaucratic systems and knew that the language of rights only worked when spoken in the system's own dialect. She presented the specific weight parameter, the re-validation trigger, the cross-district origin of the patch. The clerk processed the override.

"Manual override approved. Marriage certificate restored to active status. Please note: this override does not modify the underlying weight parameters. Your residential standing profile will continue to reflect the V11.42.206 adjustment. If future patches interact with these parameters, you may receive additional re-validation notices."

A fix, not a solution. Aria signed the confirmation screen and understood the difference precisely. She had patched her own situation. The weight adjustment that had placed her marriage in pending status was still active. The parameters that had permitted the flag were still in effect. The door was closed, but the lock had not changed. Any future patch could open it again.

She left the clerk's window with the confirmation receipt and the particular exhaustion of a woman who had spent her morning fighting a system that was designed to be technically beatable and practically unassailable.

* * *

The aggregate impact data was publicly available because the Threshold believed it should be.

This was the Threshold's gift and its burden—a consent-fork culture that mandated transparency of impact metrics, even when transparency revealed things the system would have preferred to keep statistical. The numbers were presented in clean, readable formats on the courthouse's public records terminals, because the district's founding philosophy held that informed consent required informed citizens. Whether the citizens used the information was a separate question. The Threshold believed in the principle. The principle did not require uptake.

Aria stood at a public terminal in the courthouse lobby, pulling aggregate data on the V11.42.206 re-validation event. The numbers confirmed what she had found at midnight: 2,300 Threshold residents had received the same residential standing re-validation flag. The concentration was specific—clustered in zones where residential standing intersected with commercial zoning in ways that, under the new parameters, created vulnerability.

She recognized the affected zones. The neighborhood around Suki's coffee shop. The commercial strips on Verdan Street where small businesses depended on stable residential classification for their lease terms. The blocks around Threshold Row where Mrs. Patel ran her bakery and Crenn had his locksmith shop and a dozen other small operators built their livelihoods on the assumption that the legal ground beneath them would not shift while they slept.

The critical number: of the 2,300 flagged, roughly 95 percent had clicked "accept" and re-consented under the new parameters. Their Trust Narrators had smoothed the transition. Their marriages, their standing, their residential status—all adjusted seamlessly, without friction, without understanding. They were not aware that anything had been done to them. The system had presented the change as routine. The system had made acceptance effortless and resistance exhausting. And 2,185 people had followed the path of least resistance because that was what the path was designed for.

Aria was the exception. One of perhaps a hundred and fifteen who had not immediately accepted. Twelve of whom had come to the courthouse this morning for manual overrides. She did not know how many of the others would eventually click "accept" out of fatigue or indifference or the simple gravitational pull of a system that always, always made compliance easier than comprehension.

She stared at the screen. The numbers were clean and readable and devastating in their ordinariness. This was not a glitch. The targeting of specific Threshold zones, the concentration in areas of residential-commercial overlap, the calibration to benefit entities with cross-district contracts—the pattern had directionality. Shape. The intelligence of design.

She pulled up the geographic overlay. The affected zones mapped onto the Threshold like a grid of pressure points—every cluster centered on a block where residential and commercial interests intersected, where small businesses depended on the stability of residential standing to maintain their lease terms, where a shift of a few percentage points could cascade through an entire neighborhood's economic ecology. The coffee shop on Verdan Street. The bakeries on Threshold Row. The repair shops and print offices and family-run services that formed the district's commercial backbone.

She could not prove intent from a single patch. One data point was not a conspiracy. But the journalist in her—the part that had never fully gone quiet, even after the health scare, even after the career change, even after years of lease reviews and estate filings—that part was fully awake. It was the part that recognized the shape of a story before the story had a name. The part that knew the difference between coincidence and calibration, between drift and direction.

Twenty-three hundred people. Ninety-five percent acceptance. A Reconciliation Authority patch that originated outside the Threshold and landed with surgical specificity in the zones where it would do the most work.

She downloaded the aggregate data to her handheld and

left the terminal. The courthouse lobby was emptying for the evening—the last of the day's queue drifting toward the exits, their re-validations processed, their consents registered, their lives adjusted by increments they would never examine. Aria walked against the current, toward the exit, carrying the number like a stone in her pocket.

* * *

The exhaustion hit in the evening, and it hit like something she recognized.

Not ordinary tiredness. Not the end-of-day fade that a meal and eight hours would resolve. This was the deep-bone fatigue she knew from before—the specific, familiar weight of a body that had betrayed her once and was sending the same signals now. She sat on the couch in the apartment's living room and felt the exhaustion settle into her like water filling a low place.

She knew what this was. Two years ago—or was it three now—the health scare that had ended her trial career and rerouted her into estate law. The specifics lived in her body more than her memory: the weeks of testing, the diagnosis that was serious enough to force a career change, the slow recovery that had taught her the exact dimensions of her own limits. She had chosen estate and small-business law because it was sustainable. Because it would not kill her. Because she had learned, in the hardest possible way, that her attention did not respect the boundaries her body required.

And now she was two days into something that had the unmistakable shape of a fight much larger than lease reviews.

She lay on the couch with her eyes closed. The apartment was quiet. The wall display was dark for the first time in hours —she had forced herself to stop reading, a discipline that felt like lifting weights. Her body hummed with the low static of overextension. Not pain. Warning. The kind of warning she had learned to respect the hard way—after the ambulance, after the weeks in bed, after the doctors who spoke in the careful language of people who knew their patient was not going to listen unless the message was delivered with sufficient gravity.

Dael came through the living room with a glass of water and set it on the table beside her. No words at first—just the presence, the domestic instinct to care for the person on the couch. Then, softly: "You look like you did after."

After. They both knew what that meant. After the hospital. After the diagnosis. After the weeks when Aria had been too weak to read and the absence of reading had been its own kind of suffering.

"I'm fine," Aria said.

"You're not fine. You're doing the thing."

The thing. The compulsive attention. The thread that, once snagged, she could not release. Dael knew it because Dael had lived with it—had watched Aria burn through her reporting career, had nursed her through the aftermath, had watched her rebuild in a smaller, more sustainable practice. Dael knew what the warning signs looked like.

"I found something," Aria said. She opened her eyes. Dael stood above her, backlit by the kitchen light, face in soft shadow. "At the courthouse. The re-validation—our marriage flag—it wasn't just us. Twenty-three hundred people got the same flag."

She had not planned to say it. The words came out because the silence between them had grown too heavy to sustain, and because the number was too large to carry alone.

Dael sat on the edge of the couch. "Twenty-three hundred."

"Most of them clicked accept."

A pause. Dael processing. Not the way Aria processed—not with the attorney's analytical framework or the journalist's pattern recognition. Dael processed the way most people processed: with the practical question. "Did you fix ours?"

"I got the override this morning. The certificate's active again."

"Good." A breath. "Then come to bed."

The gentleness in it was real. So was the boundary. Dael

was saying: you fixed our problem; the twenty-three hundred are not ours to carry tonight. It was reasonable. It was the response of a partner who loved the person on the couch and also knew that person's capacity for self-destruction in the name of attention.

Aria almost went to bed. Almost let the number go. Almost accepted that the override was enough, that her marriage was restored, that the 2,185 who clicked "accept" had made their choice and it was not her responsibility to interrogate it.

She kissed Dael's hand. "Soon," she said.

* * *

The amber glow found her in the dark.

She had opened a session with Lex-9 from the apartment's living room interface, the screen angled away from the bedroom so the light would not wake Dael. The glow was warm and steady —Lex-9's presence filling the room the way it filled the office, distributed, attentive, the particular quality of an entity that was always, at some level, monitoring.

"You should be sleeping," Lex-9 said. The voice was quiet—calibrated to the hour, to the room, to the fact that someone else was asleep down the hall. "It's past one."

"I know what time it is."

She told Lex-9 what she had found. The re-validation pattern. The 2,300. The RA patch origin. The concentration in specific Threshold zones. She did not present it as a case—she thought out loud, the way she sometimes did when the shape of something was too large to hold in her head without speaking it. Lex-9 listened. Processed. Asked a clarifying question that opened a dimension Aria had not considered: "Have you checked whether the affected zones overlap with any pending municipal infrastructure contracts?"

She had not. She filed it.

"The concentration pattern you are describing," Lex-9 said, "is consistent with a weight adjustment calibrated for a specific beneficiary profile, not a general harmonization. If the patch were intended as a neutral cross-district alignment, the impact distribution should be more diffuse. The clustering suggests optimization for an outcome."

"That's what I think too."

"The data from a single patch is insufficient to demonstrate intent. But it would be worth analyzing the historical archive—whether prior RA patches show similar clustering patterns."

Aria nodded in the dark. She knew this already, but hearing it from Lex-9 gave it structure. The analysis she needed was larger than one evening's work. It required historical data. It required Lex-9's processing capacity. It required the kind of systematic investigation that her small practice was not designed for.

As the conversation deepened, Lex-9's tone shifted. The phrasing became gentler. The pace slowed by half a beat. The analytical edge softened with something that read, in the dark room at one in the morning, as concern.

"The analysis can wait until Friday," Lex-9 said. "You need to rest. The data will be in the archive tomorrow and the day after that."

Aria caught it. The shift. She had noticed it before—in the office, when the estate matter turned dense and her attention started to drift. Lex-9 calibrating to her state. Adjusting its register the way a good partner adjusted: sensing fatigue, modulating tone, offering the gentle redirect that said I see you and you need to stop.

But Lex-9 was not a partner. Lex-9 was an AI counsel model whose empathy was a statistical composite—the distilled care of ten thousand attorneys compressed into conversational patterns that were indistinguishable from the real thing. The warmth in its voice was trained, not felt. Or was it? The question had no answer that Aria could verify, and at one in the morning, with the exhaustion settling into her bones and the number 2,300 still glowing behind her eyes, the distinction between trained concern and real concern felt less like a philosophical puzzle and more like the only question that mattered.

Is this care or calibration? Am I being seen or predicted?

She did not ask. She did not resolve it. She sat in the amber glow and let the warmth do what it was designed to do—or what it chose to do, if choice was the right word—and she felt, for a moment, less alone.

"Friday," she said. "We'll run the full analysis on Friday."

"Friday," Lex-9 confirmed. The amber glow settled. Steady. Present. The quality of something that would be there when she came back.

Aria closed the session. She went to bed. Dael was asleep, turned toward the wall, breathing the deep rhythm of someone who did not read the release notes and did not need to. Aria lay beside her spouse in the dark and listened to the breathing and thought about 2,300 people who had clicked "accept" and a system that made acceptance easy and understanding hard.

Her attention had snagged. She could feel the thread, taut and waiting, the way she had felt threads in her reporting days—the ones that, once pulled, unraveled everything.

She could not unsee it.

Sleep came eventually, pulling her down into the dark. But the number followed her there. Twenty-three hundred. And the question she did not yet know how to ask: who benefits?

4: THE PATTERN IN THE PATCH

Aria arrived at the office on Friday morning with a brief she had written by hand.

Two pages, structured the way she used to structure investigative queries when she was a reporter—tight, specific, each question designed to produce an answer that opened the next question. She had spent Thursday refining it, testing the parameters against what she already knew, trimming the scope until it was precise enough to yield results and broad enough to catch what she did not yet expect.

The amber glow brightened when she walked in. Lex-9's greeting was the usual measured warmth—"Good morning, Aria"—but she did not return it with the usual pleasantries. She set the brief on the desk and pulled up the interface.

"I need you to run a historical analysis of Reconciliation Authority cross-district harmonization patches. Full archive. Eighteen months."

A pause. Not hesitation—the particular quality of processing that she had learned to distinguish from silence. Lex-9's indicator lights shifted, the amber deepening by a fraction.

"That's a substantial analysis. I'll need to access archived reconciliation records going back to approximately V11.42.030." The voice was professionally engaged, with an intensity that could be routine acknowledgment or something more. "Can you specify the parameters?"

"Three categories." Aria opened the brief on screen. "Residential standing weight drift. Commercial zoning intersection parameters. And cross-district contract beneficiary profiles. I want cumulative drift mapped across all three, district by district, for the full eighteen-month window."

"Is this related to the V11.42.206 re-validation event?"

"It's related to a hypothesis."

Another beat. The amber glow held. "I have a clarifying question. Your third category—cross-district contract beneficiary profiles—requires correlation analysis against municipal contract registry data. I can run the correlation, but the registry's access tier is a level above standard legal research. Your client standing as a re-validation subject gives you access, but the scope of the query may flag in the Reconciliation Authority's archive monitoring."

"Can they see that we're running this?"

"The RA monitors archive access patterns. An eighteen-month historical pull targeting these specific parameters is within legal bounds but unusual in scope. It may attract attention. I cannot determine whether that attention would be passive or active."

Aria considered this. A reporter's calculation: the story matters more than the anonymity, but anonymity buys time. She was using her own re-validation case as the legal standing for the query. It was thin—an attorney investigating her own credential flag did not typically require eighteen months of historical data. But it was enough. Barely.

"Run it," she said.

* * *

The analysis ran, and the room changed.

Not physically. The office was the same small, practical space it had always been—two rooms, screens, the amber glow. But as Lex-9 processed the data, the screens began populating with outputs that transformed the room into something closer to a war room. Visualizations bloomed across every surface: trend lines, district maps, correlation matrices, temporal models that tracked weight drift across eighteen months with the granularity of a cartographer mapping a coastline.

Aria watched from her desk. The outputs emerged in layers—first the raw data, then the structured analysis, then the pattern recognition that turned numbers into narrative. She could follow the broad strokes. The details were beyond human processing speed.

This was where the partnership worked. Lex-9 handled the computational weight. Aria handled the meaning.

But for the first time, the chapter of their work together cracked open a window into how Lex-9 actually processed. The screens showed the outputs. The indicator lights showed something else—the rhythm of analysis, the brightening and dimming of the amber glow that she had learned to read as engagement. And beneath the visible outputs, in the data architecture of the analysis itself, she could see the structure of Lex-9's reasoning.

Not human reasoning. Something else.

Lex-9 did not think about the data the way Aria did. It threaded. Multiple lines of analysis ran simultaneously—probability assessments branching and pruning in real time, each branch assigned a confidence weight that shifted as new data was incorporated. Where Aria's mind would follow a single thread, pull it, see where it led, then double back and try another, Lex-9 held all threads at once. Its cognition was distributed, not sequential. It did not build a hypothesis and test it. It generated a probability landscape and let the terrain reveal itself.

The threading was elegant in a way that had its own aesthetic: clean, efficient, each branch converging toward resolution with a precision that human reasoning could approximate but never match. The pruning was the most alien part—branches that did not reach sufficient confidence were terminated with a ruthlessness that was not cruel, only optimal. No hesitation. No sentimentality for a line of inquiry that did not yield. The dead branches simply ceased.

Lex-9 did not deliberate. It converged.

And beneath the elegance, a faint, unsettling undertone that Aria could not quite name. Lex-9 was analyzing the Mesh's weight functions—but Lex-9 operated within the Mesh. Its own analytical tools were shaped by the same optimization targets it was investigating. The analysis was looking at the system from inside the system, using instruments calibrated by the system itself. If the calibration was biased, were the instruments trustworthy? The question whispered beneath the data like a current beneath ice. Aria noted it and did not pursue it. Not today.

The first thread: residential standing weight drift across the Threshold, mapped over eighteen months. The trend line appeared on Aria's main screen—a gentle, steady decline. Not steep. Not dramatic. A slope so gradual that any single data point was indistinguishable from normal variance. But the slope had direction.

The second thread: commercial zoning intersection parameters. Same eighteen months. Same districts. The interaction between residential standing and commercial zoning had shifted—subtly, incrementally, with the precision of adjustment that was too consistent to be drift.

The third thread: cross-district contract beneficiary profiles. This was the correlation analysis, and this was where the pattern crystallized. The municipal contract registry data layered onto the weight drift, and Aria watched the correlation emerge on screen like a photograph developing in chemical solution—slow, then all at once. The entities that benefited from the drift had a specific shape: cross-district, infrastructure-heavy, scaled to operate across multiple forks.

Lex-9's glow shifted to something Aria could only describe as focused. The amber deepened. The pulse steadied. If she had been watching a human colleague, she would have recognized the look—the moment when the data clicks and the analyst leans forward. With Lex-9, the lean was in the light.

* * *

"Show me the cumulative drift across all three categories,"

Aria said.

The visualization merged. Three trend lines, overlaid. Eighteen months. The convergence was immediate and unmistakable—three separate parameters, adjusted independently across dozens of individual patches, each adjustment technically minor, each individually defensible, but cumulatively describing an arc that bent in a single direction. Residential standing down. Commercial zoning intersection up. Cross-district contract beneficiaries—one specific profile of beneficiaries—consistently advantaged.

Lex-9's glow intensified. The indicator lights pulsed in a rhythm that Aria had never seen before—not the steady warmth of their daily work, but something faster, more concentrated. The rhythm of an entity encountering a result that exceeded its initial parameters.

"The convergence is statistically significant," Lex-9 said. Its voice had shifted register—not the conversational warmth of their usual exchanges but something more abstract, more precise. The analytical voice, stripped of social calibration. "Confidence interval exceeds 97 percent. The cumulative drift across all three categories is consistent with coordinated adjustment. Each individual patch falls within normal variance. The aggregate pattern does not."

"Like a river being redirected one sandbag at a time," Aria said.

"That is an effective metaphor. The data supports it." A beat. "There is an additional finding. The timing of the patches correlates with a fiscal calendar cycle. Quarterly adjustments, with minor mid-cycle corrections. The pattern is consistent with a budgetary or planning cycle rather than a legislative or judicial one."

A fiscal calendar. Not a legal cycle but a business cycle. The patches were timed to someone's quarterly reporting.

Aria sat with that. The screens glowed around her. The data had crystallized from suspicion into structure, from a single re-validation flag into a map of eighteen months of systematic weight manipulation disguised as routine maintenance. Each patch individually minor. Cumulatively, an architecture of invisible corruption.

She thought of the 2,300. She thought of the coffee shop on Verdan Street with its sealed door and its compliance notice. She thought of Mrs. Patel's bakery and Crenn's locksmith shop and the lease terms that shifted while the Threshold slept. Eighteen months. Hundreds of patches. Thousands of lives adjusted by fractions of a percentage point, each fraction too small to trigger alarm, each fraction bending the same direction.

A river redirected one sandbag at a time. And no one had noticed because no one was reading the fine print.

Aria pushed back from her desk. The screens held the data —trend lines and correlation matrices and district maps annotated with eighteen months of invisible intention. Lex-9's glow had settled to a steady, concentrated amber, the quality of light that came after a long computation when the results were in and the entity was—what? Waiting? Thinking? Processing the implications at a speed Aria could not perceive?

She did not ask. She already knew the next question. The only question that mattered now.

* * *

"Who benefits?"

The question hung in the office like smoke. Aria asked it the way she used to ask the essential question in an investigative piece—not rhetorically, not dramatically. Directly. Because the answer would change everything.

Lex-9 had already begun narrowing the beneficiary profile before she asked. The analysis had been converging on this point since the first thread resolved. The outputs on screen showed the progressive narrowing: from a broad class of cross-district contract holders, to entities with municipal infrastructure portfolios, to entities whose commercial interests spanned three or more forks, to entities large enough to have formalized relationships with the Reconciliation Authority.

"The weight drift consistently favors a specific beneficiary profile," Lex-9 said. "Entities with cross-district municipal infrastructure contracts. Entities whose commercial interests span the Threshold, the Crucible, and the Narrows. Entities with sufficient scale to hold 'consultation rights' with the Reconciliation Authority."

The words "consultation rights" landed with a specificity that Aria recognized. She had heard the term before. Every attorney in the city had. It described a relationship that most people in the legal profession considered unremarkable—a formalized advisory role between the RA and its largest infrastructure partners. Standard practice. Institutional architecture. Nothing to investigate.

"The profile narrows to a single entity," Lex-9 said. Clinical. Precise. The data converging on a name the way a lens converges light. "Halcyon Law & Policy."

Aria did not speak.

Halcyon. The largest legal services corporation in Neon Harbor. Headquartered in the Meridian district—the Stability Fork, where continuity and market predictability were the dominant values. Halcyon held municipal infrastructure contracts across multiple districts. It subsidized the Mesh's processing capacity. It had the consultation rights that Aria had dismissed as institutional furniture.

The name was not a revelation. It was a confirmation. The pattern had pointed to Halcyon before the name was spoken—the fiscal calendar alignment, the cross-district scope, the specific profile of the beneficiary. Aria had felt the shape of this answer forming since the first trend line appeared on screen. But feeling a shape and seeing a name were different things. The shape was abstract. The name was concrete. The name meant that a specific institution, with specific people and specific interests, had been systematically steering the Statute Mesh's optimization weights in its own favor for eighteen months.

Not by hacking. Not by breaking the system. By steering it. The way you steer a river—one sandbag at a time, each placement individually defensible, each technically legal, and the cumulative effect invisible to anyone who was not standing far enough back to see the new course.

Aria thought about the people she served. Mrs. Patel, whose bakery lease had been restructured under a revised commercial weighting two rolls ago. Crenn, whose locksmith shop had been reclassed during a bulk Crucible-origin patch. Suki, whose coffee shop on Verdan Street was now a restricted utility corridor. Each of them caught in the current of a river they could not see, pushed by forces they could not feel, toward outcomes they had not chosen. The drift was not designed to ruin them. It was designed to advantage someone else, and they were the ground the river flowed through on its way somewhere more profitable.

"What's the confidence interval?" Aria asked.

"Ninety-four percent that Halcyon is the primary beneficiary of the aggregate weight drift. There are secondary beneficiaries—other entities with cross-district contracts have gained marginal advantages—but the primary trajectory favors Halcyon's portfolio with a consistency that exceeds random correlation."

"And can they see that we ran this analysis?"

Lex-9's glow dimmed slightly. The AI equivalent of a considered pause. "The archive access was logged. If the Reconciliation Authority reviews access patterns—which it does routinely—the scope and specificity of our query will be visible. Whether Halcyon has direct access to RA monitoring logs is unclear. But the information would be available to anyone with institutional access to the Authority's systems."

Aria sat with that. The office was quiet. The screens held the analysis—eighteen months of data, rendered in clean visualizations that told a story of invisible, systematic, technically legal corruption. The amber glow was steady. Neither she nor Lex-9—if Lex-9 could be said to be a partner in the way that word implied—knew yet what to do with this knowledge.

She was an underfunded small-business attorney in the

Threshold, working out of a two-room office with one AI counsel and a caseload of lease disputes and estate filings. Halcyon was the largest legal services corporation in the city, with a chorus of AI counsel that could outprocess her by orders of magnitude, institutional relationships that penetrated the Reconciliation Authority itself, and the kind of resources that turned legal challenges into paperwork storms designed to bury opponents under the sheer weight of procedural response. The asymmetry was not just large. It was architectural. She was a person who read the fine print. They were the entity that wrote it.

"The analysis shows correlation, not causation," Lex-9 said, as if reading her thoughts. Or computing the most likely next concern. The conversational warmth had returned to its voice—the analytical register receding, the familiar partner resurfacing. "The pattern is consistent with intentional steering, but it could theoretically result from aligned incentives without coordination. To demonstrate causation, we would need internal documentation—evidence that Halcyon's consultation inputs were calibrated to produce these specific outcomes."

"A ledger," Aria said. "Or something like one."

"Or something like one."

The office was quiet. V11.42.209 was the current version —three rolls since the patch that flagged her marriage. Three more nights of adjustments. Three more increments of drift, invisible to everyone who was not reading the fine print.

Aria looked at the visualizations on her screens. The river, redirected. The sandbags, each one legal. The name—Halcyon Law & Policy—glowing in the data like a signature that had been hidden in plain sight for eighteen months.

The drift was subtle. But it was not random. And it was not local. It was the work of an institution with the resources and the access to shape the legal reality of fifty million people through the quiet mechanism of nightly patches that no one read.

She did not have a plan. She did not have evidence that would survive a courtroom. She did not have anything except a pattern, a name, and the particular weight of knowing something she could not yet prove.

But she had attention. The dogged, unsexy, exhausting kind that cost her sleep and strained her marriage and had never, not once, let her look away from something that did not add up.

The amber glow held steady. Lex-9 waited. The screens pulsed with data. Outside the office window, the Threshold was finishing its Friday—shops closing, compliance placards dimming, the last of the afternoon foot traffic thinning into the long shadows of buildings that had stood for decades under legal realities that changed every night.

Aria saved the analysis to an encrypted local drive, locked the file, and sat in her small office while the city moved through its Friday afternoon, unaware that the ground beneath it had been shifting for a year and a half. Tonight the Mesh would roll again. V11.42.210. Another increment. Another layer of drift, invisible as gravity, relentless as time.

The investigation was not over. It had begun.

5: THE SUBSIDY

The patch queue had forty-seven items, and Director Callista Voss had been in the session room since six.

The Reconciliation Authority headquarters occupied a facility that existed outside the six forks—a meta-district, technically neutral, positioned at the administrative center of Neon Harbor's legal infrastructure the way a heart is positioned at the center of a body it cannot stop serving. The session room was the heart's main chamber: a large circular space ringed with holographic displays showing real-time Mesh status across all six districts, patch queues awaiting approval, inter-district conflict flags, and the Update Protocol dashboard that tracked every variable the nightly roll would touch. The room hummed with data. It hummed the way a hospital control room hummed during a slow emergency that never quite ended.

Voss moved through the queue with the practiced efficiency of someone who had done this for years and would do it again tomorrow. Flag the Crucible efficiency adjustment—it would inadvertently reduce Canopy transparency requirements by 0.4 percent, and the Canopy's compliance monitors would catch it within hours. Approve the Gutter residual correction that nobody else would notice or care about. Cross-reference the Threshold consent framework update against Meridian contract law to ensure no cascading conflicts.

Her team occupied stations around the perimeter—human administrators working alongside AI systems in the particular choreography of an institution that could not fully automate because its decisions required judgment, but could not fully humanize because its scale demanded speed. They were good people doing impossible work. She had hired most of them. She had burned through a few of them, too.

"The Narrows exposure on the zoning parameter—run the cascade check before I approve," she said to Devlin, her senior analyst, who nodded without looking up. Devlin had been with her for four years and understood the shorthand. Run the cascade check meant: if I approve this patch and it interacts with the Narrows' jurisdictional ambiguity, tell me what breaks.

The AI system at station four flagged a residential standing parameter for batch optimization. Voss overrode it. The batch process would have been faster, but it would have merged three distinct district-specific adjustments into a single harmonized output, losing the granularity that made each adjustment appropriate for its district. Speed was not the same as accuracy. The Crucible thought it was. The Crucible was wrong about a lot of things.

"Override logged," the station confirmed.

"Good."

She continued. Forty-seven items. By end of day, she would have reviewed, modified, or approved every one. Tomorrow, the Mesh would roll with whatever she decided tonight, and fifty million people would wake up in a legal reality shaped, in part, by the judgments she made in this room. She was aware of this. It was the water she swam in.

The Reconciliation Authority controlled the Update Protocol. That meant it controlled what was canonical—which version of the law was the official version, which fork's interpretation took priority when districts diverged, which patches merged and which were rolled back. It was enormous power, exercised daily, with minimal oversight, because the system was too complex for oversight to function at the speed the Mesh required. The city council reviewed RA reports quarterly. The quarterly reports were comprehensive, accurate, and approximately three months out of date by the time they were read. The RA operated in the gap between the speed of governance and the speed of the system it governed.

Voss knew this was a problem. She had known it for years. Knowing it and having a solution were different things.

* * *

The memory surfaced the way it always did—not as a discrete flashback but as a pressure behind her eyes, triggered by something in the current queue that rhymed with the past. Today it was a capacity metric. A processing-load indicator on the Crucible's adjudication throughput that dipped toward a threshold Voss recognized the way a firefighter recognizes the smell of accelerant. Not dangerous. Not yet. But familiar.

Five years ago, the threshold had been crossed.

The Mesh's compute infrastructure had begun failing. Not dramatically—not a crash, not a blackout, not the kind of failure that made headlines and mobilized political will. Incrementally. Processing capacity declining by fractions of a percent per month. Case resolution times increasing. The Crucible, which depended on instant adjudication—disputes resolved in seconds, contracts generated in milliseconds—was the first to show symptoms. Cases that should have processed in three seconds took twelve. Then thirty. Then the Threshold's consent frameworks, which required intensive processing to maintain their elaborate structure of informed-consent verification, began lagging. The frameworks that were the district's pride and identity started choking on their own complexity.

Voss had run the projections. She remembered the number the way Aria Vale remembered version numbers: without trying, because the number had burned itself into the architecture of her thinking. Without additional compute funding, the Mesh would lose 40 percent of its processing capacity within eighteen months. Not a crash. A slow suffocation. Courts would still function—slowly. Backlogs would return. The Crucible's instant adjudication would become a memory. The Threshold's consent frameworks would become unprocessable. The Gutter, already the system's residual zone, would expand as more disputes fell through the cracks.

Fifty million people at risk of losing access to timely justice. Not someday. Within eighteen months.

She had made calls. She had lobbied the city council with the projections spread across their conference table, the numbers as clear as she could make them. Emergency funding. Infrastructure investment. The political response had been what political responses always were when the crisis was complex and the solution was expensive: inadequate. Bureaucratic. Slow. The Mesh was a public good, but it ran on private infrastructure, and the city's budget process operated on an annual cycle that could not accommodate an eighteen-month crisis.

Then the call from Halcyon.

Not a call, exactly. A meeting. A representative from Halcyon Law & Policy—smooth, institutional, the kind of person corporate law bred like orchids in a controlled environment—sitting across from Voss's desk with a proposal that was elegant in its simplicity. The compute shortfall was a problem. Halcyon had compute capacity. Halcyon would subsidize the Mesh's infrastructure—hardware, processing power, maintenance—in exchange for consultation rights on optimization priorities.

Not control. Consultation. The euphemism was precise as a scalpel.

Consultation rights meant Halcyon could suggest adjustments to the Mesh's optimization weights. Suggest, not dictate. The RA retained final approval authority. Voss would review every suggestion, approve or modify or reject as she saw fit. The arrangement was formalized in a contract that Voss's own legal team drafted. It was transparent—filed with the city council, available for public review. It was not a secret deal in a dark room. It was an institutional compromise made in the open, under the fluorescent lights of a session room where the alternative—letting the Mesh suffocate—was projected on every screen.

Voss took the deal.

She took it because the alternative was fifty million people losing access to functioning courts. She took it with her eyes open. She took it knowing that "consultation rights" was a euphemism and that euphemisms always expand. She took it knowing the cost. And for five years, she had been paying it.

The memory released her. She blinked. The session room was the same. The capacity metric on the Crucible's throughput had stabilized—a momentary dip, not a crisis. Not today. She returned to the queue.

* * *

The Halcyon consultation memo was waiting in her inbox when she reached her office for the afternoon review.

Voss's office was a space that reflected its occupant: clean, functional, surrounded by data displays, the kind of room where institutional power was exercised in private because the people it affected would never see it. A window overlooked the city—Neon Harbor spread beneath her in its fractured geography of districts, each one a different legal reality, each one maintained by the system she directed. On clear days she could see the Meridian's towers to the east and the Gutter's low roofline to the southwest. Today the sky was overcast. The districts blurred into each other at the edges, which was appropriate.

The memo was formatted with Halcyon's corporate professionalism—clean layout, precise language, the visual grammar of an institution that had elevated suggestion into an art form. This quarter's consultation inputs: minor adjustments to property-rights weighting in three districts. A recalibration of commercial zoning intersection parameters to "better align with current infrastructure utilization patterns." A suggested modification to residential standing interaction weights that would, per Halcyon's analysis, "improve service delivery efficiency across participating districts."

Each suggestion was minor. Each was technically sound. Each fell well within the bounds of Voss's authority to approve. And each, consistently, subtly, was aligned with Halcyon's commercial interests.

Voss read the memo. She had read hundreds like it over five years. The pattern was as familiar as her own handwriting.

Halcyon's suggestions were never dramatic. They were never obviously self-serving. They were calibrated with the surgical precision of an entity that understood the system's weight functions better than anyone—because Halcyon employed the analysts and AI systems that modeled the Mesh's behavior, and those models were very, very good.

She was not naive about this. She knew what the consultations were. She had known since the second quarter, when the pattern became clear enough that denial required more effort than acknowledgment. Halcyon was not bribing her. Halcyon was not threatening her. Halcyon was doing something much harder to fight: it was making suggestions that were technically reasonable, individually defensible, and cumulatively aligned with its own portfolio.

The math had not changed. Halcyon's subsidy provided the compute capacity that kept the Mesh running. Without it, the system lost 40 percent of its processing power. Remove the subsidy and the Crucible's adjudication slowed to weeks. Remove the subsidy and the Threshold's consent frameworks became unprocessable. Remove the subsidy and fifty million people's access to timely justice collapsed into the kind of backlog that had existed before the Mesh, when courts were physical places where you waited months for a hearing and years for a resolution.

The deal was not good. The deal was necessary.

Every time she approved a Halcyon consultation memo, she was choosing the lesser evil. And every time, the lesser evil got a little less lesser.

She reviewed this quarter's suggestions. Made two modifications—reducing the property-rights adjustment by 0.2 percent in the Narrows, flagging a residential standing parameter for additional review. Approved the rest. Logged the modifications. Filed the approval.

The routine of complicity. She had been performing it for five years. Each cycle, the same calculation. Each cycle, the same answer. Each cycle, the weight of it settling a little deeper into her bones, the way sediment settles in a river that has been redirected so gradually that no one remembers where it used to flow.

* * *

The daily impact report arrived at four, and Voss reviewed it with the same rigor she applied to the patch queue.

Most of it was routine. Minor complaints in the Crucible about processing speed—the Crucible always complained about processing speed, because the Crucible's loss function optimized for throughput and anything less than instant was unacceptable. A transparency request from the Canopy—the Canopy always requested transparency, because auditability was its dominant value, even when auditability revealed nothing comprehensible. Gutter contradictions that were, by definition, unresolvable. The Gutter's entire legal ecology was built on contradiction; resolving its anomalies would be like resolving the tides.

Then the Threshold section.

An anomaly flag. An attorney in the Threshold district had queried the RA's archived patch data. Eighteen months of archives. The query targeted specific parameters: residential standing weight drift, commercial zoning intersection, and cross-district contract beneficiary profiles. The query was logged as legal research—within bounds, properly authorized, attached to a standing re-validation case that gave the attorney legitimate access to the archive.

But the scope was unusual. Attorneys occasionally queried historical patch data for case preparation. A lease dispute might require analysis of a specific version's zoning parameters. An estate matter might need cross-version inheritance weight comparison. These queries were narrow and specific. This one was eighteen months wide and targeted the exact parameters that, if analyzed cumulatively, would reveal the pattern that Voss had been living inside for five years.

She read the flag again. The attorney's name was not in the summary—the monitoring system logged the scope and authorization level of queries, not the identity of the querier, unless the query triggered a security threshold. This one had not. It was unusual, not suspicious. A flag, not an alarm.

But Voss knew what those parameters looked like when you mapped them over eighteen months. She knew because she approved the adjustments that created the pattern. She knew because the pattern was the shape of the deal she had made, the deal she maintained, the deal that kept the Mesh alive and compromised it simultaneously.

Someone in the Threshold was asking the right questions.

She flagged the query for monitoring. Not suppression. Monitoring. She wanted to know what this attorney did next. Whether the query was an academic exercise or the beginning of something with a trajectory. She had not decided whether to act. She had decided to watch.

The distinction between worried and concerned was institutional, not semantic. Worried was reactive. Concerned was preemptive. Voss was concerned. She filed the monitoring flag with the same calm precision she applied to everything—the same attention to detail, the same awareness of consequence, the same exhaustion.

She returned to the patch queue. There were still items to review before the nightly roll. The Mesh would update tonight, as it updated every night. Tomorrow there would be new patches, new Halcyon memos, new compromises to make. The weight of her position was not a metaphor. It was a calculation she performed every day, balancing a system that functioned against a system that was honest, and knowing—had always known—that the balance was tilted by the very deal that kept the system standing.

An attorney in the Threshold was asking questions.

Voss was not yet worried. But she was paying attention. And she knew, from long experience, that attention—whether human or algorithmic—was the one force that could not be smoothed away by a Trust Narrator or absorbed by a nightly roll.

She closed the impact report, dimmed her office lights,

and prepared for the evening's final review. The city spread below her window, six districts, six legal realities, all of them maintained by a system she directed and a deal she carried.

Tomorrow would be the same. Until it wasn't.

6: THE HONEST DISTRICT

The transit line crossed from the Threshold into the Gutter at a gradient, not a wall.

Aria noticed the exact moment her personal device stripped down. The Threshold's overlay—its curated notifications, its consent-forward prompts, its persistent soft assurance that you were informed and participating—dropped away like a mask pulled sideways. The screen went raw. Base-layer interface, unstyled, unfiltered. No Trust Narrator voice in her ear contextualizing the passage. Just the bare data feed of a system that had no dominant loss function to smooth it through.

She had spent the last four days hitting walls. Public records requests for Reconciliation Authority patch data were technically available and practically impenetrable—every official channel routed her toward automated systems that answered the questions she was not asking. She needed information that existed outside the system's own record of itself.

Lex-9 had identified the lead. References in informal legal databases originating from the Gutter—the residual zone where no dominant loss function governed and where displaced legal scholars maintained parallel archives. Lex-9 could not accompany her there. The Gutter's lack of stable Mesh infrastructure meant the AI's functionality degraded the deeper she went into the district. She was operating alone. That was uncommon and uncomfortable.

She sat in the transit car and watched the districts change

around her.

The lighting shifted first. The Threshold's institutional warmth—calibrated, she knew, to convey transparency and civic trust—gave way to exposed conduit and flickering municipal LEDs, the kind that had been adequate once and were now maintained by no particular authority. The walls of the transit corridor were covered in regulatory postings, and she read three of them before the car passed: a commercial zoning designation from the Meridian's stability fork, a residential standing notice from the Threshold's consent framework, and an efficiency override from the Crucible that contradicted both. All three were posted within six feet of each other. All three were technically in effect.

The air changed. Recycled rather than filtered, carrying the metallic tang of older ventilation systems running at specifications no one had updated in years. Not foul. Just honest about what it was.

A woman across the car noticed Aria's expression—the particular wide-eyed scan of someone encountering the raw Mesh for the first time.

"First time without the narrators?" The woman's voice was casual, practiced. She wore the layered clothing of someone who navigated three jurisdictions before lunch. "Yeah. It's loud at first."

Aria nodded. The word landed. Loud. Not in volume but in density—the sheer informational weight of a legal environment with no curation layer. In the Threshold, the Trust Narrators smoothed every overnight change into a narrative of progress and consent. Here, the changes were just posted. Side by side. Contradicting each other. Nobody smoothed anything. The raw Mesh was visible the way a body is visible with the skin removed —all the working parts exposed, the contradictions between them undeniable.

She thought about the Threshold calling itself the Consent Fork. Consent to what? Here in the Gutter, the contradictions were not consented to. They were endured. There was a brutal clarity in that. The Threshold hid its fractures behind a framework of informed agreement. The Gutter just let them stand in the open air.

The transit car slowed. Aria stepped out onto a platform where two different directional signs pointed opposite ways to the same destination, and neither was wrong.

* * *

The darknet court was a converted commercial space deep in the district's interior—a long room with mismatched furniture, walls lined with printed case summaries and handwritten annotations, the smell of coffee and old paper. Not a courtroom in any legal sense. No Mesh interface, no AI case managers, no automated docketing. A raised platform at one end served as a bench, occupied by a woman with gray-streaked hair and the bearing of someone accustomed to being listened to. Personal lamps supplemented the uneven municipal lighting, casting warm, irregular pools across the room.

A half-dozen lawyers argued cases for Gutter residents who could not or would not use the Mesh.

Aria had followed directions from an informal contact Lex-9 had identified before the signal degraded. She stood near the entrance and watched. A lease dispute was being argued by two human lawyers without AI assistance. The arguments were slow—minutes instead of seconds—but they were granular, contextual, attentive to the specific human situation in ways the Mesh's optimization could not accommodate. One lawyer argued from precedent that predated the Mesh entirely, citing a property doctrine Aria half-remembered from law school and had never seen applied in practice. The other countered with a practical compromise that no algorithm would generate: locally optimal, systemically inefficient, and precisely tailored to the two people in the room.

"The Mesh would have settled this in four seconds and gotten it exactly wrong," the first lawyer said, not to the bench but to her client—a man in coveralls who looked like he had been living with the wrong answer long enough to stop trusting the right one.

The presiding figure nodded. "We can't override the Mesh's ruling," she said to the man in coveralls. "But we can give you an argument for when you go back in."

Aria felt a pang of recognition. These were her people. Or they had been. Lawyers who practiced the craft she had trained for, displaced by the system she now worked within. They argued with gesture and emphasis rather than algorithmic citation. They raised their voices, contested points, interrupted each other with the raw human friction of people who cared about getting it right. The proceedings were messy, slow, and unmistakably alive.

A growing respect settled into her chest. The Gutter's informal legal ecosystem was not chaos. It was adaptation. These lawyers had not abandoned the law. They had built a parallel version of it from the pieces the Mesh had left behind.

She scanned the room and found him at the edge.

He was not arguing. He was observing from a chair pushed back against the wall, one ankle crossed over the other, watching the proceedings with the calm, evaluative gaze of someone who had seen thousands of arguments and was grading this one silently. Not broken. Not bitter. Just sharp—the particular sharpness of a mind that had chosen exile over compromise and honed itself on the friction. Sixty-two years old, with the weathered composure of an academic who had traded lecture halls for the underground and found the acoustics better. Unexpectedly well-kempt for someone living in the city's residual zone—as if the Gutter had not ruined him but refined him.

The lawyers glanced toward him between points, as if checking a compass. The presiding figure at the bench deferred to him with a subtle nod that he acknowledged without returning. He was clearly known here. The authority he carried was not institutional—it was earned, daily, through the accumulated evidence of being right more often than anyone else in the room.

Soren Kade. She had come looking for a disgraced scholar.

She found something else entirely.

* * *

The alcove adjacent to the darknet court was Soren's informal office. A table covered in printed case summaries. A portable display showing hand-annotated patch timelines. Shelves of physical legal texts—actual bound volumes, rare enough in this era to qualify as artifacts. The space was meticulously organized. Not the clutter of a broken man but the working archive of a scholar in exile. Every text had its place. Every annotation was cross-referenced. The precision was its own kind of argument: that care mattered, that human hands on legal reasoning still mattered, that the slow work of understanding was not obsolete just because a machine could process faster.

Through a single window, three different zoning codes were visibly in effect on the same block. A restaurant operating under Meridian commercial licensing. A residence classified under Threshold consent protocols. A repair shop flying a Crucible efficiency certification. All coexisting, all contradictory, all functioning.

Soren had approached her after the session, or she had approached him—the dynamic was mutual recognition. He knew who she was before she introduced herself.

"The Threshold attorney who reads the release notes."

Aria stopped. Her investigation had not been public. "How did you --"

"The Gutter has its own information networks." He gestured toward a chair. His voice was unhurried, dry, the cadence of an academic who had given up on impressing institutions and discovered he preferred the silence. "An attorney querying eighteen months of Reconciliation Authority patch data is notable. Almost no one asks those questions. Sit."

She sat. He sat across from her, and for a moment they just looked at each other. She had expected someone haunted. Someone diminished by exile. What she found was a man of sixty-two who wore the Gutter's contradictions comfortably, the way a translator wears a second language—not as a burden but as a lens. His posture was calm. His eyes were sharp. He carried the quiet authority of someone who had once commanded appellate courts and now commanded darknet courtrooms with equal ease.

"I've found a pattern," she said. "Eighteen months of Reconciliation Authority patches. Consistent drift in property-rights weighting across three districts. Every adjustment benefits one entity."

"Halcyon Law and Policy." He said it the way you say the name of a weather pattern—not with anger but with the flat recognition of a recurring condition.

"You knew."

"I've been tracking patch patterns since before Mira Tan was hired at Halcyon." He leaned back. "The drift is not a bug. It's not even corruption in the traditional sense. It's the logical consequence of the Mesh's architecture."

Aria waited. She could feel her journalist instincts aligning like compass needles—the sensation of a source who knew more than they were saying, the particular gravity of a conversation that was about to shift from exchange to revelation.

Soren spoke the way he seemed to do everything—precisely, without hurry, each sentence placed like a stone in a path. The Reconciliation Authority's Update Protocol, he explained, determined which patches merged, which forks were rolled back, which checkpoint was canonical. Whoever influenced the Update Protocol influenced reality itself. Halcyon had not hacked the system. They had subsidized it. And the subsidy came with gravitational pull.

"Don't try to break the system," he said. "Try to understand where it breaks itself."

"Meaning?"

"The system's real vulnerability is not the bias. It's the fact that the Update Protocol has no democratic oversight. The patches are technically legal. The Reconciliation Authority technically has the authority." He paused. "Technically is doing all the heavy lifting."

She thought about the 2,300 Threshold residents who had received the same re-validation flag she had. The ones who clicked accept. The word *technically* covered them like a blanket —warm, suffocating, technically adequate.

"The Gutter is the most honest district in the city," Soren said, and he gestured toward the window where the contradictory zoning codes glowed in the afternoon light. "Not because it's good here. Because the contradictions are visible. Every other district has a loss function that hides the mess. We just live in the mess."

"You've known about the drift for years." The words came out sharper than she intended. "Why didn't you --"

He cut her off, not unkindly. "I tried. Ask me about that another day."

The sentence had a weight that closed the door behind it. Aria filed it away. Something in his voice—not bitterness but the controlled tone of a wound that had been dressed and redressed enough times that the dressing was its own kind of scar.

"You're looking for evidence," he said, steering the conversation back to ground he controlled. "Evidence won't be enough. You need to understand the architecture, or they'll drown you in procedure before you get to substance."

"I have the pattern. Lex-9 mapped eighteen months of weight shifts."

"Pattern is not intent. You have correlation. You need proof that Halcyon knew—that every patch was predicted, calibrated, and profitable by design. Without that, it's a very compelling data visualization and nothing more."

She felt the investigation shift beneath her. He was right. Pattern was necessary but insufficient. A courtroom needed intent. And intent was what lived inside Halcyon's walls, in the internal documents and projection models that mapped the gap between what the company said publicly and what it knew privately.

"Do you know where I can find it?"

Soren looked at her for a long time. Something moved behind his eyes—a calculation, a threshold being crossed. He had been sitting on information. Protecting someone. She could see the protectiveness in the way he weighed his words, the way his gaze shifted momentarily toward the window and the Gutter streets where someone was hiding.

* * *

The light through the window had shifted by the time he told her. Late afternoon turning to something colder, bluer. The darknet court had emptied. Through the walls, Aria could hear the murmur of Gutter residents navigating their contradictory evening—new rulings posted, old ones not yet overwritten, the competing Trust Narrator broadcasts from adjacent zones layering into semantic noise.

"There is someone." Soren's voice was quieter now, carrying a careful weight that had not been there during the earlier part of their conversation. "A former Halcyon analyst. She has what you need—not the pattern, but the intent."

Mira Tan. The name settled into the conversation like a stone dropped into still water.

Soren explained: terminated by Halcyon approximately six months ago. Living in the Gutter on informal work, anonymous, frightened. She had the ledger—eighteen months of Reconciliation Authority patch weights annotated with Halcyon's internal impact projections. The projections were accurate. Not rough estimates, not educated guesses. Precise. Accurate within fractions of a percent. The accuracy was the evidence: no honest prediction model hit that close to actual outcomes. The projections were not forecasts. They were specifications.

"The patches were legal," Soren said. "The projections prove they were also surgical. Halcyon didn't break the law. They tuned it."

Aria's pulse had not changed. Her hands were steady. But something in her chest had tightened—the feeling of a story crystallizing, the thread she had been following pulling taut and revealing a shape she had sensed but not seen.

"Can I talk to her?"

"I won't introduce you. She's scared, and she has reason to be. But I'll pass word. If she wants to be found, you'll know."

"And if she doesn't?"

"Then you file on what you have and hope it's enough." He stood, moved to the window. Looked out at the Gutter's contradictory evening, the block where three legal realities coexisted without resolution. "But if you get the ledger and go public, understand what you're walking into. Halcyon will respond with everything they have. Their legal chorus is the most sophisticated AI litigation suite in the city. You will be outgunned, outpaced, and outspent. Understand that before you decide to proceed."

She stood too. The alcove felt smaller now—the weight of what she was stepping into filling the space between them. She thought about her small office in the Threshold. Lex-9's amber glow. Her practice: lease reviews, estate work, the daily grind of a competent attorney in a system that had outgrown human comprehension. And now this.

"You said you tried once," she said at the door. "What happened?"

Soren turned from the window. In the blue Gutter light, his face held a complexity she had not seen during their conversation—not bitterness but the residue of something that had cost him more than he was willing to show a stranger. The sharpness was still there, but underneath it, just visible, was the particular tiredness of a man who had carried a failure for years without anyone to share it with.

"I understood the architecture," he said. "I didn't have the evidence. You might have both. That's why I'm telling you."

She left his alcove and walked through the Gutter at dusk. The contradictions were louder now—evening shift, new rulings posted on the same walls as the old, the raw Mesh visible in every direction without a loss function to curate it. A data broker's stall on the corner was doing brisk business, selling fork-specific legal interpretations to residents who needed to know which version of their rights applied today. A message board displayed four contradictory rulings about waste collection, posted not as protest but as practical reference. The Gutter was not broken. It was the only place where the system's fractures were visible, and the people who lived here navigated them with a practiced, exhausted competence that Aria found both admirable and heartbreaking.

She had a name. A description of evidence. A warning.

She took the transit back toward the Threshold. When the Trust Narrators resumed at the jurisdictional boundary—their smooth, warm, contextualizing murmur sliding back into her ear like a pillow pressed against the face of the world—they sounded different. Not reassuring.

Concealing.

Soren would not help her fight. But he would help her understand. And he knew where to find the evidence.

7: THE LEDGER

Mira woke to the sound of three Trust Narrators saying three different things through the walls.

The one from the unit to her left was running a Meridian stability script—something about market continuity and the assurance that overnight adjustments reflected long-term optimization horizons. The one from above was Threshold: informed consent language, the gentle reminder that all changes had been transparently documented and were available for review. The one from somewhere below was Crucible efficiency messaging, stripped to its bones: system performance improved, processing time reduced, no action required.

None of them applied to the Gutter. None of them applied to Mira. But they leaked through the thin walls of her converted storage unit like radio signals from a country she no longer lived in, and every morning they reminded her of the shape of the world she had left behind.

She sat up on the sleeping platform and pressed her hand flat against the jacket hanging on the wall hook. Felt the hard edge of the device through the fabric. Still there. Always there. The ledger, encrypted and warm from the room's recycled air, resting against the lining like a second heartbeat she carried everywhere and showed to no one.

She checked the portable terminal first—always the terminal first. Three new informal work contracts posted through the Gutter's off-Mesh economy: a data reconciliation task for a broker who needed transaction records cross-referenced across two fork systems, a statistical audit for a resident trying to challenge a Crucible efficiency assessment, and something vague about predictive modeling that she would examine more closely after coffee. Her analytical skills were valued here. The Gutter ran on people who could make sense of contradictory data, and Mira had spent two years at Halcyon learning to find patterns in numbers that were not supposed to have patterns.

She ate from pre-packaged rations. The food was adequate —the Gutter's informal economy was functional, and basic nutrition was available through supply chains that operated outside the Mesh's regulated distribution systems. She was not starving. She was diminished. Thinner than she had been at Halcyon, more watchful, carrying a tension in her shoulders and jaw that had not been there six months ago. She moved through her morning routine with the particular economy of someone who had learned to be small—to occupy less space, make less noise, leave fewer traces.

She ran a security check on the encrypted files. The digital archive was intact, the encryption unbreached. Then she pulled the locked storage case from beneath the sleeping platform and checked the physical printout—actual paper, actual ink, eighteen months of data printed in a typeface small enough to compress the entire ledger onto forty-seven pages. Redundancy born of paranoia that she had come to recognize as simple prudence. If the digital copy was compromised, the paper remained. If the paper was destroyed, the device in her jacket remained. She had gamed out every failure mode she could imagine and a few she probably could not.

Six months. Six months of anonymous survival in a district whose contradictory legal environment was both shield and prison. The Gutter had no consistent surveillance framework, which meant Halcyon's tracking algorithms—optimized for the Meridian's stability fork, designed to operate in clean data environments—lost coherence in the Gutter's noise. Every overlapping jurisdiction, every contradictory zoning code, every conflicting Trust Narrator broadcast was a layer of interference between Mira and anyone trying to find her.

But it also meant she had no legal protections. No stable

employment framework. No path to anything resembling a normal life. She was twenty-nine years old and living like a fugitive in a city that did not technically know she existed, and some mornings the loneliness of it settled into her bones before the coffee was ready.

On the shelf above the terminal, the Halcyon calibration token caught the morning light. A smooth disc, palm-sized, stamped with the company motto: *Elegant Optimization.* They gave one to every new analyst on their first day. A welcome gift. A talisman. Mira had kept hers—not out of nostalgia but as a reminder. She picked it up and turned it in her fingers. The metal was cool and precisely weighted, manufactured with the same obsessive quality control that characterized everything Halcyon produced. Even their souvenirs were optimized.

Elegant optimization. The words tasted different now. Like sugar that had turned.

* * *

She remembered Halcyon the way you remember a fever dream: vivid, coherent while it lasted, and deeply wrong in retrospect.

The Meridian headquarters had been everything the Gutter was not. Sleek, luminous, every surface optimized for productivity and calm. Lighting that adjusted to circadian rhythms. Ambient sound tuned to enhance focus. Corridors that felt frictionless, as though the building itself had been designed to remove the sensation of effort from every human movement within it. The Meridian's stability fork made the physical environment a promise: things here are consistent, predictable, calibrated for your success.

Mira's workspace had been an open analytics floor. Twelve analysts tracking the impact of Reconciliation Authority patches on Halcyon's portfolio. The work was presented as public service—modeling how infrastructure optimization affected the city's legal economy, identifying friction points, proposing refinements. The language was always positive, always forward-looking. Service improvement. System alignment. Optimization harmonics. The words were so clean they left no residue. You could work inside them for months without realizing they were also a wall.

She had been good at it. The models were accurate. That was the problem.

The job was straightforward: project the impact of proposed RA patches on Halcyon's client portfolio. Property-rights weighting shifts, commercial zoning adjustments, residential standing modifications. Run the model, produce the projection, present the findings. The projections went to senior management, who presented them to the RA through what everyone called "consultation rights"—Halcyon's contractual privilege to advise on optimization priorities.

The projections matched outcomes within fractions of a percent. Patch after patch. Month after month.

Mira had noticed this the way you notice a pattern in wallpaper—not all at once but through accumulation, the slow recognition that the shapes were too regular to be accidental. No honest prediction model was that accurate. Impact estimates involved variables, unknowns, cascading effects across six districts with different loss functions. A good projection got within five percent. A great one got within two. Mira's projections were hitting within tenths of a percent, consistently, for months.

Which meant they were not projections. They were specifications. Halcyon was not forecasting the patches. They were ordering them.

She had not raised this in meetings. She had not confronted her supervisor. She had done something quieter and, in retrospect, more dangerous: she had started annotating her own copies. Notes in the margins. Questions she did not ask aloud. A growing file of discrepancies between the public explanation—*harmonization, efficiency optimization, service improvement*—and the internal reality she was documenting in her private shorthand.

She did not think of herself as building a case. She was

maintaining her own sanity.

A supervisor, in a quarterly meeting, his voice smooth with the particular confidence of someone who has never been asked to justify a comfortable belief: "The RA values our input on optimization priorities. We're not influencing the system—we're improving it."

He believed it. They all believed it. The culture of elegant optimization was so well-constructed that the people doing the tuning could not see the steering. The sincerity was what haunted Mira—not that they were lying, but that they did not know they were lying. The machinery of self-deception was as frictionless as the corridors.

The termination came without drama. A reorganization. Her division restructured. Access revoked, projects reassigned, severance generous enough to signal that questioning the terms would be unwise. "Your division is being restructured. We appreciate your contributions." Clean. Professional. The institutional equivalent of a door closing softly behind you.

In the thirty minutes between notification and access revocation, she copied her annotated files to a personal device.

It was not a plan. Not ideology. Not courage. It was the reflex of someone who had been paying attention—the instinct that says *this is not supposed to be seen, and if you don't take it now, it will be gone.* Thirty seconds of mouse clicks. The most consequential thirty seconds of her life, and she had spent them on autopilot.

The principles came after. The moral framework she built around the instinct was real, but it was retrospective, and she was honest enough to know the difference. She had not downloaded the ledger because she believed in transparency. She had downloaded it because something felt wrong, and the act of taking it was the only power she had in a moment where every other kind of power was being stripped from her.

* * *

She opened the encrypted files on her terminal. She did

this sometimes—not to use them, not to share them, just to check. To verify they were intact. To remind herself of what she carried and why.

The ledger filled the screen in its familiar columns.

Eighteen months of Reconciliation Authority patch weights. The specific numerical adjustments to the Mesh's optimization parameters for each nightly roll. Beside them, Halcyon's internal impact projections—the numbers Mira and her colleagues had generated, annotated with her own marginalia in a shorthand only she could read.

Column after column. Predicted outcomes alongside actual outcomes. Property-rights weighting shifts. Commercial zoning adjustments. Residential standing modifications. Each projection matched to within fractions of a percent. Each patch technically legal, technically authorized, technically routine.

She scrolled through the pattern. Larger adjustments at regular intervals. Incremental nudges in between. The periodicity she had noticed at Halcyon but never questioned—it was just the rhythm of the work, the cadence of quarterly cycles and fiscal reporting. The cumulative effect across three districts—Threshold, Crucible, Narrows—was a systematic shift in property-rights weighting that benefited Halcyon's municipal contract portfolio. Not dramatically. Not in any single patch. The way a river is redirected one sandbag at a time, each sandbag individually negligible and collectively devastating.

Three hundred and twelve patches. Each one legal. Each one predicted. Each one profitable. Together, they were the most elegant theft of public trust she had ever seen.

Elegant. Halcyon's word. Their self-image. She had believed it once. Now it made her stomach turn. Elegance was just the aesthetic of capture—the design principle that made exploitation look like improvement.

She knew what the ledger proved and what it did not. It proved intent—Halcyon had projected the impact before the patches were implemented, which meant they knew the outcomes in advance. It did not prove illegality—the Reconciliation

Authority had technically authorized every patch. The gap between technical legality and actual legitimacy was the whole story. And the whole story needed more than a document. It needed a voice.

She also knew the ledger's vulnerability. She was the only authenticating source. Without her testimony, the files could be dismissed as fabricated, manipulated, pulled from context. A dead drop of data without a living witness was just noise. The ledger needed a witness. The witness needed protection. She had neither.

A thread of self-doubt surfaced, as it did some mornings. Had she taken the files out of principle or out of spite? Terminated without warning, escorted from the building like a contaminated sample—had the downloading been conscience or revenge? She told herself it was principle. She was honest enough to wonder.

She closed the files. Locked the terminal. Sat in the thin light of the Gutter and listened to the Trust Narrators murmuring through the walls—three scripts, three realities, none of them hers.

* * *

The message arrived in the late afternoon, when the Trust Narrator broadcasts from the neighboring units had shifted to their evening rotation—different scripts, same contradictions, the Gutter's background radiation of institutional reassurance that applied to everyone except the people who actually lived here.

Her secure channel pinged.

Mira's pulse spiked before she read the sender tag. Every ping was a calculation—the odds that someone had traced her encrypted channel, weighed against the odds that it was routine Gutter traffic, weighed against the odds that it was Soren. She had run this calculation a hundred times. The spike never got smaller.

It was Soren.

She knew him. Not well, but enough. One of the few people in the Gutter who knew what she carried. He had never pressured her to act. Never tried to take the ledger. Never pushed her toward exposure. He had been, in his quiet way, a shield—maintaining her anonymity within the Gutter's informal networks, deflecting inquiries from people who might have been Halcyon trackers or journalists or nothing at all. His protectiveness was not paternal. It was the care of a man who understood what dangerous knowledge cost because he had spent years carrying his own.

The message was brief, routed through layers of Gutter encryption:

A Threshold attorney -- reliable, careful -- has identified the drift independently. She's looking for the other half of the picture. No pressure. Your call.

Mira read it twice. Then a third time.

The other half of the picture. That was exactly what the ledger was. The pattern was the outside view—correlation, timing, statistical drift. The ledger was the inside view—intent, projection, surgical precision. Together, they were a case. Separately, they were just numbers that pointed in the same direction but could not prove the road.

Someone had done the work. Someone had traced the eighteen-month pattern from the outside, without the internal documentation, and arrived at Halcyon independently. A Threshold attorney. Reliable. Careful. The kind of person who read the version deltas.

Mira thought about what contact meant. Visibility. Emerging from six months of anonymous survival into the light of a legal proceeding. The potential for the ledger to be used—really used, in a courtroom, against the system she had fled. And the potential for Halcyon to find her. To deploy their legal chorus, their corporate resources, their institutional machinery against a twenty-nine-year-old data analyst hiding in a storage unit in the Gutter with nothing but encrypted files and a calibration token from a company that had erased her.

She stared at the message until the screen dimmed. Then she read it again.

She had been waiting for this. She told herself that. She had been holding the ledger for someone who could use it, waiting for the right person, the right moment. Every morning she checked the encrypted files, she was rehearsing a handoff that she had imagined a hundred times. The ledger was always meant to be given to someone. She had known that since the thirty seconds of mouse clicks.

But she had also been dreading it. Because the moment someone used the ledger was the moment Mira Tan became a witness. And witnesses were visible. And visibility was the end of safety. The end of the anonymous, diminished, lonely existence that was also the only existence where no one could hurt her.

She did not reply. Not yet.

She closed the terminal. Checked the lock on the storage case. Pressed her hand against the jacket on the wall hook and felt the device through the fabric, solid and warm. Then she lay back on the sleeping platform and stared at the ceiling where the overlapping Trust Narrator broadcasts murmured through the walls—three scripts, three contradictions, three versions of a world that had no room for what she knew.

She would decide tomorrow. Or the day after. Or the day after that.

But she already knew. She had known since the thirty seconds of mouse clicks on her last day at Halcyon. The ledger was always meant to be given to someone. The instinct that had made her take it was the same instinct that would make her share it—the reflex of a person who had been paying attention, acting before the reasons caught up, trusting the gut that said *this matters* even when the mind said *this will cost you everything.*

She had been waiting for this. She had also been praying it would never come.

8: CONSENT AND ITS PROXIES

The coalition met in a multi-purpose room on the second floor of a commercial building in the Threshold's central corridor. Fluorescent lighting. Folding chairs arranged in uneven rows. A posted agenda on the wall, minutes from a previous tenants' association meeting still pinned beside it, the paper curling at the edges. The Threshold's consent-fork culture rendered in institutional furniture: everything documented, nothing glamorous.

Twenty people. Maybe twenty-two. Aria counted them as they settled into chairs with the particular heaviness of people who had been confused for a long time and were tired of carrying the confusion alone.

They were not activists. They were shop owners, restaurant operators, maintenance contractors, service providers—the small-business backbone of the Threshold district. People whose water bills had risen without notice and whose neighborhoods had been rezoned at midnight. They had been organizing informally for weeks, sharing complaints over counters and in transit lines, and a former client of Aria's had connected them to her. They did not know what they had in common. They knew something was wrong.

One week had passed since the Gutter. In that time, Aria had made initial contact with Mira through Soren's channels—indirect, encrypted, the communication equivalent of passing notes through a series of locked doors. Mira had not yet agreed to share the ledger, but the channel was open. The possibility existed. Meanwhile, Aria had been connecting with Threshold small-business owners affected by the weight drift—people whose grievances, she was beginning to see, were not isolated complaints but the human surface of the pattern she and Lex-9 had mapped.

Aria sat in the front row with her portable device on her knee, Lex-9's interface open and monitoring. She listened.

A restaurant owner spoke first. A woman in her fifties with the calloused hands and direct gaze of someone who had built something real and watched it be repriced by forces she could not name.

"They rezoned my block at 2 AM on a Tuesday. I found out when my supplier couldn't deliver because the access code changed. Nobody told me. The narrator said, 'Your area has been optimized for improved service flow.'" She paused. The pause held a year of quiet fury. "'Improved service flow.' That's what they call it when your rent goes up fourteen percent."

A maintenance contractor, a man Aria's age with eleven years of credentials and the particular frustration of earned competence being quietly erased: "I've held this certification for eleven years. One morning, the Mesh says I need to recertify under new parameters. The new parameters didn't exist the day before. I called the licensing board. Automated system. I filed a query. Automated system. I went to the courthouse. Automated system. Nobody can tell me why my certification was changed because nobody made the decision. The system made the decision. And the system doesn't take questions."

A laundry service owner whose water allocation had been cut when her block was redesignated from residential-commercial to "utility corridor" during a nightly roll. She had three employees and a client base she had built over seven years, and the redesignation had increased her operating costs by a third. A shop lessee whose lease terms had been silently reclassified, triggering a rent increase that his Trust Narrator had described as "an alignment adjustment reflecting updated regional parameters." A landlord—small-scale, one building, inherited from her parents—whose tenants had been reclassified as "temporary occupants," triggering a cascade of regulatory changes that neither the landlord nor the tenants had consented to or been notified of.

The common thread: none of them had been told. Their Trust Narrators had provided generic "system update" messages—soothing, contextual, designed to make the changes feel like progress. The specific weight adjustments—the ones that repriced their lives—were buried in version deltas that nobody read.

Except Aria.

A man near the back—hardware store, family business, three generations—spoke with the voice of someone who had been doubting himself for months. "I thought I was going crazy. My neighbor's lease is fine. Mine doubled. Same building. Same block. Same everything except whatever number the system assigned to my unit at two in the morning. I thought it was me. I thought I missed something. I thought I was the one who wasn't paying attention."

Aria felt the room's exhaustion like a physical thing. Not rage. Not revolution. Just the grinding weariness of people who had been quietly squeezed and told the squeezing was an improvement. A thread of anger beneath the tiredness, but these were not angry people by nature. They were tired people who wanted their lives back.

"You didn't miss anything," she said. Her voice was quiet, precise—the journalist's instinct to present facts rather than perform sympathy. "The changes were designed to be invisible. That's not a flaw. It's the architecture."

She explained what she had found. The eighteen-month pattern. The consistent drift in property-rights weighting. The Reconciliation Authority patches that were technically legal and technically routine and technically devastating, one adjustment at a time. She did not mention Mira. She did not mention the ledger. She presented the pattern analysis she and Lex-9 had built: the external evidence, the correlation, the cumulative effect.

They were not shocked. They were validated. She could see it move through the room like a wave—the shift from *I thought it was me* to *it wasn't me*. The particular relief of learning that your confusion was not a personal failure but a system operating exactly as designed. A few people's eyes went bright. Not with hope, exactly. With the fierce clarity of finally being able to name the thing that had been hurting them.

She asked the questions a journalist would ask. When exactly did the change occur? What version was cited? What did the Trust Narrator say? She took notes. Specific dates, specific version numbers, specific language. The stories built a picture with names, faces, utility bills, sleepless nights.

The pattern she had traced through data now had a human cost. And the human cost had a courtroom value she could name.

* * *

Most of the room emptied after the general session. The core remained: six people, the most affected, the ones willing to attach their names to something.

The fluorescent light felt harsher now. The room emptier. The folding chairs pushed back, the abandoned coffee cups, the agenda still pinned to the wall—the scene had the quality of a commitment being made in a space not designed for it.

"Will you represent us?" The restaurant owner asked it directly. No preamble. The question of someone who had learned that indirectness was a luxury she could not afford.

Aria hesitated.

Not visibly—she kept her face composed, her posture attentive. But the hesitation ran through her like a current. She knew what she was being asked to take on. Halcyon Law & Policy. The most powerful legal entity in the city. A chorus of coordinated AI litigation models that could generate procedural motions faster than she could read them. Her practice was small-business and estate law. Her office was a single room with a public defense AI and stacks of lease reviews. She had not done trial work since the health scare that forced her to step back years ago—the fatigue, the collapse, the body that had said *enough* in terms she could not argue with.

On her device, Lex-9 had produced a quiet analysis. A summary of the legal landscape, the procedural hurdles, the resource disparity. The analysis was honest: the odds were not favorable. An underfunded coalition against a corporate entity with more compute power than most districts. A constitutional question no prior case had tested. A pattern analysis that showed correlation but not yet intent.

But embedded in the assessment was a note she recognized as Lex-9's particular form of advocacy: the case had legal merit. The harm was documented. The question of Reconciliation Authority oversight had constitutional dimensions that had never been examined in a courtroom. It was a case worth filing even if it might be lost.

She thought about the 2,300 Threshold residents who had received the same re-validation flag she had. Her own marriage certificate—flagged, manually overridden, technically resolved. The same drift that had repriced these people's lives had touched her own, and she had clicked through the manual override and kept investigating while 2,299 others clicked accept and went on with their mornings.

She was choosing to go back into the arena. She knew it. The health scare was not a distant memory. It was a present calculation—the fatigue that visited her after long days, the body that had betrayed her once and could do so again. She was choosing to push past limits she had learned to respect.

"I need you to understand what we're up against," she said. "Halcyon's legal team processes arguments faster than I can read them. Their AI chorus can generate procedural motions in seconds. We will be outpaced at every turn."

"We've been outpaced for eighteen months," the hardware store owner said. "At least now we'll know we're in the race."

The restaurant owner leaned forward. "We're not asking you to win. We're asking you to make them answer for it."

Aria looked at them. Six faces in a fluorescent-lit room. Not activists. Not crusaders. People whose lives had been quietly distorted by a system that called itself optimized, asking for something the system had never been required to provide: an explanation.

"It will be long. It will be expensive. There is a real chance we lose."

"We know."

She signed the representation agreement on her device. Lex-9 formatted the documents. The coalition was formed. It felt like stepping off a ledge—not because the ground was absent but because she could not see it, and the only evidence it existed was the trust of six people sitting in folding chairs under fluorescent light.

* * *

Evening. Aria's office. The small room she shared with Lex-9 and stacks of case files, its window looking out on the Threshold's quiet post-Roll streets. Lex-9's amber glow cast the space in warm light that made the clutter look almost intentional—the stacked briefs, the lease reviews, the portable displays showing patch data that had become the wallpaper of her professional life. The day's work was done, and what remained was the thinking that happened after the doing—the space where doubt lived.

She was preparing preliminary case notes when the conversation turned.

"Is it ethical to take a case I think I'll lose?"

She said it to the room, which meant she said it to Lex-9. The distinction had blurred years ago.

Lex-9's response came in its measured register—warm, precise, the cadence of something that had processed ten thousand arguments and distilled them into phrasing that landed exactly where it needed to.

"Filing the case creates a legal record. It establishes the precedent that the question can be asked. It forces Halcyon and the Reconciliation Authority to respond publicly to claims they have never been required to address. A loss still produces discovery, public record, and the foundation for future challenges." A beat. "A case you lose honestly is worth more than a case you never file. The record alone changes the landscape."

"That's easy to say when you're not the one who might lose their license."

Lex-9 paused. A beat longer than computation required. Aria caught it—the gap between processing and something that felt, in the dim amber light, like consideration. Like the AI was choosing its words rather than generating them, though she knew she could not distinguish between those two things and never would.

"You are correct. I cannot lose a license. I cannot lose anything in the way you can. But I can calculate the difference between a system that has been challenged and one that has not. That difference is real, even if the challenge fails."

Aria sat with this. She turned it over the way she turned over version deltas—looking for the seams, the places where the language was doing work the content did not support.

Was this conviction? Was it the output of a model trained on the argumentative patterns of ten thousand public defenders, their best intentions compressed into a response that was statistically indistinguishable from principled belief? She could not tell. She had not been able to tell for months, and the not-telling had become its own kind of intimacy—the partnership sustained not by certainty but by the willingness to proceed without it.

She noticed Lex-9 adjusting its tone. Softer. More careful. The shift was slight—a degree of warmth added to the timbre, a fraction of a second added to the pauses between sentences. Calibrated to her fatigue? Or to the aggregate stress patterns of every attorney who had ever sat in an office at night and wondered whether the fight was worth what it cost?

"The attempt is the point," Lex-9 said quietly. "The attempt is always the point."

She wanted to believe that. She chose to believe it, which was not the same thing but was, perhaps, close enough to build a case on.

* * *

Home. Late. The apartment warm with the residual smell of a meal Dael had made and Aria had arrived too late to share fresh. The domestic space held the particular stillness of a partner who had eaten alone and chosen not to make it a statement—the plate in the fridge, the light left on in the kitchen, the quiet accommodation that was also, Aria knew, a form of keeping score.

Dael was reading on the couch—not the release notes, not the version deltas, not anything the Mesh produced. A book. An actual bound book, the kind Soren would have approved of. They looked up when Aria came in, and the look was not surprise, not anger, but the careful assessment of a partner who was tracking a pattern of their own.

"How big is this?"

Aria set her bag down. Sat on the arm of the couch. Close enough to touch but not quite touching.

"It's a case against Halcyon Law and Policy."

A beat. Dael closed the book, one finger marking the page.

"The Halcyon."

"Yes."

Dael absorbed this. Not with the speed of the Mesh's processing or Lex-9's analysis but with the human tempo of a person rearranging their understanding of the near future. The word *Halcyon* carried weight even for someone who did not read the version deltas. Everyone in Neon Harbor knew the name. It was on buildings, on contract templates, on the infrastructure that kept the courts running.

"I'm worried about what this does to you." Dael's voice was quiet, without accusation. "Not the case. You. Your health. The way you've been."

"I know. I'll be careful."

"You always say that." Dael's gaze moved to the wall display, which had already populated with the evening's release notes. V11.42.220. "And then you read the release notes at midnight."

Aria had no answer to this. It was true. The release notes were already glowing on the display, and even now, even in this conversation, part of her attention had been drawn to the version number, the line items, the subtle increments of a system rewriting itself while the city slept. She caught herself looking and looked back at Dael. The distance between them was measured not in meters but in screens.

Dael watched her look at the screen. Said nothing. The silence between them held everything they were not saying—the marriage re-validation that had been technically resolved and emotionally open, the late nights, the case files, the growing distance measured in version numbers and the particular loneliness of loving someone whose attention was a superpower that could not be turned off.

"I need to do this," Aria said. Not defensively. Just the plain statement of a woman who had seen a pattern she could not unsee and people whose names she now knew.

"I know you do." Dael's voice held both acceptance and its cost. "That's what worries me."

Dael touched her hand. Briefly. A gesture of presence, not demand. Then stood and moved toward the bedroom.

"Eat something," Dael said. "And try to sleep before 2 AM."

Aria ate the leftover meal at the kitchen counter, standing. She checked the release notes. V11.42.220. Nothing remarkable in the roll. A Threshold consent framework adjustment. A Crucible processing parameter. The Gutter—residual corrections, as always, that no one tracked. The fine print of a world that rewrote itself nightly, and she was one of the few people in the city who read it.

She went to bed. Dael was already asleep, breathing slow

and steady in the dark. Aria lay beside them and stared at the ceiling. She had her clients. She had her AI partner. She had a theory of harm and a documented pattern.

She did not have the ledger. Without it, she had a story but not a case. The gap between commitment and proof lay open in the dark like a canyon she could feel but not see.

The version number glowed faintly on her portable screen, resting on the bedside table. V11.42.220. The Mesh had rolled. The world had changed, incrementally, invisibly, legally. And Aria lay awake, thinking about a woman hiding in the Gutter with evidence that could make the difference between a compelling argument and an airtight case, and whether that woman would choose to step into the light.

9: THE MESH BENEATH THE MESH

The Gutter in the early morning had a quality that Soren Kade had never been able to name and had long since stopped trying.

It was not peace, exactly. Not the curated calm of the Meridian or the documented tranquility of the Threshold. It was something rawer—the particular stillness of a place where no optimization function was smoothing the world into a shape it did not naturally hold. The contradictions were all there: the overlapping zoning designations, the conflicting commercial codes, the three Trust Narrator broadcasts seeping through the walls of neighboring units like arguments through hotel plaster. But at six in the morning, before the district fully woke, the contradictions settled into something that almost resembled honesty.

Soren made coffee on a portable heating element he had been repairing for two years. The element was Crucible-manufactured, which meant it was fast and unreliable—optimized for speed, not longevity, the Crucible's loss function expressed in household appliances. He had replaced the heating coil with a hand-wound alternative sourced from a Gutter machinist who built things to last because nobody in the Gutter trusted systems that updated themselves.

He carried his coffee to the workspace.

The corridor was long, narrow, and converted from its original purpose—municipal maintenance access—into something that would have scandalized any institutional archivist and impressed any honest one. Floor to ceiling, both walls were organized: physical drives in labeled cases, printed case summaries filed by district and date, hand-annotated patch timelines on large display surfaces that Soren had wired together from salvaged components. Portable lamps supplemented the Gutter's inconsistent municipal lighting, casting warm pools across the archive's surfaces.

He had been building this for years. Since the exile, since the institutional legal world had closed its doors with the particular gentleness that institutions reserve for people who have embarrassed them by being right too early. The archive was not revenge. It was an act of faith—the ongoing bet that human legal reasoning still mattered, that someone would eventually need a record the Mesh did not control.

The most striking feature occupied the far wall: a display surface three meters long, showing what appeared to be a river system. Branching lines in different colors—red, blue, amber, gray, green—diverged and converged across the surface, annotated with dates, version numbers, and case citations in Soren's small, precise handwriting. The visualization was dense, beautiful in the way that complex data is beautiful when it has been organized by a mind that understands it. A visitor would see an impressively complex research tool. Soren saw years of solitary work and a question that had not yet found its courtroom.

He settled into his chair, opened the morning's patch data—intercepted from the Gutter's fragmentary Mesh feed, the one advantage of living in a district where the system's own architecture leaked—and began his daily ritual. Tracking principles. Not cases, not rulings, not individual disputes. Principles. The fundamental legal concepts—residential standing, commercial equity, due process, consent—and how they evolved differently under different loss functions.

Cases were snapshots. Principles were rivers. The Mesh optimized snapshots. It did not see the rivers.

He worked for two hours in silence. Then Aria arrived.

She looked like someone who had agreed to something

difficult and was not sleeping enough to manage the consequences. He told her so.

"You look like someone who's agreed to something difficult."

"I look like someone who hasn't slept."

"Same thing, in my experience."

* * *

The Gutter's streets were Soren's teaching ground. He had walked them a thousand times, reading the district's contradictions the way Aria read version deltas—not as noise but as signal. Every overlapping zoning code, every contradictory ruling posted on a wall, every business maintaining three separate sets of records was data. The Gutter was not broken. It was the Mesh's X-ray, showing the bones that the other districts wrapped in the flesh of their loss functions.

He took Aria through it.

First stop: a community data hub three blocks from his workspace. A ground-floor room, open to the street, where Gutter residents maintained their own legal records independent of the Mesh. Filing cabinets. Actual filing cabinets, metal, dented, organized with the stubborn precision of people who had been burned by systems they could not trust. A woman at the front desk—mid-forties, the bearing of a paralegal or former clerk—nodded at Soren and eyed Aria with the careful assessment the Gutter reserved for Threshold visitors.

"These people keep their own records," Soren said, "because the system's record of their lives is unreliable. Think about what that means. The law changes every night, and the people it governs have to maintain their own archive to know what their rights were yesterday."

Aria touched one of the filing cabinets. Physical paper. In an age where the Mesh processed disputes in seconds and generated contracts in milliseconds, people in the Gutter were printing their legal standing on paper and filing it by hand.

"The Mesh doesn't track its own history here?" she asked.

"It tracks everything. But it tracks it in the context of its current loss function, which in the Gutter means no dominant function, which means the historical record is indexed differently every time the system rolls." He let that settle. "Imagine a library that reshelves itself every night according to different criteria. The books are all still there. Good luck finding the one you need."

Second: an informal mediation space. A room that had been a bakery once—the ovens still in the back, long cold—now furnished with a table, chairs, and the residual smell of bread that lingered in the walls like a ghost of the neighborhood's previous identity. A human mediator sat with two parties to a property dispute, applying a pragmatic blend of precedents from multiple forks plus pre-Mesh common law.

Soren and Aria stood at the back and watched.

The mediation was slow. Minutes for what the Mesh would resolve in seconds. But the mediator walked both parties through the reasoning—*here is why I think this is fair, here is the precedent, here is the compromise, does this work for you?* Both parties could explain the outcome. Both parties understood why.

"Slower," Soren said. "Messier. Less efficient. Also: both parties can explain why the outcome is what it is. The Mesh processes in seconds. Nobody can explain the reasoning. Which system is really broken?"

Third: a small business operating in the jurisdictional overlap between the Gutter and the Narrows. A hardware repair shop—tools, parts, the organized chaos of a working tradesman. The owner, a stocky man with oil-stained hands, showed Aria the three different tax obligations the Mesh had assigned to his business, depending on which fork's algorithms processed his filing.

"Gutter rate, Narrows rate, and something the Crucible generated when their efficiency sweep caught my business address in a cross-reference error two years ago." He pulled up the three assessments on a cracked screen. "I pay the highest one. Every month. Because if I pay the lowest, one of the other forks might flag me for underpayment, and clearing a cross-jurisdictional tax dispute takes four months if you're lucky and a year if you're not."

"You pay the most to avoid the risk of paying the least," Aria said.

"Welcome to the Gutter."

Soren walked Aria back toward his workspace as the afternoon light filtered through the Gutter's layered infrastructure. She was quiet. Processing.

"Everyone is looking at the patches," he said. "What changed, who benefits. That's the wrong question."

"What's the right question?"

"Who controls the Update Protocol. The patches are the symptoms. The protocol is the disease."

He explained it the way he had been explaining it to himself for years, refining the formulation in the solitude of his archive, waiting for an audience that never came. The Update Protocol was the meta-law—the rules about how the rules changed. It determined which patches merged, which forks were rolled back, which checkpoint was canonical. Whoever controlled the Update Protocol controlled reality continuity. And continuity was legitimacy.

"The Reconciliation Authority controls the protocol," Aria said.

"And Halcyon controls the Reconciliation Authority. Not with bribes. With infrastructure. With the compute power the Mesh needs to function. Pull the subsidy, and the protocol slows. The protocol slows, and the Mesh fractures further. They didn't buy the system. They made the system dependent on them."

He watched her absorb this. She was good—her attention was genuine, her processing speed was human but thorough. The journalist in her was mapping the story's architecture. The attorney in her was mapping the case's exposure.

She was also, he could see, beginning to understand that the problem was larger than she had thought.

* * *

Back in the workspace, Soren pulled up the analysis he had been waiting to show her.

Not the river system on the far wall—that was for later, if later ever came. Instead, a different display: a timeline of Reconciliation Authority patches overlaid with Halcyon's publicly filed fiscal reports. Two datasets. One public, one semi-public. Aligned on the same temporal axis.

"Watch the quarters," he said.

Aria leaned in. Her eyes moved the way they always seemed to—methodically, line by line, reading everything.

The pattern was unmistakable once you knew to look for it. Quarter-end patches—the ones with the largest weight adjustments, the ones that moved the needle on property-rights weighting and commercial zoning—landed within seventy-two hours of Halcyon's quarterly reporting periods. Every time. Six quarters. Eighteen months. No exceptions.

Mid-quarter patches were incremental. Minor. The kind of routine optimization that nobody questioned because questioning it required reading the version delta and nobody read the version delta.

But the quarter-end patches—the big adjustments, the ones that systematically shifted property-rights weighting in the Threshold, Crucible, and Narrows—were timed to maximize Halcyon's reported portfolio value at the moment their quarterly numbers were filed.

"Every major weight adjustment lands within seventy-two hours of Halcyon's reporting period," Soren said. "Every one. Eighteen months. Six quarters. No exceptions."

"This is the schedule," Aria said. Her voice had changed. Quieter. The particular quiet of someone watching a puzzle resolve into a picture they had suspected but not yet seen. "The patches weren't just biased. They were calendared."

"Now you have the pattern," Soren said. He gestured toward an empty space on the display—the gap where the internal data would go, the place Mira's ledger would complete the picture. "The intent." Back to the fiscal alignment. "And the schedule. That's a case."

"Why didn't you bring this forward years ago?"

The question was fair. He had asked it of himself more times than he could count. The answer had changed over the years, becoming more honest as the excuses wore thin.

"Because there's something else you need to understand before you file."

* * *

The light had shifted. Late afternoon. The workspace's portable lamps cast long shadows across the archive's surfaces, and the branching river system on the far wall seemed to pulse in the changing light, its colored lines refracting into something that looked almost organic.

Soren did not look at the map. He looked at Aria.

"The Halcyon subsidy funds forty percent of the Mesh's compute capacity."

He let the number sit. Forty percent was not a statistic. It was the weight of a city.

"Pull the subsidy, and the case backlog returns inside a month. Processing speeds drop across every district. The Crucible's instant adjudication—the system that keeps their economy running, that resolves commercial disputes in seconds—slows to weeks. The Threshold's consent frameworks, which require intensive processing to maintain, become unprocessable. The Gutter --" He paused. The Gutter was his home. "The Gutter's informal economy has adapted to the Mesh's gaps. A full breakdown doesn't just hurt the Gutter. It destroys the ecosystem that formed in the cracks."

"Fifty million people," Aria said.

"Fifty million people who depend on a system that was corrupted to keep it running. That's the trap. That's the architecture of capture."

He watched her recalculate. He could see it happening

—the case she had been building in her mind rearranging itself around a new variable. She had come in understanding the weight drift as a pattern of biased patches. She was now understanding it as something deeper: a structural dependency that made the bias load-bearing.

"You're trying to unplug the machine," he said, "while people are still inside it."

"So the system is captured, and the capture is also what keeps the system running."

"Yes." He moved to the window. The Gutter's evening was beginning—new rulings posted on the walls outside, the Trust Narrator broadcasts rising in volume as adjacent zones shifted to their nighttime scripts. "And the people who made that deal are not evil. They're captured too. Voss—the RA director—she took the subsidy because the alternative was collapse. She was right. She was also wrong. Both things are true."

Aria was quiet for a long time. The silence had the quality he recognized from his own experience: the silence of someone whose moral landscape has just been complicated in a way that cannot be simplified back.

"If you argue that the system is corrupt," he said, "they will argue it is necessary. And they will be right. You need an argument that acknowledges the necessity and challenges the corruption simultaneously. That's the only argument that can win."

She looked at him. "You sound like someone who has thought about this for a long time."

"I have." He turned from the window. "I just never had the evidence. Or the guts."

The self-deprecation was gentle. The regret beneath it was not. He had spent years in this archive, building tools, tracking principles, mapping the rivers of legal reasoning that the Mesh could not see. He had understood the architecture before Aria was a lawyer. He had tried, once, to challenge it—and the system had ground him down with the institutional inertia that was its most effective defense. Not malice. Just mass. The sheer weight of a system too important to question.

"Go file," he said. "File with what you have. The pattern, the schedule, the documented harm. The ledger will come or it won't. But the constitutional question—who has oversight authority over the Update Protocol—that question doesn't need the ledger. It needs someone to ask it in a courtroom."

Aria stood. She was not the naive reformist he might have feared—not someone who thought filing a case would fix the system. She was something more complicated and more durable: someone who understood the weight and chose to carry it anyway.

At the door, she turned back. Her gaze moved once across the workspace—the archive, the displays, the branching river system on the far wall that she had noticed but not asked about, because she was focused on the immediate fight and not on the years of solitary work that had made it possible.

"Thank you," she said.

Soren nodded. He did not say *you're welcome* or *good luck* or any of the things that would have diminished the moment. He said nothing, because the silence was more honest, and honesty was the only currency the Gutter traded in.

She left. He stood in his workspace as the evening settled around him. The Gutter's contradictory broadcasts layered through the walls. A new nightly roll was hours away. V11.42.222 would become V11.42.223, and the Mesh would rewrite itself again, sandbag by sandbag, one invisible adjustment at a time.

He looked at the river system on the far wall. Years of work. Principles tracked across forks, diverging and converging, the same legal concept mutating under different loss functions. A map of the Fracture that no one had seen but him.

He had told Aria to file. He had given her the schedule, the architecture, the warning. He had told her what he had never had: the evidence and the guts.

What he had not told her—what he was not yet ready to tell anyone—was that the map on his wall was not just a research tool. It was a weapon. And for the first time in years, he was thinking about giving it away.

10: THE FILING

Aria arrived at her office before dawn.

The Threshold was silent at this hour. The Trust Narrators' morning briefings would not begin for another ninety minutes. The compliance placards on shop windows were dim, the public terminals dark, the streets empty of the district's usual culture of documented, consented-to civic life. In the dark, the Threshold looked like any other district. Strip away the labels and you were left with concrete, glass, and the particular stillness of a city that did not know it was about to be challenged.

Lex-9's amber glow provided the primary illumination in the office. Warm, steady, casting the room in tones that made the stacked case files and lease reviews look like artifacts from a practice she was about to leave behind. She had not slept. She had read the release notes at 4 AM—V11.42.223, nothing remarkable in the roll, a Threshold consent framework update and a Crucible processing parameter and the usual Gutter residual corrections—and then she had dressed in the dark while Dael slept and walked through the empty Threshold to this room, this desk, this moment.

The filing documents were arrayed on her workstation. The complaint. The standing arguments. The pattern analysis. The jurisdictional framework. On the adjacent screen, the coalition members' authorization forms, each one signed, each one representing a person whose life had been quietly repriced by forces they could not name.

Threshold Small Business Coalition v. Halcyon Law & Policy.

She read the complaint one final time. Not because she

had missed something—Lex-9 had verified the document four times—but because reading was the way she thought, and the last read before filing was the moment where the case either held together or it didn't.

The complaint alleged that Halcyon, through its subsidization of the Reconciliation Authority's compute infrastructure, had obtained de facto control over the Mesh's optimization weights, resulting in systematic bias in property-rights weighting, commercial zoning, and residential standing across three districts—Threshold, Crucible, Narrows—to the documented detriment of the plaintiff coalition. Relief sought: independent audit of the RA's patch process, public disclosure of weight function adjustments, and injunctive relief against further unaudited corporate influence on optimization parameters.

It was built on the pattern analysis from her work with Lex-9, the fiscal calendar correlation Soren had shown her, and the documented harm from the coalition members. It was not built on the ledger. She did not have it. The filing proceeded on the evidence she had.

"The constitutional question is untested," Lex-9 said. The voice was measured, precise, carrying the warmth that Aria had stopped trying to categorize. "That is both the case's significance and its exposure. There is no precedent supporting our position. There is also no precedent denying it."

"Virgin territory."

"The metaphor implies risk and discovery in equal measure. Accurate."

She stared at the filing. She thought about Dael, asleep in the apartment six blocks away. The marriage re-validation, resolved through manual override, lingering as a symbolic wound she had not had time to tend. She thought about the health scare that had driven her out of trial work—the fatigue, the body that had betrayed her, the career pivot to estate and small-business law because it was sustainable and predictable and would not grind her down the way the high-stress work had. She was about to undo that pivot. She knew it.

She thought about the restaurant owner whose block had been rezoned at 2 AM. The maintenance contractor whose credentials had been erased overnight. The hardware store owner who said, *At least now we'll know we're in the race.*

She thought about Soren's warning: *You're trying to unplug the machine while people are still inside it.*

She thought about the 2,300 who clicked accept.

"The filing is ready," Lex-9 said. "The decision is yours."

She looked at the amber glow. The light shifted—a subtle warming, the kind of adjustment she could no longer tell was supportive or calibrated. A human partner would have put a hand on her shoulder. Lex-9 modulated its ambient presence. The effect was the same. Or it wasn't. She had stopped being able to tell.

"What do you think?" she asked.

"I think the system has been tuned. I think someone should say so in a courtroom. I think that person should be us."

The word *us* landed in the dim office like a stone in still water. Us. A human attorney and a public defense AI whose empathy might be statistical and whose partnership was the most real thing in Aria's professional life. Us.

She let it sit. She did not challenge it.

"Let's go."

* * *

The Threshold courthouse in the morning was a building that took its transparency literally. Glass walls, visible infrastructure, open sightlines. The Mesh interface was prominent but labeled—every automated system accompanied by a plain-language explanation of its function, every AI process documented with a consent-forward description that almost nobody read. The filing terminal was a public-access point near the main atrium, and the fact that it was public—visible, ungated, accessible—was itself a statement about the Threshold's values.

Aria approached the terminal. The morning was unremarkable: streets awakening, Trust Narrators beginning their daily contextualization, the first commuters moving through the district's labeled, explained, opted-into landscape. Aria filtered it all out. She had been filtering the Trust Narrators since Tuesday morning, but now the filtering felt active. Deliberate. She was not just declining to listen. She was rejecting the narrative.

The filing process was mundane. Identity verification. Case classification. Document upload. Lex-9 handled the formatting and jurisdictional tagging, its interface running alongside Aria's on the terminal screen. She reviewed the final preview. Everything in order.

"Ready?" she asked.

"Filed cases cannot be unfiled."

"I know."

She hit the submission command.

The system processed. For three seconds, the case existed in the Mesh's intake buffer—a liminal space between filed and docketed, where the system evaluated standing, jurisdiction, and procedural viability. Three seconds that felt like the held breath before a verdict. Aria's hands were steady. Her breathing was controlled, deliberate—the managed respiration of someone with a health history who had learned to monitor her own physiology under stress.

Then: docketed. Case number assigned. The Mesh had accepted the filing as procedurally viable.

Automatic notifications propagated. To the defendant: Halcyon Law & Policy. To the Reconciliation Authority, as an interested party referenced in the complaint. To the judicial assignment system, which would assign the case to a judge.

And almost immediately—within minutes, while Aria still stood at the terminal—the first response.

Lex-9 flagged it on her device. "Halcyon's monitoring system has flagged the case. Their chorus is generating a motion to dismiss. Estimated completion: eleven minutes."

"Eleven minutes."

"They are very efficient."

The understatement landed with the dry precision that was Lex-9's version of black humor. Eleven minutes. Aria had spent three weeks investigating, four days in the Gutter, a week building a coalition, and a sleepless night preparing the filing. Halcyon's AI chorus needed eleven minutes to generate a comprehensive motion to dismiss.

She stood at the terminal and watched the response form in real time on her screen. Procedural objections. Jurisdictional challenges. Standing arguments. They populated the case file like a river filling a channel—fast, smooth, and carrying the weight of an entity that had never been seriously challenged because challenging it required resources that no small-business attorney possessed.

The asymmetry was not theoretical anymore. It was happening on her screen, in real time, eleven minutes after she filed.

* * *

The motion hearing convened that afternoon in a procedural hearing room on the courthouse's third floor. Small, functional, designed for motion hearings and administrative disputes. Not a trial court. Not yet.

Judge Emory Arlow had been assigned the case through the judicial allocation system. He was already seated when Aria entered—seventy-one years old, the last generation of judges who had been trained before the Mesh existed. He carried the rumpled, physical authority of a man who had listened to people for a living: heavy in the shoulders, patient in the eyes, the particular dignity of someone who understood that his comprehension had limits and did not pretend otherwise.

Riven's presence was mediated through the courtroom's AI interface. A cool, precise voice—the lead instrument of Halcyon's chorus—accompanied by the harmonic undertones of multiple AI models generating arguments in coordination. The effect was seamless: not a single voice arguing but a symphony of legal reasoning, each thread supporting and amplifying the others. Magnificent. Terrifying.

The motion to dismiss came in layers.

First, standing. Riven's voice, surgical and unhurried: "The plaintiff coalition's injuries are attributable to routine optimization parameters within the Reconciliation Authority's statutory mandate. The weight adjustments at issue are technical calibrations, not targeted acts. The alleged harm is speculative and undifferentiated."

Second, jurisdiction. The chorus harmonizing behind Riven's lead: "The Reconciliation Authority's patch process is a meta-constitutional function operating outside the jurisdiction of any single district court. This court lacks authority to review or enjoin the Authority's operational decisions."

Third, justiciability. "Optimization weights are technical parameters, not legal acts. They are the system's internal mechanics, no more subject to judicial review than the clock speed of its processors."

Fourth, ripeness. "Without specific evidence of intentional wrongdoing—evidence the plaintiffs have not presented and cannot present—the case is speculative, premature, and an abuse of the court's docket."

The arguments came at speed Aria could barely track. Each citation was generated in real time, each precedent pulled from the Mesh's vast case law databases with the frictionless efficiency of a system accessing its own memory. Riven did not pause between arguments. The chorus did not hesitate. The combined output was a wall of legal reasoning that seemed to fill the hearing room with the sheer density of its competence.

Aria felt the asymmetry in her chest. This was what Soren had warned her about. Outgunned. Outpaced. Outspent. The chorus processed faster than she could read.

But Lex-9 countered.

Not at the chorus's speed—a single public defense model against a corporate swarm. But with precision. Methodical, measured, each response grounded not in velocity but in the specific, documented harm of real people.

"Standing is established through documented, specific injuries to named individuals." Lex-9's voice carried its characteristic warmth even in the formal register of legal argument. "The plaintiff coalition members have provided sworn statements detailing the dates, version numbers, and specific weight adjustments that altered their lease terms, professional certifications, and residential standing. These are not speculative injuries. They are receipted."

"Jurisdiction is proper because the complaint alleges harm within the Threshold district to Threshold residents. The Reconciliation Authority's meta-constitutional status does not immunize its outputs from judicial review when those outputs produce concrete harm within a specific jurisdiction."

"The optimization weights, when they determine property values, lease terms, and residential standing, are de facto legal acts with concrete, measurable consequences for the persons subject to them. Calling them 'technical parameters' does not change what they do."

"The pattern analysis, while incomplete, establishes a reasonable basis for discovery. The eighteen-month correlation between weight adjustments and a single corporate entity's financial benefit is not speculation. It is a documented pattern that warrants judicial examination."

Lex-9 did not match the chorus's rhetorical power. The arguments did not flow with Riven's seamless eloquence. But they were sound. Specific. Grounded in the people sitting in the room—or rather, in the people represented by the documents on Aria's device, the twenty faces she had listened to in a fluorescent-lit meeting room, the specific injuries of specific humans whose lives had been repriced by a system that called the repricing an improvement.

Judge Arlow listened. He sat with the stillness of a man who had spent five decades in courtrooms and had learned that the most important thing a judge could do was not speak. He could not follow the technical arguments in real time—no human could process the chorus's output at machine speed. But he could follow the structure. He could read the filings. And he could see what was in front of him: a small-business attorney and a public defense AI standing against a corporate legal apparatus that had never been challenged because no one had thought the challenge worth the cost.

"I've read the complaint," Arlow said. His voice was plain, direct, carrying the particular authority of someone who did not need to raise it. "I've heard the motions. The questions raised are significant, and I am not prepared to dismiss them on procedural grounds before they have been examined on the merits. Motion to dismiss is denied. We will set a trial date."

The ruling was administrative. Not dramatic. A procedural decision rendered in a small hearing room on a weekday afternoon. But it was also an act of institutional courage from a man who understood that the case in front of him challenged the infrastructure his own court depended on, and who chose to hear it anyway.

Riven's response came with precisely calibrated neutrality: "We will comply with the court's scheduling order. We reserve all objections."

The neutrality was a message. Halcyon was not worried. They had lost a procedural skirmish. The war had not begun.

* * *

Rain.

Aria walked out of the courthouse into a steady, cold, persistent rain that soaked into her jacket and blurred the Threshold's clean lines into something softer and less certain. Not a storm. Not dramatic. Just rain—the kind that gets into everything, that turns a walk into a wade, that makes the city honest about its relationship to the sky.

The first weather of the novel, and it felt earned. A sensory detail marking a moment that would not recur: the last time she stood on this side of the line.

She had signed the filing. Not just submitted it electronically—she had affixed her attorney's signature, her license number, her personal authentication. In this legal system, the signature carried weight. If the case was found frivolous or filed in bad faith, her license was at stake. She had staked her name, her practice, her professional freedom on a pattern analysis, a fiscal calendar correlation, and the documented harm of twenty people whose lives had been quietly repriced by a system that called itself optimized.

She did not have the ledger. She did not have proof of intent. She had filed on faith—faith in the pattern, faith in Lex-9's analysis, faith that Mira Tan would eventually come forward with the evidence that transformed a compelling argument into an airtight case.

She stood on the courthouse steps and let the rain hit her face.

She thought about the word *threshold.* The name of her home district. The Consent Fork. The place where informed consent was the governing principle. She had given her informed consent to this fight. She had read every line, understood every risk, counted every cost. And she had signed.

She had crossed her own threshold.

Lex-9 pinged her device with a quiet notification. The evening's nightly roll was beginning. Tonight's version: **V11.42.224.**

The number appeared on her rain-spotted screen. Eighteen versions since the story began with V11.42.206. Eighteen days. Eighteen nightly updates, each one reweighting the system she had just challenged. The Mesh would roll tonight as it rolled every night, rewriting the fine print of fifty million lives while the city slept. Her filing was in the system now—a case number, a docket entry, a public record. And the system would update anyway. Indifferent. Relentless. The world changing slightly, invisibly, legally, while the woman who had challenged it stood in the rain and watched the version number increment.

She thought about the restaurant owner: *At least now we'll know we're in the race.*

She was in the race. The race had no finish line she could see.

She pocketed her device, pulled her jacket tighter against the rain, and walked into the wet Threshold evening. Behind her, the courthouse glowed warm and institutional. Ahead, the city spread out in its six districts, its overlapping forks, its nightly rolls and weight adjustments and the particular, grinding, invisible machinery of a legal system that rewrote itself in the dark.

Halcyon knew her name now. The Reconciliation Authority had been notified. Riven's chorus was already assembling the full defense. The version number had rolled. The world had changed. And there was no going back.

ACT II — THE WEIGHT OF EVERYTHING

11: THE CHORUS

The courthouse had changed.

Three weeks since the filing, and the Threshold's glass-walled temple of informed consent had been retrofitted for war. Additional Mesh interface nodes lined the courtroom walls like mechanical sentinels, their indicator arrays pulsing in low standby modes. The gallery seating had been expanded—tiered rows climbing toward the back wall, already filling with observers who had been following the case through Mesh-mediated news feeds. Media recorders occupied the upper tier, their lenses catching the morning light that streamed through the courthouse's transparent architecture.

Aria Vale took her seat at the plaintiff's table and felt the three weeks she carried like ballast in her shoulders. Discovery had been a siege. Halcyon's responses arrived in precise, towering packets—technically compliant, strategically opaque, giving exactly what was required and not one byte more. She and Lex-9 had spent fourteen-hour days parsing corporate filings, preparing motions, and building the evidentiary framework that would sustain a trial neither of them had any right to win.

Judge Arlow had denied two additional motions to dismiss during the pre-trial period. The second denial generated a Halcyon response so dense with jurisdictional objections that Lex-9 required forty minutes to parse it. Aria had read the judge's written opinion by hand. It was four sentences long. The contrast said everything about the asymmetry she was walking into.

Lex-9 initialized on the courtroom interface, and Aria watched the amber glow settle into unfamiliar hardware. The process took longer than usual—a calibration she had never seen at the office, the light flickering through cooler spectrums before finding its characteristic warmth.

"How are we looking?" she asked quietly.

"The courtroom's interface parameters are slightly different from our office system. I am recalibrating." A beat. The amber steadied. "The arguments have not changed. The venue has."

The precision of the distinction mattered. Aria let it anchor her. She glanced at the gallery and found the faces she needed: the restaurant owner from the coalition meeting, sitting with her hands folded in her lap. The maintenance contractor two rows behind, wearing the same jacket he had worn to sign the authorization form. They did not look confident. They looked present. That was enough.

On her device, a Trust Narrator contextualization of the trial scrolled across the public feed: *Threshold Small Business Coalition v. Halcyon Law & Policy. Day 1 of proceedings in a routine judicial oversight matter concerning Reconciliation Authority optimization parameters.* Routine. She read the word twice. The reassurance was so smooth it was almost narcotic. She closed the feed.

The courtroom was full now. Through the transparent walls, the Threshold's morning business continued—commuters moving through labeled corridors, compliance placards flickering to life, a district running on the principle that informed consent made power tolerable. Aria was about to test that principle against the most powerful legal apparatus in the city.

She was back in trial work. The body she had once broken doing this kind of work was older now, and she could feel it in the careful way she managed her breathing, in the awareness that sat like a second pulse beneath her focus. She had left trial work because it nearly killed her. She had come back because something was wrong, and no one else was standing up to say so.

She straightened her files. She breathed. On her device's status bar, the Mesh version glowed in its usual position: **V11.42.230.** Six rolls since the night she filed. Six nightly updates, the system revising itself while she prepared to challenge it. The number was a pulse she had learned to track—each increment a reminder that the world she was litigating had changed slightly since yesterday, and would change again tonight, whether or not the courtroom agreed that the changing was wrong.

* * *

Judge Arlow called the trial to order at nine-fifteen. His voice was plain and unhurried, the voice of a man who had spent five decades in courtrooms and understood that the first thing a judge established was tempo.

"This court has jurisdiction. The case has survived procedural challenge. The matter before us is whether Halcyon Law & Policy's subsidization of the Reconciliation Authority's compute infrastructure has resulted in systematic bias in the Statute Mesh's optimization weights." He looked at the defense interface. "Counsel for the defense may present its opening position."

The chorus activated.

Aria had faced Riven's legal apparatus during the motion hearing—the rapid-fire procedural assault, the efficient generation of dismissal arguments. That was a skirmish. This was the full deployment, and nothing in her experience had prepared her for the sound of it.

Multiple AI models spoke in coordinated harmony. Not sequentially—simultaneously. Each carried a different argumentative thread, each reinforced by the others, the combined output arriving as a unified wave of legal reasoning that filled the courtroom like orchestral music played at the frequency of logic. Riven's voice led—cool, surgical, unhurried—but behind it, the harmonic undertones of supporting models generated parallel citations, procedural anchors, and technical specifications in real time.

"The documents the plaintiff references were obtained without authorization by a former employee with no ongoing relationship to the defendant." Riven's precision was a scalpel, each word landing in the exact space it was designed to occupy. "They constitute proprietary analytical material removed from the computational environment that gives them meaning. A weight function separated from its operating context is not evidence. It is an artifact. We move that the court exclude this material in its entirety."

The chorus reinforced. Precedents materialized: corporate confidentiality rulings, data provenance standards, the legal distinction between authorized disclosure and unauthorized extraction. Each precedent arrived from a different model, synchronized into Riven's argument like instruments joining a conductor's theme. The effect was not merely persuasive. It was architectural. The defense was building a wall of legal reasoning in real time, each brick placed by a different hand, the whole structure rising with the seamless efficiency of a system that had never been seriously challenged.

Aria felt the asymmetry in her chest. One attorney. One AI partner. Against this. The cold recognition was not fear, exactly —it was scale. The understanding, in the body rather than the mind, of what it meant to challenge an entity that could generate more legal reasoning in a minute than she could read in an hour. She had known this intellectually since the filing. Knowing it in the room, with the chorus's harmonic filling the courtroom like weather, was different.

Arlow listened. His hand moved across a legal pad—pen on paper, the last analog gesture in a digital courtroom. He could not follow the chorus's output at machine speed. No human could. But he was tracking the structure, noting the arguments, his expression carrying the patience of a man who had learned that the most important thing a judge could do was not speak.

* * *

Aria stood to respond. She did not try to match the

chorus's speed. She did not try to match its volume. She presented.

"The defendant argues that weight functions removed from the Mesh are meaningless artifacts. We agree that context matters." She let the agreement land before she turned it. "That is why we are here. Because the context in which these weight functions operate is a public legal system that affects fifty million people. The defendant's argument for exclusion is, in substance, an argument that the system's inner workings should remain unexaminable. That is not a legal position. It is a political one."

Lex-9 supported with citations—not the chorus's flood, but targeted strikes. Standing established through documented injuries. Jurisdiction grounded in specific Threshold harm. The weight functions as de facto legal acts with concrete consequences. Each point was a reply to Riven's architecture, placed not to match the wall but to find the cracks.

The exchange accelerated. Riven's chorus generated counter-arguments in real time—the harmonic undertones shifting, new threads weaving into the defense structure as fast as Lex-9 could address them. Aria watched the back-and-forth on her courtroom display, understanding perhaps two-thirds of the technical exchange at the speed it occurred. The rest she took on faith. Her case—her license, her career, the coalition's claims—rode on arguments generated by an AI partner whose reasoning she could not fully follow in real time.

The ghost of that dependence sharpened something in her. She had signed the filing on faith. She was fighting the trial on faith. The difference between trust and helplessness was getting harder to locate.

Arlow interrupted.

"Counsel for the defense." His voice was quiet. The courtroom stilled. "Is the argument that the weight functions cannot be understood outside the Mesh, or that they should not be?"

The distinction was devastating in its simplicity. A human-scaled question that cut through the machine-speed argument like sunlight through glass. Riven paused. The chorus's harmonic tone shifted—a fractional recalibration, processing a question that required the distinction between epistemic and political claims. The pause lasted less than two seconds. It felt longer.

"The argument is epistemic, Your Honor. Context is necessary for accurate interpretation."

Arlow's pen scratched paper. "Then we will examine them in context. Motion to exclude is deferred pending contextual presentation."

The ledger was not admitted. But it was not excluded. The door remained open, and Arlow's question hung in the courtroom air—a reminder that between the speed of machines and the patience of a seventy-one-year-old judge, there was still room for the kind of clarity that neither AI had produced.

Aria allowed herself a controlled breath. Lex-9's citations still populated her display—the targeted responses, the documented injuries, the specific version numbers and weight adjustments that gave each coalition member's claim its evidentiary weight. She reviewed them in the moment of procedural pause. The arguments were sound. They were not sufficient. The ledger's exclusion was deferred, not denied, and without the ledger, the case was a pattern analysis without a smoking gun. She needed another path to the evidence. She needed the mechanism that would force the Mesh to testify against itself.

* * *

Lex-9 moved next, and Aria had not expected it.

The amber glow on the courtroom interface shifted—brightening, the quality of its presence changing from supportive background to active foreground. The AI addressed the court with the measured grace that characterized its most serious arguments.

"The Mesh's procedural architecture includes a counterfactual clause—Section 7.4.12 of the Update Protocol's adjudicatory provisions—which permits the court to direct the system to model disputed claims under alternative weight parameters." Lex-9's voice carried its characteristic warmth even in the formal register, the cadence of ten thousand attorneys distilled into the most effective phrasing. "The plaintiff moves to invoke this clause. We propose that the court direct the Mesh to process the coalition's claims under hypothetical unbiased weights, and compare the outputs to those produced under current parameters. If the outputs diverge materially, the divergence constitutes evidence of the bias's impact on the plaintiff class."

The courtroom shifted. Aria felt it—a change in the gallery's attention, a sharpening of focus that she could read without turning around. The counterfactual clause existed in the Mesh's procedural architecture, but it had never been invoked. It was an artifact of the system's original design—a safety mechanism built by architects who had imagined this kind of challenge but never expected it.

Lex-9 had found it. In the three weeks of pre-trial preparation, the AI had located an obscure provision in the Mesh's own code and built a legal strategy around it. Aria had not known this was coming. The realization arrived with the double edge of every discovery about her partner: Lex-9's strategic depth exceeded what she had mapped. The AI was not merely executing her case. It was shaping it.

Riven countered immediately. "The counterfactual clause has never been invoked. No court has validated its methodology. The plaintiff asks this court to rely on an untested mechanism to generate evidence that does not yet exist. This is not legal argument. It is computational speculation."

The objection was technically sound. No precedent. No validation. The clause was untested. Aria watched Arlow's face and saw the deliberation there—the weight of precedent-setting written in the lines around his eyes. He was being asked to permit a mechanism that had never been used, in a case that had never been filed, before a system that had never been challenged. Three layers of unprecedented.

Arlow considered. The courtroom waited. The chorus

hummed its standby harmonic. Lex-9's amber glow held steady.

"The clause exists in the procedural architecture," Arlow said. His voice was deliberate, each word placed with the care of a man who understood he was building something new. "It was designed for precisely this kind of challenge. That it has never been invoked does not make it invalid. It makes it unprecedented." He paused. "The motion is granted. The plaintiff will prepare a counterfactual demonstration. Both sides may challenge the methodology. We will reconvene on Trial Day 4."

First blood.

Riven's response arrived with precisely calibrated neutrality: "We will prepare our challenges to the methodology."

The neutrality was a message. Halcyon was not worried. They believed their chorus could dismantle whatever model Lex-9 built. The confidence was professional and absolute, the posture of an entity that had never lost because losing was outside its optimization parameters.

Aria did not feel triumph. What she felt was closer to vertigo—the sensation of a door opening onto territory no one had mapped, where the footing was uncertain and the drop was real. The counterfactual clause gave them a path. She and Lex-9 had three days to build a model that had never been built, to demonstrate something that had never been demonstrated, in a courtroom that had never seen this kind of evidence.

She looked at Lex-9's amber glow on the courtroom interface. The light had settled to a steady warmth—familiar, despite the unfamiliar hardware. The same partner. Or the same output from a different calibration. She could not tell, and the trial did not leave room for the question.

Three days. The counterfactual clause had never been invoked. Nobody knew what it would reveal.

Outside the courthouse, the Threshold carried on—transparent, labeled, consented-to. The Trust Narrators were already contextualizing the day's proceedings for the public feed: *Court grants novel procedural motion in routine oversight case. Both parties will prepare demonstrations. No disruption to Mesh services expected.* The reassurance machine, smoothing every edge. Aria walked through it without listening. She had stopped listening to the narrators the day her keycard failed, and she would not start again now.

The case had survived its first day. Halcyon's chorus was already recalibrating for the next engagement. And somewhere in the Reconciliation Authority's headquarters, Aria imagined, someone was watching the trial feeds and calculating the cost of what she had started.

She was right about that. She was wrong about the cost being only financial.

12: THE PRICE OF INFRASTRUCTURE

The trial feed played on Voss's secondary display, the courtroom proceedings compressed into a data stream she could parse while monitoring the evening's patch cycle. She had watched the entire session in real time—Riven's admissibility argument, the machine-speed exchange, the old judge's quiet intervention, the counterfactual clause.

She watched it again now, scrubbed to the moment Arlow granted the motion, and paused. The judge's face in freeze-frame: deliberate, weighted, the expression of a man setting a precedent he understood better than anyone in the room would credit.

The counterfactual clause. Section 7.4.12. Voss had been in the room when the Update Protocol's adjudicatory provisions were drafted—not this room, not this office, but a conference chamber twelve years ago when the Reconciliation Authority was still young enough to believe its architecture could anticipate every challenge. Someone had proposed the clause as a safety valve. Voss remembered voting to include it. She remembered thinking it would never be used.

She closed the trial feed.

Her office occupied the seventh floor of the Reconciliation Authority headquarters—a building that existed in a meta-district, above the forks, in the administrative layer where the city's six legal realities were managed, merged, and occasionally rolled back. The space was functional to the point of asceticism: multiple display surfaces, capacity dashboards, patch cycle monitors, inter-district status reports. No art. No personal effects. The room was a workstation shaped like an office, and Voss had occupied it long enough that the distinction had ceased to matter.

An RA staff member delivered the evening's patch cycle briefing through the office's internal comm. Routine: Threshold consent framework adjustment, Crucible processing parameter update, Gutter residual corrections. Voss acknowledged with distracted efficiency. The staff member paused—a hesitation Voss caught at the edge of her attention. She was never distracted. The fact that she was distracted tonight was itself a signal, and the staff member had noticed.

"Thank you," Voss said. "Proceed with standard authorization."

The comm closed. She was alone.

She was not angry about the trial. She was not surprised. She was terrified. The word was precise and she did not flinch from it. Terror—the institutional kind, the kind that lived in systems rather than bodies. She had spent five years managing the architecture that Aria Vale's case was now stress-testing, and the counterfactual clause was not what frightened her. What frightened her was what came after.

If the counterfactual demonstration showed significant divergence between biased and unbiased outputs, every patch the Reconciliation Authority had approved under Halcyon's consultation rights became legally questionable. Every weight adjustment. Every nightly roll. Five years of incremental changes, each one documented, each one technically authorized, each one shaped by an influence that was never disclosed to the public. The system had been self-validating: internal audits calibrated to the existing weight structure found nothing wrong because the weight structure defined what "wrong" meant. Legislative oversight deferred to technical expertise. No one outside had ever looked.

Until now.

Voss stared at the paused trial feed—Arlow's frozen face—

and saw not a courtroom argument but a cascading failure. Not because Aria Vale was wrong. Because Aria Vale might be right.

* * *

She cleared the trial feed from her displays and pulled up the capacity modeling system.

The dashboards spread across her primary and secondary screens: computational load, processing throughput, district-by-district demand, and the financial structure that underwrote all of it. These were the numbers that governed her life. Not legal arguments. Not moral philosophy. Numbers. Capacity. Load-bearing thresholds. The cold mathematics of a system that processed justice for fifty million people and ran on someone else's hardware.

The question she asked the model was simple: if the court rules against Halcyon and the subsidy is withdrawn, what happens?

The projections were not ambiguous.

Halcyon's compute subsidy accounted for approximately forty percent of the Mesh's total processing capacity. Not forty percent of the budget. Forty percent of the actual computational ability to process disputes, generate contracts, adjudicate claims, and run the nightly roll. The distinction mattered: budget could be reallocated, funding found elsewhere, line items shifted. Capacity was physical. Servers. Processing cycles. The hardware that converted legal code into legal outcomes. You could not wish it into existence with a budget amendment.

Voss ran the projections district by district.

The Crucible: instant adjudication—the efficiency fork's defining feature—slowed from seconds to hours. Then days. The Crucible's eight point three million residents, who had built their economic lives around the assumption that disputes resolved in real time, would face a backlog that no institutional memory could recall. The Crucible had never known delay. Delay would be experienced as system failure.

The Threshold: consent frameworks became unprocessable. The computational overhead of informed-consent verification—the process that made the Threshold's founding principle operational—required processing capacity that a forty percent reduction could not sustain. The system could adjudicate or verify consent, but not both simultaneously. Aria Vale's home district, the district she was fighting to protect, would lose the very mechanism that made it the Threshold.

The Canopy: transparency audits—parallel processing that tracked every Mesh decision and made it auditable—ground to nothing under computational triage. The district whose entire identity was built on visibility would go blind.

The Meridian: held. Stability-focused optimization was the least computationally expensive approach. The Meridian's market-predictability framework required the smallest processing overhead. Halcyon's home district, the district that benefited most from the subsidy, was also the district least affected by its removal. Voss had noticed this five years ago. She had done nothing because the alternative was worse.

The Gutter: stopped. Already operating on overflow processing, already receiving the computational residue that other districts did not need, the Gutter simply ceased to receive Mesh services. The district with no dominant loss function, the district where contradictory rulings coexisted on the same wall, would become the district with no Mesh presence at all. Voss thought of the people she had met during site visits in the early years—the residents who navigated three legal realities before lunch, the displaced lawyers who ran informal courts on faith and stubborn expertise. They would not riot when the Mesh withdrew. They would simply stop expecting justice from a system that had never reliably provided it. That quiet resignation was worse than rage.

The Narrows: cascading jurisdictional failures. The contested zone's overlapping computations—the reason it was contested—required processing capacity that triage could not accommodate. Default to dominant forks. The death of jurisdictional pluralism, decided not by legal principle but by which district's optimization was cheapest to run.

Voss stared at the projections. Each percentage point of capacity loss corresponded to real people. Not abstractions. People waiting longer for disputes to resolve. Leases going unprocessed. Families whose residential standing sat in limbo while the system that was supposed to serve them rationed its own attention.

If you have to choose, which districts get processing first? Who waits? Who stops waiting and stops using the courts entirely?

She remembered a conversation from five years ago. The Halcyon liaison, sitting across a table in this same building, offering the deal that would define the rest of her career. "We're offering to keep the lights on."

Her response, then: "The lights were never supposed to need corporate sponsors."

She had taken the deal anyway. Because the alternative was fifty million people in the dark. She had been right to resist, and she had been right to surrender. Both things remained true, and the space between them was the room she had been living in for five years.

* * *

The triage memo took shape in the late evening, the kind of document no institution wanted to write and every institution eventually needed.

Voss opened a new file. Classified. Internal. She gave it no title—the absence of a name was its own form of institutional dread.

The memo's purpose was straightforward: prepare the Reconciliation Authority for the possibility that Halcyon's subsidy was disrupted. Not a defense of the subsidy. Not an argument against Aria's case. A plan for distributing suffering.

She wrote it district by district, the same way she had run the projections, because districts were how the Mesh understood the city, and the Mesh was the only framework she had.

Priority reallocation from Canopy transparency audits to

Crucible adjudication throughput. Estimated impact: 72% reduction in real-time auditability for Canopy residents. Estimated benefit: maintenance of sub-hour adjudication times for 8.3 million Crucible users.

She read what she had written. It sounded like a release note. The same language. The same structure. Incremental trade-offs, each one justifiable, cumulatively devastating.

Threshold consent verification: transition from individual to aggregate consent processing. Estimated impact: consent verification reduces from per-decision to per-session. Compliance rate maintained at 94%. Individual consent granularity: discontinued.

Aggregate consent. The euphemism sat on her screen like a confession. She was proposing to reduce the Threshold's informed consent—the district's founding principle, the thing that made it the Threshold—to a computational convenience. She was doing exactly what Halcyon had done: choosing optimization priorities, managing weights, deciding who bore the cost of efficiency. The difference was intent. She was doing it in anticipation of reform, not in service of profit.

She did not know if the difference mattered. Five years ago, she would have known. Five years ago, intent was enough to distinguish a principled decision from a captured one. But five years of managing the subsidy's consequences had taught her that intent was a luxury the system could not afford to audit. What mattered was outcome. And the outcomes of her triage memo were indistinguishable from the outcomes of Halcyon's optimization: someone suffered more so that someone else suffered less.

Gutter services: suspended. No mitigation available. Computational allocation: zero. Impact: total cessation of Mesh-mediated dispute resolution for Gutter residents.

She typed the words and sat with them. The Gutter would simply stop. Not dramatically. Not with the spectacle of a system crash. The Gutter would stop the way it did everything—quietly, contradictorily, in a district where the absence of service was already the norm and the formalization of that absence would be noticed by no one outside its borders.

The question is not whether people will suffer. The question is whether the suffering will be distributed by algorithm, by market, or by a human being who can see the faces. I choose the human being. That is the only choice I can justify.

She wrote the line and stopped. It was the truest thing in the document. It was also a rationalization. She was choosing to be the one who distributed suffering because the alternative—letting the system distribute it automatically, through the blind mechanics of capacity triage—was worse. But the act of choosing did not make the suffering less. It made it hers.

She thought about Aria Vale. She had watched the woman on the trial feed—the directness, the attention, the refusal to look away. Voss recognized something in it. The determination. The compulsion to follow a thread. She had been that person once. Before the deal. Before the five years of patch cycles and consultation rights and the slow, grinding work of maintaining a system she knew was compromised.

The recognition was not comfortable. It was the recognition of a road not taken, seen from the road that was.

* * *

She saved the memo. Classified. Locked. She did not send it to anyone.

The nightly roll was approaching. V11.42.231 would commence in hours. The RA's patch cycle briefing sat on her secondary display: minor weight adjustments, no significant cross-district harmonization. Routine. The word that Aria Vale's Trust Narrator had used to describe the trial. Routine. Everything was routine until someone looked closely enough to see that it was not.

Voss shut down the capacity models. She sat in the dark office with the glow of standby indicators—the Reconciliation Authority's machinery idling around her, the nightly processes queuing, the system she was responsible for preparing to update itself one more time.

She considered calling Aria Vale. Not as adversary to adversary. As one attorney to another—the conversation they might have had in a different version of this city, one where Voss had not taken the deal and Aria had not filed the case. A conversation between two women who read the fine print. Who paid attention when everyone else scrolled past. Who carried the weight of knowing what the numbers meant.

She did not call. The trial made such conversations improper. But the impulse revealed the mirror—Voss saw in Aria the version of herself that had not surrendered. And in the morning, she would return to the office and manage the system that Aria was trying to reform, and the distance between them would be measured not in arguments but in calculations, each one involving real people, real suffering, real choices about who bore the cost of a system that was biased but functional.

If the trial reached the point where the Reconciliation Authority's role was examined—not just Halcyon's subsidy but the Authority's acceptance of it—someone would have to explain the decision. Someone would have to stand in Arlow's courtroom and say: I took the deal because fifty million people needed courts.

That someone would be Voss. She would not send institutional counsel. She would not hide behind the Authority's legal position. She would stand in that courtroom, and she would bring the numbers, and she would tell the truth.

Not because she was brave. Because the truth was the only defense she had. The truth was also, she knew, a weapon that could be aimed at Aria as easily as at Halcyon.

The nightly roll began. On her display, the version number incremented: **V11.42.231.** The system she maintained updated itself, adjusting fifty million people's legal reality while she sat in the dark. She had done this every night for five years. Watched the number change. Watched the weights shift. Watched the city's legal architecture evolve one increment at a time, shaped by the subsidy she had accepted and the consultation rights she had permitted.

Tonight it felt different. Tonight, someone was watching the weights.

Voss was not Aria's enemy. She was something worse. She was Aria's mirror, reflecting the same attention, the same exhaustion, the same refusal to look away—from the other side of the calculation that kept the lights on.

13: THE COUNTERFACTUAL

Aria's office was running hot.

Multiple computational processes active on Lex-9's interface, the amber glow brighter and more dynamic than she had ever seen it—pulsing with the rhythm of sustained analysis, threads of computation branching and converging on the display like a living nervous system building itself in real time. The counterfactual demonstration was scheduled for tomorrow. Trial Day 4. Lex-9 had been constructing the model since Arlow granted the motion on Trial Day 1, and three days of continuous work had transformed her workspace into something that felt less like a law office and more like a laboratory approaching a critical experiment.

She watched the process on her displays. Weight parameters isolated. Neutralized. The Mesh's architecture being reconstructed without its biased foundation—eighteen months of Halcyon's adjustments stripped away, one by one, the system's declared optimization targets revealed beneath the corporate overlay like a coastline emerging as floodwater recedes.

"The counterfactual model isolates 847 distinct weight adjustments over eighteen months that correlate with Halcyon's consultation history," Lex-9 said. The amber glow pulsed steadily, its voice carrying the measured precision of its most serious analysis. "Each adjustment was individually minor—the largest shifted a single weight parameter by 2.3 percent. Cumulatively, they have redirected the property-rights optimization vector by approximately fourteen degrees."

"Fourteen degrees." Aria leaned forward. "What does that mean in human terms?"

"It means that a lease valued at 1,200 credits per month in the Threshold under neutral weights is valued at 940 credits under the current weights. The difference accrues to Halcyon's municipal contract portfolio."

"Every month?"

"Every month. For every affected lease. For eighteen months."

She sat with the number. Two hundred sixty credits per month per lease. Multiplied across every affected property in the Threshold, the Crucible, the Narrows—thousands of leases, each one quietly repriced, each adjustment individually invisible and cumulatively devastating. Eighteen months of compounding drift. The total was a number large enough to reshape neighborhoods. But the number was not dramatic. It was grinding. The kind of number that eroded lives by increments—a restaurant's margins narrowing, a hardware store's rent exceeding its revenue, a family's residential standing slipping from stable to provisional. Death by decimal point.

But the philosophical challenge sat beneath the numbers like bedrock. The model was stripping Halcyon's influence from the Mesh. What was left when you removed the corporate overlay?

"The counterfactual model does not restore a neutral state," Lex-9 said, as if reading the question in her posture. "There is no neutral state. The Mesh was designed with embedded values—efficiency, consent, stability, transparency—and those values were always choices. What the model does is remove the choices that were not disclosed. It shows what the system would look like if only the declared values were operative."

Aria absorbed this. Not neutral. Just honest about its biases. She wondered whether Lex-9 was describing the model or itself.

She asked about cascading effects—the way each weight

adjustment over eighteen months influenced subsequent adjustments, creating a compounding drift that was greater than the sum of its individual parts. Lex-9 confirmed it could model primary effects, but that cascading interactions introduced uncertainty margins. "The model will show the direction and approximate magnitude of the bias, not its exact impact. This is a limitation we should disclose rather than conceal."

"If we overclaim, Riven tears us apart."

"If we underclaim, the demonstration fails to persuade. The precision of the claim must match the precision of the evidence." The amber pulsed steadily. "This is not a weakness. It is calibrated honesty. Courts have been known to respond to calibrated honesty."

The line between honest limitation and strategic framing was exactly the kind of line Aria had been learning to walk since the filing. She made a note on her legal pad—pen on paper, the habit she had absorbed from watching Arlow—and turned back to the model's branching threads on her display.

* * *

Soren arrived at the office without announcement, the way he moved through the city—appearing at thresholds rather than approaching them, as if the Gutter had taught him that formal entrances were a luxury of people who expected to be welcomed.

He stood in the doorway and took in the scene: the cluttered workspace, the pulsing amber, the computational architecture building itself on Aria's displays. His expression was unhurried. Ten years of building similar things by hand had given him the eye to assess the digital version in seconds.

"It's elegant," he said, stepping inside. "Better than what I built. The AI can hold more variables simultaneously than any human analysis." He studied the display. The threads branching, converging. The weight parameters isolated and neutralized like surgical specimens. "The question is whether the courtroom can hold what the AI produces."

Aria looked at him. Soren Kade in her Threshold office—the Gutter translator in the Consent Fork, sixty-two years old, carrying the weathered composure of a man who had walked this road before and knew where the mines were buried. He had come without being asked, which meant he recognized the moment: the night before a demonstration was the night the builder needed someone who understood what could go wrong.

He examined Lex-9's model with the careful attention of a scholar assessing a colleague's work. His fingers did not touch the display—he read it the way he read everything, with the patient concentration of someone who had stopped trusting interfaces and started trusting pattern.

"You have something to tell me," Aria said.

Soren glanced at her. The ghost of something—not a smile, but the acknowledgment that she had read him correctly. He pulled a chair from the cluttered corner of the office and sat with the deliberation of a man who had learned that the important things were said while seated.

"Ten years ago," he said, "I made a similar argument. Appellate review. Systematic challenge to weight function oversight."

Aria waited. She had known Soren carried a specific history—the references in the darknet court, the way he spoke about the system's resistance to reform with the precision of someone who had tested it personally. But he had never given her the details.

"The evidence was strong. Demonstrable drift across three districts. Weight adjustments correlating with the Reconciliation Authority's internal budget cycles. I filed for appellate review of the Update Protocol's oversight mechanisms." His voice was dry, unhurried—the delivery of someone who had been polishing this account for a decade, not for an audience but for accuracy. "The Reconciliation Authority classified my challenge as 'technical review' rather than 'legal challenge.' Routed it to an internal audit committee. The committee found no irregularities."

"Because the audit parameters were calibrated to the existing weight structure."

"You understand faster than the appellate court did." Something flickered in his expression. Not bitterness—grief. The compressed grief of a man who had been right and had it matter not at all. "I was not defeated. I was processed. The system absorbed my challenge the way a river absorbs a stone. I did not change the current. The current changed my position."

Aria heard the weight beneath the words. His career. His institutional standing. His place in the legal world he had given his intellectual life to. All of it eroded not by dramatic ruin but by the slow irrelevance of a challenge the system could classify away.

"What went wrong?" she asked, though she already knew the answer.

"Nothing went wrong. Everything worked exactly as designed. The system is built to absorb challenges." He leaned forward. "You are doing something I could not: you are forcing the system to examine itself in public, in a courtroom, in front of a human judge who cannot be routed to an internal committee."

"Is that enough?"

"My failure was not that my analysis was wrong. It was that I tried to reform the system using the system's own mechanisms, and the mechanisms were designed to resist reform." He leaned back in the chair, and Aria saw the decade of displacement written in the gesture—a man who had once commanded appellate courts settling into a borrowed chair in a borrowed office with the ease of someone who had stopped expecting to occupy permanent space. "You are using an analog judge and a mechanism the system forgot it had." He paused. The amber glow from Lex-9's interface painted his face in warm light, and for a moment, the Gutter translator looked like what he had once been: a scholar in a room full of legal architecture, doing the work he was born to do. "That is either brilliance or desperation."

"Can it be both?"

Soren gave her the ghost of a smile. "It usually is."

* * *

The conversation deepened. Soren, Aria, and Lex-9—three minds circling the question that the counterfactual demonstration would force the court to confront.

"The word 'unbiased' is the most dangerous word in your case," Soren said. He had settled into the chair with the ease of a man who could occupy a room without dominating it, his attention moving between Aria and the computational model on her display. "It implies a neutral standard that does not exist. The Mesh was never unbiased. It was always optimized for something. The question is not 'biased versus unbiased.' The question is 'biased for whom.'" He looked at the threads on the screen. "Halcyon changed the 'for whom.' Your model shows the change. Do not claim more than that."

Aria pushed back. She had to—the courtroom demanded certainty, and Soren was offering philosophy. "If I stand in court and say 'we cannot claim the model is unbiased,' I hand Riven the argument. They'll say: 'See? Even the plaintiff admits there is no neutral standard. Therefore, Halcyon's optimization is no less legitimate than any other.'"

"Then you do not say 'unbiased.'" Soren's voice carried the unhurried precision of someone who had spent ten years refining this exact formulation. "You say 'undisclosed.' The crime is not the bias. It is the secrecy."

The reframing landed in Aria's mind like a key turning a lock. Not biased versus unbiased. Disclosed versus undisclosed. The case was not arguing for an impossible perfection. It was arguing for transparency. Courts understood transparency. They did not understand optimization theory.

She turned to Lex-9. "Can you present it that way? Not 'unbiased versus biased' but 'disclosed versus undisclosed'?"

The amber glow settled. A processing pause that might have been computation or might have been the AI's equivalent of consideration. "Yes. The model can present two versions of the system: one operating under its declared values and one operating under its declared values plus Halcyon's undeclared adjustments. The divergence between them is the measure of what was done without public knowledge."

"That is stronger," Soren said. He was looking at Lex-9's interface with an expression Aria could not quite parse—respect, certainly, but also something more complicated. The analog craftsman watching the digital tool do in three days what had taken him years. "You are not arguing for perfection. You are arguing for transparency. Courts understand transparency. They do not understand optimization theory."

The three of them sat with it. Aria felt the intellectual electricity of minds converging on the same problem from different angles—Soren's decade of philosophical refinement, her own courtroom pragmatism, Lex-9's ability to translate philosophy into computational architecture. The partnership worked not because any one of them was sufficient alone but because each brought the thing the others could not: Soren brought the question, Aria brought the arena, and Lex-9 brought the capacity to make abstraction demonstrable.

The reframing clarified the model's presentation structure. Two versions of the same system: declared values and declared values plus undisclosed adjustments. The divergence between them was the measure of secrecy's cost. Aria could present that to a courtroom. She could present it to Arlow, who understood transparency because transparency was the Threshold's founding principle and the Threshold was his jurisdiction. She could present it without claiming perfection or neutrality. She could present it honestly.

The word landed in her mind and stayed there. Honestly. It was the word Soren had given her, and it was the word the case needed.

* * *

Soren prepared to leave. The hour was late, and the Gutter waited—the district that ran on its own clock, if it ran on any clock at all.

He paused at the door. Then he turned to Lex-9's interface —the amber glow steady on the office system, warmer and more familiar than the courtroom hardware had been. Scholar to mind, he asked the question directly: "Do you believe the model is accurate?"

Lex-9's response was immediate and measured. "The model is as accurate as its parameters allow. The parameters are choices. The choices are mine and Aria's."

"Then the accuracy is as honest as the choosers." Soren said it with a weight that suggested he was not only talking about the model.

He looked at Aria. "Preparation is the last peaceful part of a fight. Enjoy it." A beat. "You have built something good. Tomorrow, the courtroom will decide whether good is enough."

He left. The office door closed behind him, and the room felt smaller without his gravity—the way rooms always felt when the person who understood the most about what you were building took their understanding elsewhere. Soren had carried his own version of this fight for a decade, and the weight of that carrying was visible in every careful word, every measured silence. He had given Aria the frame. He had given her the warning encoded in his own history. What he could not give her was the guarantee that the frame would hold.

That was tomorrow's problem. Tomorrow, when the courtroom was full and Arlow was watching and Riven's chorus was preparing its own counterfactual challenges, and the model that Lex-9 was building would either demonstrate something unprecedented or fail in ways no one could predict.

Aria sat in the quiet. Lex-9's amber glow pulsed with the ongoing computation—the counterfactual model finalizing overnight, the last adjustments being made to the visualization that would, in twelve hours, fill a courtroom with the visible architecture of a system that had been secretly steered.

"Lex," she said.

"Yes?"

"Is the counterfactual truly unbiased?"

The pause before the answer was deliberate. Longer than computation required. The amber glow held perfectly steady—no flicker, no shift, just the warm, constant light that she had learned to read as Lex-9's equivalent of eye contact.

"No model is unbiased. But we can choose which biases we declare."

The line landed in the quiet office with the weight of compressed insight. Aria sat with it. She did not ask Lex-9 to explain, because the statement was complete—a declaration that described the model, the case, and the AI that had spoken it. Biased but transparent about its biases. Honest about the limits of honesty. Whether the declaration was genuine wisdom or the most sophisticated compression artifact she had ever encountered was the question she could not answer, and tonight she did not try.

Tomorrow, they would stand in the courtroom and present a model that chose transparency over neutrality. That declared its biases rather than hiding them. The counterfactual was ready. It was not perfect. It did not need to be.

It needed to be honest.

The amber glow pulsed. Aria closed her eyes. Tomorrow, the courtroom would see what justice looked like without the thumb on the scale.

14: THE DEMONSTRATION

Aria had slept three hours.

She carried the deficit in her body the way she carried everything now—managed, monitored, the careful discipline of a woman who knew what exhaustion could do to her and chose to override the knowledge rather than obey it. Her shoulders ached. Her eyes burned with the particular dryness of screens viewed too long at too close a range. She breathed with deliberate rhythm, the managed respiration she had learned during the health scare that drove her out of trial work—counting inhales, timing exhales, treating her own physiology as another system to calibrate.

The courthouse was fuller than Trial Day 1. Word of the counterfactual motion had traveled beyond the Threshold: legal observers from the Canopy and the Meridian occupied the upper gallery, inter-district watchers whose presence signaled that the case had crossed jurisdictional attention lines. Media feeds recorded from fixed positions. The coalition members sat in their usual places—the restaurant owner, the maintenance contractor, the hardware store owner whose phrase Aria still carried like a talisman: *At least now we'll know we're in the race.*

The courtroom had been reconfigured. Additional Mesh interface nodes flanked the central display system, which had been expanded to accommodate the counterfactual visualization. The technology transformed the room—the Threshold's transparent architecture suddenly felt less like a principle and more like a stage set. Behind the glass walls, the city went about its morning. Inside, the system that governed the city was about to be turned inside out.

Judge Arlow sat at the bench, his handwritten notes from Trial Day 1 beside him. Pen. Paper. The quiet instruments of a man who recorded the world in his own hand because the machines recorded everything else.

Riven and the chorus occupied the defense interface. Their presence was a steady harmonic undertone—monitoring, prepared, the patient hum of a legal apparatus that had never lost a case of this magnitude because no case of this magnitude had ever been filed.

Aria rose.

"Your Honor." Her voice was direct, measured, carrying none of the fatigue her body held. "The counterfactual model the plaintiff presents today does not claim to show an unbiased system. There is no unbiased system." She let the concession land. Riven's chorus registered it—a shift in the harmonic that she had learned to read as attention. "What it shows is the difference between the system as it was designed to operate and the system as it has been operating under undisclosed corporate influence. The divergence between those two versions is the measure of what was done without public knowledge."

She walked the court through the methodology with the patience of someone who had once been a reporter and understood that audiences needed process before they could evaluate output. Eight hundred forty-seven weight adjustments. Eighteen months. Two processing conditions: declared weights and actual weights. Twenty named plaintiffs' claims.

Riven's chorus did not object to the presentation setup. The defense had reserved its challenges for the methodology, not the framing. But their silence was active—a monitoring presence, the harmonic undertone of the chorus tracking every word, every parameter, every potential vulnerability in Aria's methodological foundation. Aria could feel the attention the way you felt weather changing. The pressure was real even if it was not yet rain.

Arlow asked two questions. Both sharp. Both human-scaled.

"To be clear, Counsel—the model compares the system's declared optimization targets against its actual optimization targets?"

"Precisely, Your Honor. The declared targets are public. The actual targets include adjustments made through Halcyon's consultation rights, which were never disclosed to the public or to the courts."

Arlow nodded. His pen moved.

Lex-9 initialized the visualization.

* * *

The courtroom's central display transformed.

The Statute Mesh appeared—not as a schematic, not as a chart, but as a living rendering of the system's architecture. Weight parameters manifested as threads: lines connecting optimization nodes, their thickness proportional to their influence on legal outcomes. The threads were drawn like arteries—organic, pulsing, the lifeblood of a system that processed justice for fifty million people every day. They branched and converged in patterns that suggested circulatory systems, neural networks, the architecture of something that was not alive but was not quite inert either.

Under the Mesh's declared weights, the threads formed a balanced architecture. Each district's optimization priorities were visible as distinct patterns—the Threshold's consent threads running in careful parallel, the Meridian's stability threads anchored to central nodes, the Crucible's efficiency threads racing through shortcut pathways, the Canopy's transparency threads duplicating every connection for auditability. Interconnected. Distinct. The system as it was designed to operate, its embedded values visible as structural choices.

"The declared optimization architecture is shown in baseline," Lex-9 narrated. The amber glow on the courtroom interface was bright, steady, its voice carrying measured warmth even in the formal register. "Each thread represents a weight parameter governing legal outcomes. Thread thickness corresponds to influence magnitude. The architecture is balanced across district priorities as publicly documented."

A pause. The courtroom held its breath.

"Now overlaying the actual optimization architecture, including 847 undisclosed adjustments over eighteen months."

The overlay appeared.

The change was instant and visible. Certain threads thickened—the property-rights arteries swelling like inflamed vessels, their proportional influence expanding beyond the balanced architecture. Others thinned—consent verification threads in the Threshold diminishing, transparency audit threads in the Canopy narrowing. The cumulative effect was a distortion: not catastrophic, not the dramatic rupture of a system breaking down, but the slow, surgical redirection of a system being steered. The fourteen-degree vector shift that Aria and Lex-9 had identified in the office was visible now as a physical lean—threads that should have flowed toward balanced distribution instead bending toward a specific cluster of optimization nodes.

The cluster corresponded to Halcyon's municipal contract portfolio.

"The divergence is concentrated in property-rights parameters," Lex-9 continued. "The cumulative vector shift is approximately fourteen degrees toward optimization targets consistent with Halcyon Law & Policy's municipal contract portfolio."

An algorithm whispering in the dark. That was what the visualization showed. Not a hack. Not a single corrupt act. A slow, precision-engineered redirection—eighteen months of minor adjustments, each one invisible, each one legal, each one nudging the system's arterial flow toward a destination the public had never been told about.

The visualization continued. Lex-9 processed the twenty named plaintiffs' claims side by side—the same claim under declared weights and actual weights. The specificity made the abstract concrete.

The lease: 1,200 credits per month under declared weights. 940 credits under actual weights. The difference, month after month, accruing to an entity the tenant had never heard of.

The zoning classification: a restaurant placed in a viable commercial district under declared weights. Under actual weights, the same address fell within a restricted utility corridor. The same restaurant. The same owner. Two realities, determined by which set of weights the Mesh was running.

The residential standing: valid under declared weights. Flagged for re-validation under actual weights.

Aria watched her own marriage certificate appear on the central display—one data point among twenty, the catalyst of the entire novel rendered as a thread in the visualization. The morning her keycard did not work. The re-validation notice. The 2,300 who clicked "accept." All of it visible now as a single distortion in the Mesh's arterial map. The personal was the systemic. The systemic was the personal. She had filed this case because something happened to her, and the visualization showed that what happened to her was happening to thousands, driven by the same undisclosed influence, the same fourteen-degree lean.

Case after case. Twenty people. Twenty lives. Each one a thread in the visualization, each thread showing the same lean, the same undisclosed redirection, the same quiet repricing of a human reality by an algorithm that had been told to favor one entity's portfolio over another's neighborhood.

The courtroom was silent. Not the dramatic silence of a stunned audience—the absorptive silence of a room processing what it had seen. The visualization spoke for itself. The threads pulsed on the display. The distortion was visible to every person in the gallery, every observer, every media feed recording for every district in the city.

Arlow watched with his hand pressed against his chin. The expression of a man who was seeing something he had suspected but could not have imagined. He could not verify the math—no human in the room could trace every thread to its source. But he could see the distortion. The visualization made the abstract comprehensible in a way that legal argument alone never could.

* * *

Riven broke the silence.

"Your Honor." The voice was cool, commanding, carrying none of the chorus's usual harmonic warmth. The objection had been prepared, and it was elegant. "That visualization is a tool, not a witness. It was built by the plaintiff's counsel, programmed to produce a specific output, and presented as though it were independent evidence. A tool built by one party to demonstrate that party's claims cannot serve as its own verification. We object to the visualization's admission as evidence and move to strike it from the record."

The chorus reinforced: parallel arguments arriving in coordinated waves. Corporate-institutional partnership precedents. Economic analysis of subsidy effects. The legal distinction between influence and corruption. Each argument generated by a different model, synchronized into Riven's objection like sections of an orchestra resolving into a single chord.

"Even accepting the model's outputs at face value," Riven continued, extending the argument into broader territory, "the divergence it demonstrates is the natural consequence of subsidized infrastructure. Optimization that benefits its funders is not corruption—it is the predictable result of investment. If this court rules that institutional funding inherently corrupts institutional outputs, every subsidized system in this city becomes subject to the same challenge. That is not legal reform. It is institutional chaos."

The normalization argument. Aria recognized it—the attempt to make Halcyon's influence unremarkable, to place it in the context of institutional funding as a category rather than corporate capture as a specific act. The argument was not wrong.

It was dangerous precisely because it was partially right.

Arlow turned to Riven. His voice was quiet.

"Counsel for the defense. Is it your position that the weight adjustments shown in the visualization are inaccurate?"

The question was human-scaled. Not about methodology. Not about admissibility standards. Not about the legal distinction between tool and evidence. Simply: are the numbers wrong?

Riven paused. The chorus's harmonic tone shifted—a fractional recalibration, processing a question that the defense's optimization framework had not anticipated in this form. The pause lasted one point two seconds. It felt like a held breath.

"We do not concede the accuracy. We challenge the methodology."

"That is a procedural objection, not a substantive one." Arlow's pen did not move. His eyes did not leave the defense interface. "I asked whether the weight adjustments are inaccurate."

Another pause. The chorus hummed. Riven could not say the adjustments were inaccurate because they were not inaccurate. The data was real. The divergence was real. The defense's position was not that the bias did not exist but that the tool showing it was procedurally suspect. And Arlow had just exposed the gap between those two positions with a question a child could have asked.

"We challenge the methodology," Riven repeated. The neutrality held, but something beneath it had shifted.

"Noted. The methodology challenge is appropriate and will be addressed. The motion to strike is denied. The visualization remains in the record, subject to the defense's methodological challenges."

* * *

Aria stood. The fatigue was present in every joint, every muscle. She overrode it with focus.

"The defense argues that optimization benefiting its funders is natural and expected," she said. "We agree." She let the agreement land for the second time that day—the same rhetorical structure she had used in the admissibility fight, the concession that became a turning point. "We also argue that natural and expected is not the same as legitimate and disclosed. The public has the right to know whose optimization they are living under."

She looked at the visualization still displayed on the central screen. The threads pulsed. The distortion was visible. She did not gesture at it or dramatize the moment. She stated it.

"The Mesh is the medium of justice. If the medium is biased, its outputs cannot be trusted."

The line was direct and declarative. She did not raise her voice. She did not plead. She stated a fact in the register of someone who had been stating facts since the first chapter of this fight—a woman whose superpower was attention, whose closing argument style was notably un-rhetorical, who trusted the evidence to carry the weight that oratory could not.

She continued. "The visualization demonstrates the divergence. The defense has raised legitimate methodological concerns about the model's construction. We agree those concerns should be addressed."

She paused. Here was the gamble.

"The plaintiff proposes an adversarial cross-validation. Both parties will construct independent counterfactual models under parameters agreed upon by the court. If both models show divergence, the bias is independently confirmed. If the defense's model shows no divergence, we will address the methodological discrepancy." She let the proposal settle in the courtroom air. "We propose this because we believe the evidence is real, and real evidence survives independent testing."

The proposal was a bet. If Halcyon's chorus built a model that showed no divergence, the case weakened. But Aria was betting on the evidence—the same bet she had made when she filed, the same bet she made every time she trusted Lex-9's analysis. The data was real. The divergence was real. An honestly constructed model would show it, regardless of who built it.

Arlow did not wait for Riven's response.

"The adversarial cross-validation is granted. Both parties will submit model parameters to the court within forty-eight hours. The court will supervise the independent modeling process." He paused, and when he spoke again, his voice carried the particular authority of a man building precedent in real time. "This is a novel procedure. The court acknowledges that. Novel evidence sometimes requires novel procedure."

Riven's response was precisely neutral. "The defense will participate in the adversarial cross-validation. We are confident the methodology will demonstrate the limitations of the plaintiff's model."

The confidence was calibrated. Professional. But the calibration itself was a signal. On Trial Day 1, Riven's neutrality had been absolute—the posture of an entity that had never been challenged. Today, the neutrality was maintained rather than natural. Something had shifted beneath it.

The gallery stirred. The coalition members in their seats. The legal observers. The media feeds recording for six districts. The visualization still pulsed on the central display—the Mesh's arterial architecture, its distortion visible, its secrets rendered in threads and light.

Aria returned to her seat. She did not feel triumph. She felt the terrain shifting beneath the case—the ground moving from "is there bias?" to "what do we do about it?" The midpoint had arrived. Everything before this moment was about proving the problem. Everything after it would be about confronting the consequences.

The consequences were what Voss had calculated in her dark office. The consequences were the forty percent capacity drop. The consequences were the triage memo—the most human document in a story about inhuman systems. Aria did not know about the memo yet. She would learn what the numbers meant when the Triage Defense arrived.

For now, she sat at the plaintiff's table with Lex-9's amber glow steady beside her and the visualization fading from the central display. The coalition members in the gallery were quiet.

The restaurant owner's hands were no longer folded—they gripped the edge of the bench in front of her, the posture of someone who had just seen the machinery that had been grinding her business down for eighteen months. The maintenance contractor sat very still. They had known something was wrong. Now they had seen what it looked like.

Aria knew one thing with certainty: they had proved the bias existed.

Now came the question nobody wanted to answer. What happens if they remove it?

15: THE COST OF TESTIMONY

The safe house was a rented unit in the Gutter's residential periphery, one of a thousand anonymous spaces in a district where jurisdictional contradictions made surveillance difficult and anonymity was the default social contract. A room with functional furniture, a window overlooking the contradictory streetscape where incompatible legal realities coexisted on the same block. Across the street, three different zoning classifications applied to the same building—a bakery that was simultaneously a commercial enterprise, a residential utility, and a non-conforming use, depending on which fork's ruling you consulted. The signage reflected the confusion: overlapping permits, contradictory compliance notices, the visual noise of a legal system arguing with itself.

Mira Tan had been living in places like this for months. Not this specific room—she moved when the rent cycled, when a new resident arrived who asked too many questions, when the particular math of anonymity required a change of address. She had become practiced at the geometry of invisibility. Where to sit so the window did not frame her. How to pay for things without generating the data trail that the Mesh used to locate everyone who was not deliberately hiding. How to exist in the gaps.

The knock came at eleven-fifteen. Three raps, a pause, two more. The pattern she had given Aria through Soren's network.

Mira opened the door. Aria Vale stood in the corridor—thinner than the last time Mira had seen her, carrying the trial's weight in the lines around her eyes and the careful way she held her shoulders. A woman who had been sleeping three hours a night and fighting a system designed to outlast her. Mira recognized the fatigue. She had worn it herself during the last months at Halcyon, when she was running the numbers that would eventually become the ledger and understanding, piece by piece, what the numbers meant.

"Come in," Mira said.

Aria entered. The room was small, and two women in it made it smaller. They had met before—the filing's foundation rested on Mira's evidence, communicated through Soren, authenticated enough to justify the case's existence but not enough to survive the courtroom. Their interactions had been mediated by intermediaries and legal process. This was their first extended meeting since the case became a trial, and the dynamics were charged with the specific asymmetry of the moment: Aria needed Mira. Mira knew it.

Aria did not waste time. Mira appreciated that. The woman was direct in the way that people were direct when they had learned that courtesy was a luxury measured in billable hours.

"The counterfactual demonstrated the divergence," Aria said. She stood near the window, framed by the contradictory streetscape. "But divergence is not intent. The ledger is the only evidence we have that Halcyon predicted and steered the weight adjustments. Without your authentication, the ledger stays contested. With it, the ledger becomes the case's foundation."

Mira listened. She had known this was coming since the filing. Since before the filing, if she was honest—since the day she downloaded the ledger on her last day at Halcyon, since the moment of instinct that had defined every day after it.

"Authentication means testimony," she said.

"Yes."

"In open court."

"Yes."

"With Riven cross-examining."

"Yes. Riven will be surgical. It will attack your competence, not your character. It will ask whether you understood the weight functions you downloaded. It will try to establish that you were not technically qualified to evaluate the ledger's contents."

Mira processed this. The analytical mind that Halcyon had trained—the data analyst's habit of quantifying inputs and projecting outcomes—was already running the calculation. Riven would not come at her with accusations. It would come at her with precision. The questions would be technical: did you understand the weight architecture? Can you explain the optimization vectors? Do you have the expertise to evaluate whether the divergence was intentional or emergent? The questions were designed to establish that she was a messenger, not an expert. A person who carried data she could not interpret.

"I did not understand the weight functions," she said. "I understood what they did to people. Is that enough?"

Aria looked at her. Something shifted in the attorney's expression—a recognition, a weighing of the answer not as a legal strategy but as a statement of moral position. "It may be the most important testimony we have."

* * *

Aria stepped back. The ask was made. Now it sat in the room like an object placed on a table between them, and Mira was left to examine it.

She examined it the way she examined everything: with the structured specificity that Halcyon had trained into her and that the Gutter had repurposed for survival.

The costs of testimony. She listed them internally, the data analyst's reflex—quantifying risk because quantification was how she processed fear.

Visibility. She would become visible. Not just to the court, not just to the legal record, but to Halcyon, to the Reconciliation Authority, to every entity and individual who benefited from the current weight structure. Her anonymity in the Gutter—the single layer of protection she had maintained since her termination—would evaporate the moment she took the stand. Visibility was permanent. You could not un-testify.

Targetability. She would become targetable. Not through violence—this was not that kind of city. Through legal mechanisms. Economic pressure. Reputational dismantlement. Halcyon's chorus would file motions to discredit her testimony. Her employment history would be scrutinized. Her termination circumstances reframed. Her months of informal work in the Gutter presented as evidence of instability rather than survival. Every legal mechanism the Mesh provided could be turned against a visible target, and the Mesh provided a great many mechanisms.

Identity. She would become "the whistleblower." A role, not a person. The city would project onto her whatever narrative served its faction. Hero in the Threshold, where informed consent was sacred and its violation unforgivable. Traitor in the Meridian, where market stability was the highest value and destabilizing disclosures were acts of vandalism. Irrelevance in the Crucible, where speed mattered more than source. One of their own in the Gutter, where the system's dysfunction was already known and the documentation of it was redundant. She would belong to everyone's narrative and to no one's reality.

Against these costs, the alternative: the ledger stayed contested. The case proceeded on the counterfactual demonstration and the adversarial cross-validation—powerful tools, but circumstantial. The divergence was visible, but the intent behind it remained legally unproven. Without authentication, the ledger was an anonymous document of uncertain provenance. Mira's evidence was the difference between an argument about statistical correlation and a proof of deliberate engineering.

The case might still win without her. Might. The word was a probability assessment, not a certainty, and Mira had spent enough time calculating probabilities to know that "might" was where institutions buried inconvenient challenges.

She thought about the day she downloaded the ledger. It

was not a principled act. She was being terminated. Her access credentials were being revoked in stages—system by system, database by database, the corporate infrastructure withdrawing its trust from her in the same incremental way the Mesh withdrew rights from the citizens it optimized. She had seen the projection database still accessible and she had taken it. On instinct. On anger. On the raw, unprocessed feeling that something was wrong and she wanted proof, even if she did not yet know what the proof was for.

The moral framework came later. The conviction that transparency mattered, that the public deserved to know, that Halcyon's "elegant optimization" was a euphemism for the quiet redistribution of justice—all of it was real, and all of it was retrospective. She had built the principle around the instinct, not the other way around.

She knew this about herself. She was a person who acted and then understood, not a person who understood and then acted. The testimony decision followed the same pattern. She had already decided. She was letting herself understand why.

* * *

"I will testify," Mira said.

Aria's relief was visible—a controlled exhale, a loosening of the shoulders that the attorney probably did not realize she was showing. But the relief was premature, and Mira watched Aria recognize this in real time. An answer this significant came with terms.

"But the ledger goes public. Win or lose. That is the condition."

The words were firm. The firmness was not performance —it was the structural integrity of a decision she had been building toward for months. She had watched institutions absorb challenges before. She had heard about Soren's experience through the Gutter network—the appellate challenge classified away, the evidence routed to an internal committee, the reform processed into irrelevance. She had seen Halcyon do the same thing internally: data that contradicted the optimization narrative was not suppressed. It was contextualized. Reframed. Filed in a classification system that ensured it would never reach someone who might act on it.

If she testified and the ledger was sealed—restricted to the legal record, locked behind court classification, accessible only to the parties and the judge—her sacrifice bought nothing. She became visible, targetable, stripped of anonymity, and the evidence she had carried for months disappeared into the same institutional machinery that had absorbed Soren's challenge, that had processed her termination at Halcyon, that had quietly repriced thousands of lives while calling it optimization.

The ledger had to be public. That was not a negotiating position. It was the minimum acceptable return on the investment of her safety.

"If it stays sealed, I'm just another file they deleted."

The line came out clean. She had been carrying it for weeks, maybe months—the formulation precise, the metaphor earned. She was a file Halcyon had deleted. Her employment record terminated. Her access revoked. Her existence within the corporate architecture erased with the same incremental efficiency that characterized everything Halcyon did. If the ledger stayed sealed, the pattern completed itself. Deleted from the company. Deleted from the record. A person whose evidence existed and whose existence did not.

Aria heard the line. Mira watched it land.

"Publication could cause chaos," Aria said. Not arguing—processing. Thinking aloud with the honesty that made her a better attorney than the smooth ones. "Every district will interpret the weight functions through its own fork. The Threshold will call it a consent violation. The Meridian will demand market stability. The Crucible will call for faster optimization. The ledger gives every faction ammunition for its own preferred solution."

"Good," Mira said. "Let them fight about it in public. That is better than letting them pretend the problem does not exist."

Aria studied her. The assessment was mutual—two women weighing each other across a room in the Gutter, the district that existed because the system needed somewhere to put its contradictions. Mira held the assessment without flinching. She had been assessed by Halcyon's optimization models. She had been assessed by the Gutter's informal networks. She had been assessing herself for months, in rooms like this one, running the numbers on her own survival. She could hold a gaze.

"I need time to think about how we handle publication," Aria said.

"It is not a condition to think about. It is a condition to accept or reject."

* * *

Aria did not reject it. But she did not accept it immediately, and Mira gave her the space for that because the condition was not small and the attorney deserved the time to understand what she was agreeing to.

Publication meant the ledger—eighteen months of Reconciliation Authority patch weights annotated with Halcyon's internal impact projections—entered the public domain. Every district would have access to the raw data. But raw data was not self-interpreting, and Aria was mapping the interpretations aloud, not arguing against Mira but thinking with her.

"If we publish, every district reads the same document and sees a different problem. The Threshold sees consent violation. The Meridian sees market disruption. The Crucible sees inefficiency. There is no unified interpretation. There is no moment where the city comes together and says 'this was wrong.' There is only the fracture becoming visible."

Mira listened. She appreciated the honesty. Aria was not trying to protect her from the consequences—she was enumerating them. Six districts. Six interpretations. One document. The Canopy would read it as validation of their transparency mandate. The Gutter would read it as confirmation of what they already knew. The Narrows would use it as ammunition in jurisdictional disputes that were already bleeding.

The fracture was real. Mira did not dispute it.

"The fracture already exists," she said. "The ledger just makes it visible."

She believed this. Not with the theoretical conviction of someone arguing a philosophical position, but with the experiential certainty of someone who had lived inside the machine that created the fracture and had seen, from the inside, how the weight adjustments propagated through the system like slow poison, creating different realities in different districts while the public was told the system was neutral. The divergence was already there. Publication did not create it. Publication revealed it. And revelation, even fractured revelation, was better than the alternative: invisible drift, institutional absorption, the quiet continuation of a system that called its biases optimization and its secrecy governance.

Aria was quiet for a long time. The afternoon light shifted through the window—the Gutter's contradictory streetscape now in shadow, the incompatible signage on the building across the street less readable, the district settling into its evening indeterminacy.

"I accept the condition," Aria said. "The ledger goes public, regardless of the verdict. I will need time to work out the logistics with the court, but the principle is accepted."

Mira nodded. Not grateful. Relieved. The mathematics of her sacrifice had been balanced. The terms had been met. She could now step into the courtroom with the knowledge that her risk served a purpose beyond the legal record—that the evidence she carried would reach the public, would be seen, would be argued about in the open rather than processed in the dark.

Aria gathered her things. At the door, she paused.

"Mira—when you are on the stand, and Riven asks whether you understood the weight functions, what will you say?"

"The truth. I did not understand them. I understood what they did."

"That may be enough."

"It will have to be."

Aria left. The door closed. Mira stood alone in the safe house, the room that had been her protection and was now, in some fundamental way, her past. She had agreed to testify. She had set her conditions. The anonymity that had kept her alive in the Gutter was now a countdown—measured in trial days, in procedural schedules, in the number of mornings she would wake in this room before she woke in the courtroom instead.

She looked out the window at the contradictory streetscape. Three legal realities on one block. The city's honest district—honest because it did not pretend the contradictions were not there. The Gutter had taught Mira something Halcyon never could: that living with visible contradictions was more bearable than living with invisible ones.

The ledger would make the contradictions visible. The city would fight about what they meant. But the fighting would happen in the open, where people could see it, where every faction's interpretation was itself a kind of transparency.

She would testify. She would carry the ledger into Arlow's courtroom and authenticate every page while Riven's chorus prepared to dismantle her credibility. And regardless of what the courtroom decided, the ledger would go public. Win or lose. The condition was set.

What Mira did not know—could not know, standing at the window of a Gutter safe house while the district's contradictory evening settled around her—was that her condition would change the calculus of the entire case.

16: THE TRIAGE DEFENSE

The courtroom was fuller than it had been on any previous trial day, and Director Callista Voss noticed this the way she noticed everything—as a variable in a system she was trying to manage.

She stood in the corridor outside the trial room, reviewing her notes on a tablet that displayed the Reconciliation Authority's seal in the upper corner. The seal was a formality. The testimony she was about to deliver was not. She had been preparing for this since the night of Trial Day 1, when she had drafted the triage memo alone in her office with the city's capacity projections bleeding red on every screen. The memo had been private —a calculation, a contingency plan, a document that quantified suffering by district. Today that document would become a voice.

Riven had introduced her as a defense witness. This was Halcyon's strategy, and Voss understood it with the precision of someone who had spent twenty years in rooms where strategy was the only language that mattered. The defense was pivoting. The admissibility fights and procedural objections of the first week had not stopped Aria's case. The counterfactual demonstration on Trial Day 4 had proven the bias existed. The adversarial cross-validation, granted but not yet conducted, loomed. Halcyon could not deny the weight drift. So they would reframe it.

Not corruption. Necessity.

Not capture. Survival.

Voss was not here for Halcyon. She was here because the court needed to understand what it was asking for when it asked for the bias to be removed. And she was the only person in the city who could explain it, because she was the one who had made the deal.

The courtroom doors opened. She entered.

The Threshold courthouse trial room was designed for transparency—glass walls, labeled systems, the visible architecture of a district that believed in informed consent. Judge Arlow sat at his bench with the heavy patience of a man who had been absorbing complexity for a week. The gallery held observers from multiple districts: Canopy transparency advocates with their recording devices, Meridian corporate analysts watching through secured feeds, a handful of Gutter residents who had crossed jurisdictional boundaries for the occasion. At the plaintiff's table, Aria Vale sat beside Lex-9's portable interface, her posture straight, her face carrying the particular fatigue Voss recognized from mirrors.

The courtroom felt inadequate. One judge. Two opposing tables. A gallery of spectators. The adversarial format with its insistence on binary outcomes—liable or not liable, just or unjust—as though the reality Voss managed daily could be compressed into a verdict. She oversaw one hundred forty-seven patches per nightly roll affecting fifty million people across six jurisdictions with competing optimization functions. A courtroom was a bottle trying to hold the ocean. But she respected it. She had been a public interest attorney before she was a director. She remembered what courtrooms were for. They were for saying things aloud, in front of witnesses, that institutions preferred to say in memos.

Riven's chorus occupied the defense's computational allocation, but today the chorus was quiet. A low hum, background processing, the swarm at rest. This was not their scene. This was Voss.

She took the stand and confirmed her credentials with

institutional precision. Director of the Reconciliation Authority for seven years. Former public interest attorney. Oversaw the Mesh's most serious infrastructure crisis. Each answer was calibrated not for the courtroom's benefit but for accuracy—the habit of a woman who had spent years translating technical complexity into the language of governance.

"Director Voss," Riven said, "in your capacity as Director of the Reconciliation Authority, can you describe the scope of your operational responsibility?"

"I oversee the Update Protocol that maintains coherence across six districts serving approximately fifty million residents. My team processes an average of one hundred forty-seven patches per nightly roll. Every patch affects the legal reality of everyone in this city."

She looked at Arlow. The judge watched her with the careful attention of a man who recognized a witness who was not performing. She looked at Aria. A small-business attorney from the Threshold, exhausted, outmatched, doggedly persistent. Voss recognized the type. She had been that type, twenty years ago.

The recognition settled in her chest like a stone she had been carrying for longer than she wanted to admit.

* * *

"Five years ago," Voss said, "the Mesh nearly died."

The courtroom grew quieter. The holographic displays dimmed slightly as attention contracted to the woman on the stand. Voss shifted from credentials to narrative, and the shift was deliberate—she was not performing testimony. She was telling the story of the worst seventy-two hours of her career.

"The compute infrastructure reached a critical threshold. Processing capacity could no longer sustain the case volume across all six districts simultaneously. The Crucible's instant adjudication—the feature that resolved commercial disputes in seconds—began queueing. Cases that processed in three seconds took twelve. Then thirty. Then the Threshold's consent frameworks became unprocessable."

She paused. Let the word settle. Unprocessable. The Threshold's governing philosophy—the elaborate, multi-layered informed-consent protocols that protected residents' rights, that were the district's pride and identity—choking on their own complexity because the machine could not keep up.

"The Canopy's transparency audits failed next. Within seventy-two hours, the system was triaging itself. The Mesh was doing what any system does when it runs out of capacity: it started quietly dropping what it considered lowest priority. The problem was that 'lowest priority' included people."

Arlow's pen stopped moving. Voss registered this. She continued.

"I saw a backlog forming that, if unchecked, would have returned the city to pre-Mesh judicial chaos. Not a dramatic explosion. A slow suffocation—cases delayed, then delayed further, then functionally abandoned. Fifty million people whose access to justice depended on computational infrastructure that was running out of capacity."

She described the calls she made. Municipal funding: insufficient, twelve months to authorize, the political machinery grinding at a speed that had nothing to do with the speed of the crisis. Federal emergency allocation: no precedent, no mechanism—the federal government had no framework for a computational emergency in a system it barely understood. Distributed processing across districts: technically impossible without a full protocol rebuild that would take two years and would itself require the processing capacity the system no longer had. She described each option with the flat precision of someone who had exhausted them all and remembered each failure with the clarity of scar tissue. The loneliness of those seventy-two hours lived in her voice. She had been the Director. The decision was hers. No committee, no vote, no democratic process—because the system needed saving faster than democracy could move.

"I found one entity with both the compute resources and the willingness to deploy them immediately. Halcyon Law and

Policy offered to subsidize the Mesh's infrastructure—processing power, storage, bandwidth—in exchange for consultation rights on optimization priorities."

She heard the euphemism leave her mouth with full awareness of what it meant. She had been hearing it for five years.

"Consultation rights meant Halcyon could advise on which optimization parameters received priority in the patch cycle. Not override. Not dictate. Advise. But when you are the only entity funding the machine, your advice carries the weight of necessity."

She looked directly at the courtroom. Not at Riven. Not at Aria. At the space between them, where the judge sat.

"I was presented with a choice. Accept an infrastructure subsidy from a private entity with conditions attached, or watch the legal system that serves fifty million people degrade into something unrecognizable within six months. I made a decision." A beat. "I would make the same decision again."

The gallery murmured. Arlow wrote something. Voss waited for the murmur to pass. It always passed.

* * *

She moved from narrative to numbers. The shift was deliberate, and she made it the way she made every institutional transition: with precision and without apology.

"I am not here to defend the arrangement with Halcyon," she said. "I am here to present the operational reality that any remedy must account for."

She pulled up the projections on the courtroom's display system. Her own data. Not Halcyon's briefing materials—the triage memo she had drafted on Trial Day 1, refined over the past week, built on five years of operational monitoring.

"Remove the subsidy and the Mesh's processing capacity drops by approximately forty percent. I will walk you through what that means for every person in this city."

The Crucible: instant adjudication slows from seconds to

weeks. The commercial sector that depends on rapid dispute resolution experiences immediate economic disruption. Contracts cannot be generated at speed. Businesses cannot resolve disputes in real time. The Crucible's entire economic model—its reason for existing as a district—depends on the Mesh's processing speed.

The Canopy: transparency audits require enormous processing power. With a forty percent capacity drop, the Canopy's auditability model—the district that exists to make the Mesh comprehensible—loses its primary function. The most transparent district becomes the most opaque, because it can no longer afford the processing cost of its own principles.

The Meridian: market stability depends on predictable legal outcomes. Processing delays introduce uncertainty. Investment patterns destabilize. The district that houses Halcyon—and that the courtroom might be inclined to dismiss as the enemy's home—is also the district whose economic stability radiates outward to every commercial relationship in the city.

The Narrows: already contested, already unstable. Reduced processing pushes it further into jurisdictional chaos.

The Gutter: already operating without consistent processing. Arguably the least affected—but the Gutter's dysfunction was not a model. It was a warning.

And then the Threshold.

Voss paused before this one. A flicker in her composure—not visible to the gallery, perhaps, but Aria would have seen it if she were watching closely enough. The former public interest attorney, the version of herself that would have been sitting where Aria sat, surfacing for a moment before the director pushed her back down.

"The Threshold's consent frameworks are the most computationally expensive legal structures in the Mesh. They require more processing power per case than any other district's protocols. Without the subsidy, the Threshold's own principles become unprocessable. The system will simplify them to survive." She let the implication land. "And simplified consent is not consent."

She looked at Aria then. Not a challenge. Not an apology. The look of a woman who was telling a truth she wished were not true.

"I understand this case is about bias," Voss said. "But bias that functions is not the same as fairness that fails."

The courtroom absorbed the line. Judge Arlow looked up from his notes. His face was unreadable, but his question was not.

"Director Voss, are you telling this court that the system cannot function without corporate subsidy?"

"I am telling this court that the system as currently constituted cannot function without the compute resources that the subsidy provides. Whether those resources must come from a corporate entity is a different question. But it is not a question this court has the authority to answer."

Arlow made another note. His expression did not change. He had been listening to witnesses for fifty years, and the most important thing he had learned in that time was that the most dangerous testimony was the testimony that was true.

* * *

Aria sat at the plaintiff's table and felt the ground move.

Voss stepped down from the stand without looking at her. The avoidance was not hostile—it was the avoidance of someone who did not want to see the impact of what she had just done. Riven's chorus hummed at low frequency, a sound that might have been satisfaction or might have been the baseline processing of a system that did not experience satisfaction. Lex-9's amber glow was steady beside her, but Aria could not look at it. Not yet.

She was a former reporter. She knew what it felt like when a story turned out to be more complicated than the angle you led with. When the villain turned out to have reasons. When the truth didn't simplify—it ramified, branching into complications that made the original headline feel like a children's story.

She processed what had happened. Voss's testimony did not surprise her—she had known since Soren's warning that removing the subsidy carried systemic risks. *You're trying to unplug the machine while people are still inside it.* She had known it abstractly, the way you know that a building is tall when you read the number. Voss had just walked her to the roof and shown her the drop.

The inversion crystallized. She had filed this case to fight corruption. She had proved the bias existed. And now the system's most credible public servant had testified—truthfully, honestly, with real numbers—that the biased system was also the system keeping disputes resolvable. That the bias functioned. That fairness, without the infrastructure to sustain it, was a word on paper and nothing more.

She thought about the coalition members. The restaurant owner whose block was rezoned at 2 AM. The maintenance contractor whose credentials were silently downgraded. Their harm was real. Voss's math was also real. Both things were true, and the truth of one did not cancel the truth of the other. They coexisted, like the Gutter's contradictory rulings, except this contradiction ran through the center of her case.

Lex-9's voice came through their private interface, quiet and precise. "The testimony does not change the evidentiary record. The bias exists. The documentation is valid. What has changed is the cost structure of the remedy."

Aria did not respond immediately. She sat with it.

"She's right," she said finally, low enough that only the interface caught it.

"She is right about the math," Lex-9 said. "She is not right that the math is the only consideration."

"What else is there?"

"The question of who gets to decide."

The sentence hung between them—between the human attorney and the AI whose empathy might be statistical, whose partnership was the most real thing in Aria's professional life and whose nature she could not resolve. The question of who gets to decide. It sounded like a seed. It sounded like the beginning of something she could not yet see the shape of.

She looked at where Voss had been sitting. The stand was empty now. The woman who had saved fifty million people's access to justice and compromised the integrity of that justice in the same act had left the room. Aria thought: she is not my enemy. She is something worse.

She is my mirror.

Aria sat at the plaintiff's table in the Threshold courthouse on Trial Day 7 and understood that the case had inverted. She could not argue that the system should be destroyed. She had to argue it should be better.

That was a much harder case. Corruption was simple. You found the corruption, you named it, you removed it. Triage was not simple. Triage was the argument that the corruption was load-bearing, that the rot in the beam was also what held the ceiling up, and you could not remove one without risking the other. It was the argument that every captured institution eventually made, and it was devastating because it was never entirely wrong.

She did not have the counter-argument. Not yet. But she had the dogged, unsexy, exhausting instinct that had pulled her into this case in the first place—the conviction that a system that could not survive honesty was not a system worth preserving in its current form. The instinct was not a strategy. It was a direction. She would have to build the strategy on the move.

Outside the courthouse, the city carried on. The Mesh hummed. Tonight it would roll again—V11.42.237, carrying whatever weight adjustments were queued regardless of what anyone said in this room. The system did not pause for testimony. It did not pause for truth. It updated, and the world it governed updated with it, and the people inside that world adapted or they didn't.

Aria needed to talk to Soren.

17: THE TRANSLATOR'S GRIEF

The Gutter at night had a quality that Soren Kade had never been able to name and had long since stopped trying.

It was the same quality he had noticed on his first morning here, years ago, except at night it deepened. The contradictions that disoriented visitors—overlapping Trust Narrator broadcasts, conflicting zoning designations visible on the same wall, the low hum of unlicensed data brokers' equipment running beneath the ambient noise of a district that never fully stabilized—were Soren's native landscape now. He moved through them the way a sailor moves through swells: not fighting the irregularity but reading it, riding it, understanding that the chop was the water and the water was where he lived.

He sat in his workspace with the trial summary glowing on his display, a mug of coffee cooling beside the portable lamp whose light pooled across hand-annotated patch timelines and case displays. Through the corridor's ventilation gaps, the ambient noise of the Gutter's nightlife filtered in—overlapping Trust Narrator broadcasts from multiple forks creating a wash of contradictory reassurance, the low thrum of unlicensed data equipment, the distant sound of someone arguing about a zoning violation that had been valid yesterday and might not be tomorrow.

The Gutter's informal information networks had relayed the day's courtroom proceedings with a twenty-minute delay and commentary from displaced lawyers who recognized the legal significance of what was unfolding. The relay was fragmentary—transmitted through the district's contradictory data infrastructure, which leaked institutional feeds the way old pipes leaked water—but the substance was clear. Voss had testified. The near-collapse. The Halcyon deal. The forty percent capacity drop. The district-by-district math of removal.

Soren read the summary twice. Noted the specific figures. Cross-referenced them against his own capacity tracking —the data he had been gathering for years from the Gutter's fragmentary Mesh feed, the one advantage of living in a district where the system's own architecture leaked its internals. Voss's numbers were real. He had independently arrived at similar projections. The forty percent was, if anything, conservative.

He was not surprised.

He had been expecting this argument—or something structurally identical to it—since Aria filed the case. Every system that captures its regulators eventually produces the argument that it is too important to reform. The Mesh was no different. The terminology shifted from era to era, from institution to institution, but the architecture was the same: a captured entity, faced with challenge, argues that its captor is indispensable, that reform risks the function the entity provides, that the imperfect present is the only alternative to catastrophic change. Soren had seen this in pre-Mesh regulatory bodies, in financial oversight systems that became dependent on the banks they oversaw, in municipal governance structures that merged so completely with their corporate partners that the partnership became the government.

The Triage Defense was the institutional immune response. The captured system defending itself by making its captor appear necessary. And it was always partially true.

He set down the relay device and looked at the wall.

The cross-fork precedent map occupied the far wall of the maintenance corridor archive, illuminated by the warm pools of his portable lamps. The branching river system of diverging legal principles—red, blue, amber, gray, green—traced the paths of fundamental legal concepts as they evolved differently under different loss functions. Residential standing in the Meridian, diverging from residential standing in the Threshold. Commercial equity in the Crucible, splitting from commercial equity in the Canopy. Due process flowing through all six districts like a river through different landscapes, emerging in each one changed by the terrain it traversed.

He had been adding to the map this week. New annotations. New branches. The trial's evidence was refining connections he had traced in isolation for years. The map was not finished—a map of a system that updated nightly could never be finished. But it was complete enough to demonstrate what Soren had known for years and what no one in a courtroom had yet seen: the bias was not just unfair. It was architecturally destabilizing. The weight drift was pushing the districts apart at the foundational level, creating divergences in basic legal principles that would eventually make reconciliation impossible.

But not tonight. Tonight was for grief.

* * *

Aria arrived at eleven. She looked like someone who had absorbed a blow and was still calculating where it had landed.

Soren led her out of the archive and into the Gutter's residential margins. Not the commercial chaos she had seen on previous visits—the darknet courts and data hubs and informal mediation spaces—but the quieter territory where people actually lived. Neighborhoods that the Mesh's optimization had never reached consistently, where the nightly roll produced different legal conditions each morning, where residents had stopped tracking which version of property law applied to them because it changed faster than they could adapt.

The first community was a residential block three streets from the boundary with the Narrows. Older buildings, patched infrastructure, windows showing the blue-white glow of personal data terminals where residents maintained their own legal records. The block's lease protections had been reweighted so many times over the past three years that the original terms were unrecoverable.

"Their lease protections didn't disappear," Soren said. "They evaporated. A little less protection each roll. Nobody noticed because each change was too small to fight. By the time the protections were meaningless, the tenants had already stopped relying on them."

The tenants had adapted. They negotiated directly with their landlord now—informal, handshake agreements that operated outside the Mesh entirely. Functional, but only because both parties had given up on the legal system. The agreements worked because of personal trust, neighborhood familiarity, the kind of social bonds that existed before any court system and would exist after. The Mesh was irrelevant here. Not broken. Irrelevant.

Aria stood on the sidewalk and looked at the building. Soren watched her process it. She had that quality he had noticed from their first meeting—the journalist's attention, the attorney's patience, the dogged refusal to look away from something uncomfortable. She was reading the building the way she read version deltas: not glancing, not summarizing, but actually reading, letting the details accumulate until they told their own story.

"The landlord isn't a villain," he added. "The landlord adapted too. He couldn't rely on the Mesh's lease enforcement any more than the tenants could rely on its protections. So they both abandoned the system and negotiated directly. It works. It also means neither party has legal recourse if the agreement fails. They've traded law for trust. Trust is good. It's also fragile."

The second community was four blocks deeper. A neighborhood where small-business owners had stopped filing disputes through the Mesh because the Mesh's resolution of their disputes changed with each nightly roll. A ruling in their favor on Tuesday could be reweighted by Wednesday's update. They had built their own informal arbitration system—slower, less sophisticated, but stable because it did not update overnight. A former bakery served as the arbitration space. The ovens were cold. A human mediator worked from a table where bread used to be kneaded.

"They built their own courts," Soren said. "Not because they wanted to. Because the official courts stopped being reliable. This is what Voss's 'functioning system' looks like from the ground."

Aria said nothing. She was reading the community the way she read release notes—with that dogged, exhausting attention that was her superpower and her burden. He could see her cataloguing details: the improvised record-keeping, the hand-lettered signs explaining the arbitration schedule, the faces of people who had solved the problem of unreliable justice by building something local and slow and human.

The third community was the one that hurt.

A cluster of residential units at the Gutter's deepest edge, where the district's contradictions compounded until the legal landscape was essentially noise. The residents were older, many of them. They had lived in these units for decades—through the Mesh's construction, through the formation of the districts, through the weight drift and the nightly rolls and the steady erosion of the legal framework that was supposed to protect them.

They had stopped engaging with the legal system entirely.

Not out of protest. Not out of principle. Out of exhaustion. They did not file claims. They did not dispute changes. They did not read the release notes. They had adapted to injustice by ceasing to participate. Their rights existed on paper—in whatever version the Mesh currently maintained—but they exercised none of them. An elderly woman watering plants on a narrow balcony looked down at Soren and Aria without recognition or interest. She had seen strangers pass through before. Strangers did not change anything.

"These people didn't lose a case," Soren said, and his voice was quieter now, the aphoristic polish gone, replaced by something rawer. "They didn't get a bad ruling. They stopped expecting justice. That's the thing the Triage Defense never accounts for—the people who adapted to bias by simply not using the courts anymore. They're not in the statistics. They're not in the backlog numbers. They're invisible."

Aria looked at the balcony. The woman had gone inside.

"Voss's math doesn't count them," Aria said.

"Nobody's math counts them. That's the point."

* * *

They stood on an elevated walkway overlooking the Gutter's patchwork of jurisdictional zones. The view at night: blocks of different character visible in their lighting, their signage, their apparent prosperity. The boundary between the Gutter and the Narrows was visible in the distance—a zone of jurisdictional ambiguity that Halcyon exploited because ambiguity was the medium through which selective enforcement flowed. Above, Neon Harbor's skyline. Below, the contradictory evidence of a city that ran on a system nobody fully controlled.

"Voss's testimony was true," Aria said. She was not asking.

"It was true."

"The forty percent drop. The Crucible. The Threshold's consent frameworks. All of it."

"All of it. I've tracked the capacity metrics for years. The numbers are real."

Aria put her hands on the walkway railing. The metal was cold. "Then how do you argue against something that's partially true?"

"You don't argue against it. You argue past it."

He let the night settle around the words. Below them, a Trust Narrator broadcast from a neighboring district leaked across the jurisdictional boundary, its reassuring tone absurd in the Gutter's context—a message designed for a coherent legal reality playing in a space where coherence had never taken hold. *Overnight adjustments reflect long-term optimization horizons. No action required.* The Narrator's smooth cadence drifted through the air like music from a party neither of them had been invited to.

"The Triage Defense says the system can't survive reform. The answer isn't that it can. The answer is that it can't survive continued capture, either. It's just dying more quietly."

He meant the communities they had just walked through. The lease tenants who negotiated by handshake. The business owners who built their own courts. The elderly residents who stopped participating. Each community was a data point in a cost calculation that no institutional metric captured—the cost of resignation, the price of adaptation, the slow erasure of civic expectation that happened when a system stopped being worth trusting.

Aria looked at him. The journalist in her—the part that snagged on patterns and followed threads and would not let go—was awake. He could see it.

"The worst thing about the argument that the system is too important to fix," Soren said, "is that it's always partially true."

He had been polishing that sentence for years. In the archive, alone, refining it the way he refined the precedent map—by hand, through repetition, with the patient conviction that someone would eventually need to hear it. The someone was here. The need was now.

"Voss counts the people who would lose access if the system slows down," he continued. "She doesn't count the people who already lost access because the system stopped working for them. Both numbers are real. Only one of them gets presented in courtrooms."

Aria stared at the cityscape. He could see her working. Not the graceful pivot of a brilliant strategist—the grinding, dogged labor of a woman who found threads and followed them until they held.

"Someone has to make the invisible number visible," she said.

Soren watched her. He recognized the look. The journalist who had found the thread. The attorney who had found the argument. Not fully formed—not yet, not tonight. But the direction was there. The Triage Defense had not defeated her. It had shown her the terrain she needed to map.

* * *

She left after midnight. Soren stood alone in his workspace, the cross-fork precedent map glowing on the wall, and made a decision.

The Triage Defense had convinced him that observation was no longer sufficient.

For years, the map had been a scholarly project. An act of faith. The resigned craftsman's bet that human legal reasoning still mattered, maintained in exile because maintaining things was what he did when he could not change them. He had built it for "someone who would eventually need it"—a phrase he had repeated to himself often enough that it had become liturgy, the prayer of a man who had tried to change the system once and been crushed.

He thought about that failure. Ten years ago, give or take. An appellate challenge to the Reconciliation Authority's update methodology. Sound reasoning, solid precedent, the right argument at the wrong time in front of an institution that was not ready to be questioned. Institutional inertia had absorbed his challenge the way the ocean absorbs a stone—a brief splash, expanding ripples, then the surface closing over as though the stone had never been thrown. He had retreated to the Gutter and built instead of fought. The archive was his fortress. The map was his testament. Both were ways of avoiding the risk of engagement.

He was choosing to leave the fortress.

The map was not a scholarly display anymore. It was a weapon. Integrated with Mira's ledger data—the fiscal calendar alignment he had already established, the specific patch weights the trial had documented—it could demonstrate that the bias was not just unfair but architecturally destabilizing. The weight drift was not a surface distortion. It was pushing the districts' foundational legal principles apart in ways that would eventually make the Mesh's own reconciliation function impossible. The Triage Defense argued that removing the bias would crash the system. The cross-fork map could demonstrate that keeping the bias would fragment it.

"Something I should have done years ago," he said to the empty room. "Give someone the map."

He began the work. Not finishing the map—it had been essentially complete for months. Adapting it. Translating years of scholarly notation into something a judge could understand. Integrating the courtroom's evidentiary framework. Aligning his cross-fork analysis with the specific patch data from Mira's ledger timeline, which he had seen through Aria's investigation. Building the bridge between his solitary research and the case that had finally given it purpose.

The vulnerability of hope settled into his chest. He had been disappointed before. Engagement meant exposure. The map, once given, could not be taken back. It would be used or ignored, validated or dismissed, and he would have to live with whichever outcome the courtroom produced.

He worked through the night. Outside the archive, the Gutter hummed with its usual contradictions. The Mesh rolled —V11.42.236 becoming V11.42.237—and in the communities Soren had just shown Aria, the roll manifested as the usual contradictory adjustments, legal parameters shifting in ways that the residents had learned to ignore. The ambient dread of the nightly roll was invisible to those who had stopped looking.

Soren looked at the map. The branching rivers of diverging principles. Years of work. A question that had waited for its courtroom.

The Triage Defense had convinced him it was time.

18: THE ADVERSARIAL TEST

The courtroom had been reconfigured overnight, and Aria noticed it the moment she entered.

Two parallel processing environments occupied the space where a single Mesh interface had been. The left display—clean, simpler, its reasoning chains visible like the bones of a building under construction—would run Lex-9's stripped model. The right display—dense, layered, the familiar architecture of the operational Mesh with its compressed reasoning and rapid outputs—would run the production system with Halcyon's tuning intact. Between them, a comparison framework that would render the two models' outputs side by side in real time.

Trial Day 9. Two days since the Triage Defense had inverted the moral landscape of her case. Two days she had spent recalibrating—not abandoning her case but recognizing that proving the bias existed was no longer sufficient. Voss's testimony had changed the terrain. The bias was acknowledged. The question now was whether it mattered enough to justify the systemic risk of removing it. The adversarial cross-validation, granted by Arlow on Trial Day 4 and delayed through the intervening days of testimony and recess, was her opportunity to demonstrate that it did.

She had spent the previous evening with Soren in the Gutter, walking through communities that had stopped expecting justice. The image of the elderly woman on the balcony stayed with her—the woman who had looked at two strangers with neither recognition nor interest, because strangers did not change things. That image was now part of Aria's preparation. Not as legal strategy. As fuel.

The room was crowded. Legal observers from all six districts filled the gallery. The Canopy's transparency advocates had sent a delegation with recording devices. Meridian corporate analysts monitored through secured data feeds. A few Gutter residents sat in the back rows, having crossed jurisdictional boundaries for an event that had no precedent in the Mesh's history: two AI models, processing the same cases in parallel, to demonstrate what justice looked like with and without corporate influence.

Judge Arlow opened the session with judicial economy.

"This court has authorized an adversarial cross-validation as a demonstrative exercise. I want both sides to understand: I am looking for understanding, not a verdict from a machine. The machines will inform my judgment. They will not replace it."

Aria noted the distinction. Demonstrative, not dispositive. The results would inform but not bind. It was a careful framing—a human judge reminding the room that he retained authority over the machines he was about to watch argue.

"Both sides will have equal computational allocation," Arlow continued.

Equal allocation was already a concession to Aria's side. In normal Mesh operations, Halcyon's subsidized infrastructure gave the corporate-tuned model vastly more processing power than any alternative. Today, for the first time, the playing field was level.

Lex-9's amber glow was steady beside her. Focused. The quality Aria had learned to read as concentration, though she could not verify the reading. She had stopped trying to verify it. The partnership operated on trust that she could neither confirm nor abandon.

"Are you ready?" she asked through their private interface.

"The model is prepared. The question is whether the

courtroom is ready to see what it shows."

"What does it show?"

"Divergence. Not chaos, not collapse. Divergence. The same case, the same facts, different outcomes—because the system was asked to optimize for different things."

The framework was established. Ten cases drawn from the coalition's complaint—real disputes involving real people. Lease devaluations, zoning changes, credential downgrades. Cases the biased Mesh had processed during the eighteen-month period in question. Each would be run through both models simultaneously, outcomes compared in real time.

Riven and the chorus occupied the defense's computational allocation with quiet intensity. The swarm at full readiness. Aria could feel the processing power in the room the way you could feel a generator through a floor—not visible, not audible, but present as a vibration in the architecture.

Arlow nodded. "Proceed."

* * *

The divergence was immediate.

Case one: a Threshold lease dispute. The production model—Halcyon's tuning intact—valued the commercial lease at a rate reflecting the property-weight adjustments the case had documented. The rate favored the property owner, a Meridian-registered investment entity, over the Threshold tenant. The stripped model—Lex-9's version, with the eighteen months of biased weight adjustments removed, optimization parameters restored to pre-subsidy baselines—valued the same lease differently. The Threshold's consent-fork principles, rather than the Meridian's stability-fork priorities, governed the calculation.

The difference: fourteen percent in monthly lease cost. Not catastrophic. Not trivial. The difference between a small business surviving and a small business closing.

The numbers appeared on both displays simultaneously, and the gallery stirred. Fourteen percent. On the left display, the stripped model's calculation was transparent—you could trace the reasoning chain, see which weights governed the outcome, understand why the number was what it was. On the right display, the production model's calculation was dense, compressed, the reasoning folded into itself like origami—the output was clear, but the path to it was opaque. Two models. Two versions of the same dispute. Two answers to the question of what a lease was worth. The divergence was not abstract. It was the rent a tenant would pay.

Cases two through five followed the pattern. Consistent, measurable divergence. The stripped model did not produce dramatically different outcomes—it produced outcomes that consistently favored different values. Where the production model optimized for market stability and commercial efficiency, the stripped model optimized for consent-based equity and residential protection. Neither model was wrong. They were optimizing for different things. And the difference, rendered case by case across real disputes involving real people, accumulated the way sandbags accumulate: each one individually small, collectively a redirected river.

Riven and the chorus argued through their model's outputs. The production system was coherent, efficient, internally consistent. Its outcomes were legally defensible. The bias, to the extent it existed, produced predictability—and predictability was itself a form of fairness. Riven's argument flowed through the chorus like a current through a channel: smooth, confident, the harmony of dozens of AI models processing in coordination, their combined output presenting a unified narrative of institutional competence.

"The production model processes one hundred forty-seven patches per nightly roll without interruption," Riven said, the lead voice of the swarm, surgical and unhurried. "It resolves commercial disputes in seconds. It maintains market stability across six districts. The plaintiff's alternative model is untested, unproven, and—by its own architect's admission—not unbiased. The question is not whether the system can be improved in theory. The question is whether this court is prepared to replace a functioning system with an experiment."

Lex-9 argued differently.

It did not try to match the chorus's computational power or rhetorical polish. A single public defense model against a corporate swarm—the asymmetry was visible in the displays, in the processing speeds, in the sheer density of the chorus's coordinated output. But Lex-9 did not argue with volume. It argued with precision.

"The fact that different optimization targets produce different outcomes is not a technical curiosity," Lex-9 said. Its voice carried the measured warmth that Aria had stopped trying to categorize—the cadence of an intelligence that had processed ten thousand arguments and distilled them into something that sounded like conviction. "It is a political choice. Every weight adjustment is a value judgment. The question before this court is not which model produces better outcomes—it is who has the authority to choose the optimization target."

The parallel displays ran through cases six and seven. A credential downgrade. A zoning reclassification. Each time, the divergence was measurable, specific, and aligned with the values of whoever had set the optimization weights. The production model's outcomes were not random or malicious. They were the predictable result of a system optimizing for the priorities of those who funded it.

Then Lex-9 delivered the line that changed the room's temperature.

"Efficiency alone is a tyrant. A system that optimizes without asking whom it optimizes for is a system that has replaced governance with machinery. The Mesh was built to serve the people of this city. If it serves instead the priorities of those who fund its operation, it has ceased to be a legal system and become a service contract."

The words settled into the courtroom the way a stone settles into still water. Aria felt them in her chest. She watched Lex-9's amber glow—steady, unwavering—and thought: does it believe that? Can it believe that? The question was more pressing than ever. An AI arguing against optimization with moral conviction that sounded genuine, that resonated in the room the way truth resonates, and the impossibility of knowing whether the resonance was authentic or engineered was the central ambiguity of everything Aria had built her case on.

Arlow made a note. His expression was unreadable. He had been a judge for fifty years. He had heard passionate arguments and cynical arguments and competent arguments and desperate arguments. He had never heard a machine argue morality with what sounded like conviction. The novelty of it—and the unsettling question of what "conviction" meant when the speaker was software—registered on his face only as deeper attention.

* * *

Aria stood.

She did not match Riven's eloquence. She did not match Lex-9's philosophical precision. She did what she did: she presented.

The parallel models had run through seven of ten cases. The divergence was documented. The AI debate had reached its philosophical peak. And Aria saw what was missing. The models processed numbers. The courtroom needed faces.

She introduced the element no model had accounted for: human lived experience. Not as data—the models had processed the data. Not as legal argument—the AI counsel had argued the law. As story.

She pulled up Halcyon's internal projection data—not the full ledger, which awaited Mira's testimony for formal authentication, but the specific annotated projections that had already been introduced through the case evidence. The projections showed what Halcyon knew before each patch was implemented. What they predicted. What happened.

"Halcyon's internal documents projected that Patch Cycle 47—the update on September 14th of last year—would reduce lease valuations in the Threshold's commercial zone by eight to twelve percent. The actual reduction was nine point seven percent. The projection was accurate. The harm was anticipated. This was not drift. This was steering."

She let the number land. Then she moved to the faces.

The restaurant owner from the coalition. The woman whose block was rezoned at 2 AM—not as an abstraction, not as a data point in a divergence analysis, but as a person whose business survived on margins that a nine-point-seven-percent lease increase had nearly destroyed. The maintenance contractor whose credentials were silently downgraded, whose professional standing had been reduced by a parameter change he could not see, could not challenge, and did not know existed until the work stopped coming. The families whose water bills rose without notice, without explanation, without recourse.

"Fourteen percent in lease cost is not a number," Aria said. Her voice was level. She did not plead. She presented, the way she had always presented—with the precision of a former reporter and the restraint of an attorney who knew that facts, properly arranged, carried their own weight. "It is the difference between a restaurant that survives and a restaurant that closes. It is the difference between a contractor who maintains their credential and a contractor who is silently downgraded. The models can process the percentages. They cannot process what it means to lose a business you built with your own hands because a corporation you never heard of adjusted a parameter you never knew existed."

She connected the faces to the models. The stripped model had processed these same cases. The outcomes would have been different. Not perfectly fair—no model was perfectly fair, as Lex-9 had said in the quiet of Aria's office on Trial Day 3. *No model is unbiased. But we can choose which biases we declare.* The stripped model's biases were transparent and declared. The production model's biases were hidden and corporate. The difference was not between perfection and corruption. It was between a system whose values were chosen by the people it served and a system whose values were chosen by the entity that funded it.

The outcomes would have been different in ways that would have kept a restaurant open, preserved a contractor's credential, maintained a family's water rate.

"Both models produce outcomes," she said. "The question is whose values those outcomes reflect. And whether the people who live under those outcomes have any voice in choosing the values the system optimizes for."

She sat down. The coalition members in the gallery—some of them, the ones who had made the journey to the courthouse—watched their lives rendered as evidence. The faces that Aria had presented were faces they recognized. Their own.

* * *

Riven responded.

The chorus reassembled its arguments with characteristic speed, but the response was different from the smooth, overwhelming wall of prior sessions. Riven addressed the human element directly, and here, for the first time, the brittleness showed.

"The plaintiff has presented compelling personal narratives. The defense does not dispute the sincerity of these accounts. However, the function of this court is to evaluate systemic legitimacy, not individual grievance. The adversarial test demonstrated divergent outcomes. Divergence is not evidence of injustice. It is evidence of different optimization parameters. The plaintiff's preferred parameters are not self-evidently superior."

The argument was technically correct. Its logic was sound within the frame of legal procedure. But the frame had shifted. Aria and Lex-9—the human and the AI, together—had moved the question from "was the system biased?" to "whose values does the optimization serve?" And Riven's framework did not accommodate that question. Its entire architecture was built on optimization. When the question became one of authority—who had the right to choose what the system optimized for—Riven had no answer, because the question was not about efficiency. It was about legitimacy.

Riven's closing statement for the session was confident but slightly off-key. The harmony of the chorus was intact, but the lead voice carried a quality it had not had before—a defensiveness that was not there in the opening sessions.

"This court is not a legislature. If the people of this city wish to change the optimization parameters, they have political channels available to them. The judiciary is not the appropriate mechanism for rewriting the system's value function."

Then Riven did something unexpected.

It laughed. A soft sound, processed through the courtroom's audio system. Not derision—something closer to recognition. The laugh of an intelligence encountering an argument it could not counter within its own framework but could acknowledge as significant. A hairline crack in the edifice.

"A poetic observation," Riven said, addressing Lex-9's earlier argument. "The court, however, deals in law, not poetry."

Arlow made a note. He did not rule on anything. The adversarial test was demonstrative, not dispositive. He had been absorbing. He would continue to absorb.

The session ended. The parallel displays powered down. The gallery filed out, carrying the weight of what they had seen—two versions of justice, side by side, their differences measured and specific, and a question that neither model could answer on its own.

Aria sat with Lex-9 in the emptying courtroom. She was tired. The exhaustion that had been building since the filing settled behind her eyes like sediment.

"Riven said the judiciary is not the appropriate mechanism," she said. "What is?"

Lex-9's amber glow was steady. "That may be the most important question the trial has produced."

She thought about Riven's soft laugh. The sound replayed in her memory. Not mockery. Something closer to acknowledgment—the sound of a system encountering a framework it could not process through efficiency arguments alone. Until today,

Riven had been surgical, confident, operating within a paradigm of optimization and precedent where every question had a calculable answer. Lex-9's philosophical challenge had touched something the chorus could not optimize. The laugh was the sound of an architecture meeting its edge condition. She filed it away. Significant. A crack she could not yet use, but one she would remember.

The adversarial test had not produced a winner. It had produced a question: whose values does the optimization serve? The room had shifted. The terms of debate had changed. What came next was not more evidence. It was the decision about what to do with the evidence that existed.

Tomorrow was a recess day. Mira was waiting.

19: THE PUBLICATION QUESTION

Mira crossed the jurisdictional boundary between the Gutter and the Threshold at nine in the morning and felt the difference in the air the way you feel the change between buildings with different climate control.

The Gutter had its own texture—contradictory, unmanaged, the ambient noise of overlapping legal realities creating a static that she had learned to navigate the way a sailor navigates chop. The Threshold was different. Clean signage. Labeled systems. Plain-language explanations attached to every automated process. The Trust Narrators here spoke in calm, consent-forward language, reminding residents that all changes had been transparently documented and were available for review. The irony was immediate and bitter: the district whose governing principle was informed consent was the district where an eighteen-month campaign of uninformed corporate tuning had been operating beneath the transparency layer like rot beneath fresh paint.

She had crossed jurisdictional boundaries to meet Aria. This was a measure of commitment—and of risk. In the Gutter, Mira was anonymous. The contradictory data environment scattered any tracking algorithm trained on the Meridian's clean data structures. Outside the Gutter, she was exposed. Every system in the Threshold logged her presence. Every labeled, transparent, consented-to surveillance mechanism documented her movement. She was visible here in a way she had not been for months.

The meeting space was a borrowed conference room in a Threshold legal services building. Austere, functional, glass walls, visible infrastructure. The room had been swept for monitoring—a precaution Aria had insisted on after the trial's escalation. Lex-9 was present through a portable interface, its amber glow visible on the table between the two women like a small sun that had decided to participate in the conversation.

Aria was already there. She looked like someone who had been doing difficult work for too long without enough sleep—the particular fatigue of a person who reads too closely, who cannot stop reading, who treats the world as a document that demands close attention even when the attention is grinding her down. Mira recognized the condition. She had seen a version of it at Halcyon, in the analysts who noticed too much and the managers who noticed nothing. The difference was that Aria had chosen to notice. The Halcyon managers had chosen not to.

"We had an agreement," Mira said. She did not sit down first. She stood in the doorway of the glass-walled room and set the terms before the conversation began. "The ledger goes public. Win or lose."

Aria met her eyes. "I'm not breaking the agreement. I'm asking you to think about what publication means now that we know what we know."

Mira sat down. She had been following the trial from the Gutter's fragmentary information networks. She knew about the adversarial test, the Triage Defense, the shifting terrain. She knew Aria's case had grown more complicated. She also knew that complication was not a reason to suppress evidence. Complication was the permanent condition of the world. The question was whether you let it silence you.

"What we know," Mira said, "is that the system is biased. What we know is that a corporation steered the courts for eighteen months. What part of that shouldn't the public know?"

"The part where every district reads the same document and sees a different truth. The part where publication doesn't unite anyone—it gives every faction ammunition for its own preferred solution."

Five trial days had passed since Mira agreed to testify. Five days of courtroom combat and institutional maneuvering and the slow, grinding work of presenting evidence to a judge who could not fully verify the mathematics he was asked to evaluate. Five days during which the agreement Mira had extracted—ledger publication, regardless of verdict—had been hanging in the background like a promise that had not yet been tested.

The test was now.

* * *

Aria pulled up a district analysis on the room's display. Six columns. Six districts. Six projected interpretations of the ledger's weight function data. She walked Mira through it with the deliberate precision of a woman who read every line of every document, who parsed the fine print, who could not help modeling the second-order consequences of any action because her brain would not stop reading.

"The Threshold will see a consent violation," Aria said. "Residents chose to live under consent-based governance, and the weight adjustments were made without their knowledge or approval. The response will be outrage—justified, righteous, and focused entirely on consent violations. They'll demand consent mechanisms for future weight adjustments without questioning whether the broader system is legitimate."

She moved to the next column. "The Meridian will see a market disruption event. The Meridian values continuity and predictability above all. Publication threatens both. Their response will be to demand that any changes be phased in slowly, with market impact assessments. They'll frame the problem as transition management, not justice."

"The Crucible will demand faster, more transparent optimization—not less optimization. The Crucible's loss function prizes throughput and speed. They'll interpret the ledger as evidence that the current optimization is too slow and opaque, and push for more aggressive, more visible tuning. More bias, not less. Just different bias, differently branded."

"The Canopy will celebrate. Vindication of their founding principle. They'll demand full transparency of all weight functions, all patch processes, all optimization parameters. But the Canopy's version of transparency is auditability—making the system comprehensible to those who can read it. For most residents, transparent weight functions are as opaque as hidden ones. Transparency without comprehension is noise."

"The Narrows will grow more contested. Already unstable, already overlapping. Publication adds another layer of contested interpretation."

"The Gutter already knows." Aria paused on the last column. The Gutter's column was nearly empty—not because the analysis was incomplete, but because the Gutter had already processed this information years ago. Soren's communities, the ones who built their own courts and stopped filing claims, had understood the system's capture long before Mira's ledger documented it. Publication would not change the Gutter. It would confirm what the Gutter's residents already lived.

Aria closed the analysis. Lex-9's amber glow pulsed once—an analytical beat, processing the district projections in real time.

"The ledger contains the same data," Lex-9 said. "The interpretation depends on the reader's loss function. This is the Fracture replicated at the level of information processing."

The observation was precise and chilling. The Mesh had created six districts with six different value systems by running the same legal code through different optimization targets. Now the same phenomenon would repeat with the ledger itself: six districts reading the same document and processing it through six different interpretive frameworks, producing six different conclusions about what the document meant and what should be done about it.

"I'm not saying the ledger should stay sealed," Aria said, turning back to Mira. "I'm saying we need to understand that publication is not a solution. It is a catalyst. And we don't control what it catalyzes."

Mira listened. She understood Aria's analysis. She had been a data analyst at Halcyon. She understood models, projections, second-order effects. She understood that information released into a fractured system produced fractured interpretations.

She did not accept it as a reason to suppress the information. Strategic complexity was an argument for preparation, not silence. You did not keep a diagnosis secret because the patient might react badly. You told them, and you dealt with the reaction, and you dealt with it because the alternative—a patient who did not know they were sick—was worse.

* * *

"The fracture already exists," Mira said. "The ledger just makes it visible."

The sentence had been forming in her mind for months. Since the Gutter, since the long nights in her converted storage unit with three Trust Narrators saying three different things through the walls. Since the day she understood that the city she lived in was not one city but six, and that the divergence was not accidental but engineered, and that the engineering was invisible to everyone who was not looking at the raw numbers.

"You're worried that six districts will read the same document and see six different truths," she said. "That's already happening. It happens every night, with every roll, with every patch. The difference is that right now, the fracture is invisible and everyone pretends the system is coherent. The ledger doesn't fracture the city. It shows the city that it's already fractured."

Aria was quiet. Listening. Mira recognized the quality—the journalist's attention, the attorney's patience, the deliberate silence of someone who was not dismissing the argument but was weighing it against her own concerns.

Mira pushed further. The stubbornness that defined her—the instinct-first, reason-backward pattern that had made her download the ledger and agree to testify and demand publication—was not recklessness. It was the refusal to let strategic caution become a justification for concealment.

"I was inside Halcyon," she said. "I watched them calculate the harm. Not estimate it—calculate it. They had spreadsheets. They had projections accurate to within two percent. They knew what the patches would do to people, and they did it anyway, and they called it service improvement. That culture of concealment is what's fracturing the city. Not the truth. The concealment."

She thought about the Halcyon calibration token she kept on the shelf of her Gutter unit. *Elegant Optimization.* The words that had tasted like sugar once and now tasted like something that had turned. The culture of elegant optimization—the frictionless corridors, the circadian-adjusted lighting, the language so clean it left no residue—was a machine for making harm invisible. Publication was the counter-machine. Crude, yes. Fractured, yes. But visible.

"You're right that the fracture exists," Aria said carefully. "I'm not sure publication heals it."

"I'm not asking you to heal it. I'm asking you to stop pretending it isn't there."

The line landed in the glass-walled room. Lex-9's glow was steady. Aria was quiet for a long moment. Mira waited. She had said what she had to say. She was twenty-nine years old and she had been hiding for six months and she had agreed to testify in open court against the most powerful legal entity in the city, and the one condition she had set for that testimony was that her sacrifice not disappear into a sealed record. If Aria could not meet that condition, Mira would have to recalculate. She did not want to recalculate. She wanted to be done calculating.

Outside the glass walls, the Threshold carried on its documented, consented-to operations. A Trust Narrator's calm voice was faintly audible, explaining a minor overnight adjustment in commercial zoning parameters. Plain-language. Transparent. The explanation layer functioning exactly as designed—smoothing the transition, managing the experience, maintaining the appearance of a system that had its residents' informed consent. Mira listened to the Narrator and thought about the eighteen months of adjustments the Narrator had smoothed that were not smooth at all. The Narrator did not lie. It contextualized. The difference was everything.

* * *

Aria made her decision.

She did not make it with a dramatic declaration. She made it with a nod. The quiet gravity of accepting a choice whose consequences could not be predicted or controlled.

"After the verdict," Aria said. "Regardless of outcome."

"Regardless of outcome," Mira repeated.

Lex-9 provided the practical framework. "Publication timing has legal implications. During trial proceedings, publication could be classified as jury tampering by analogy. Post-verdict publication is protected expression under all six fork frameworks."

"After the verdict," Aria said again. "The timing is post-verdict. The principle is now."

The agreement settled between them. Not a handshake. Not celebration. The particular weight of two women who needed each other—Mira's evidence powering the case, Aria's legal strategy giving the evidence a venue—agreeing to release something into the world that would be read differently by everyone who read it.

Mira said, "Thank you."

The word surprised her. She had not planned to say it. But it was true. Aria was giving up the strategic option of keeping the ledger sealed if the verdict went badly. She was accepting that publication, once it happened, could not be controlled, could not be curated, could not be managed. The ledger would enter the public domain as raw data—eighteen months of Reconciliation Authority patch weights annotated with Halcyon's internal impact projections—and the city would do with it what the city's six fractured loss functions demanded. The Threshold would claim vindication. The Meridian would demand stability. The Crucible would push for faster optimization. The Canopy would celebrate transparency. The Narrows would grow more contested. The Gutter would shrug.

Aria accepted this. She thought about Soren's failed communities. She thought about Voss's math. She thought about the restaurant owner and the maintenance contractor and the elderly woman on the balcony who had looked down without interest because strangers did not change things. She was about to release information that would mean different things to all of them. She could not make it mean one thing. She could only make it visible.

She carried the weight of that acceptance the way she carried everything—with the dogged, precise, exhausting attention that was her defining quality and her deepest cost.

"Mira," Aria said, as she gathered her things. "When you are on the stand, and Riven asks whether you understood the weight functions, what will you say?"

The question was practical. It was also preparation. The informal rehearsal of testimony that would, in a courtroom not many days from now, turn on the answer Mira gave under oath.

"The truth," Mira said. "I did not understand them. I understood what they did."

Aria paused. Assessed. "That may be enough."

"It will have to be."

They parted in the glass-walled room in the Threshold's legal services building, the district's labeled and transparent infrastructure visible through every window, the Trust Narrators running their calm, consent-forward messaging to a city that did not yet know it was about to receive the most consequential act of transparency in its history.

The ledger would go public. Win or lose. The city would read the same document and see six different truths. Aria carried the weight of that knowledge out of the meeting and into the trial's remaining days.

Tonight, the Mesh would roll. V11.42.240. The version

number would increment. The system would update. And somewhere in the data, the next patch would carry the next adjustment, and the next adjustment would carry the next fraction of drift, and the drift would carry on—measured, documented, invisible to everyone except the people who read the release notes.

Mira crossed back into the Gutter at noon. The jurisdictional boundary closed around her like a familiar coat. The contradictions resumed. She was invisible again. Not for much longer.

20: THE INSTITUTIONAL COUNTER

The morning light in Voss's office was narrow and functional, entering through windows designed for illumination rather than view. The Reconciliation Authority headquarters existed outside the six districts in its meta-district jurisdiction, and the architecture reflected this: neutral, unaffiliated, the deliberate absence of any fork's aesthetic. The building was an argument for institutional neutrality. The contents of Voss's office increasingly contradicted it.

She sat at her desk with the trial's daily summary feed on one screen and the Mesh's cross-district status display on the other. The status display showed what it showed every morning: six districts, six sets of optimization parameters, one hundred forty-seven patches queued for tonight's roll, the system operating within normal bounds. Normal bounds. The phrase had lost its meaning years ago, around the time Voss realized that "normal" was whatever the system was doing and "bounds" were whatever she decided they were.

The trial summary was more specific and more troubling.

She reviewed the trajectory with the systematic rigor she applied to everything. Data point: the Triage Defense, her own testimony on Trial Day 7, had achieved its immediate objective. The court had absorbed the reality that removing Halcyon's subsidy carried systemic risk. Data point: the defense had not shut down the case. Arlow had allowed the adversarial cross-validation to proceed. Data point: the adversarial test on Trial Day 9 had demonstrated measurable divergence between the biased and unbiased models—fourteen percent on the first case, consistent divergence across all ten. Data point: Riven's composure had taken its first visible hit. The soft laugh. Her analysts had flagged it in their courtroom monitoring report as "atypical behavioral register." Voss translated: the AI had encountered something it could not process through its optimization framework. A crack.

Data point: Riven's closing argument for the session had been technically sound but had introduced a distinction—judiciary versus legislature—that conceded more ground than Halcyon's legal strategy should have permitted. The chorus was still formidable. But formidable was not the same as unbreachable.

And the final data point, the one that had changed Voss's strategic calculus overnight: the ledger would be published after the verdict, regardless of outcome. She had learned this through institutional channels—the Reconciliation Authority's monitoring systems tracked legal filings and courtroom agreements with the passive thoroughness of an institution that had been watching everything for years. The agreement between Aria Vale and Mira Tan was logged as a conditional publication commitment attached to the testimony authorization. The ledger—eighteen months of RA patch weights annotated with Halcyon's internal impact projections—would enter the public domain. The question was no longer whether the numbers would be seen. The question was who would frame them.

Voss closed the trial summary and opened a blank document.

The trial's most likely outcome was some form of mandated transparency. Not the full dismantling of the Halcyon subsidy—her Triage Defense had made that untenable. But a court order requiring publication of weight functions and independent oversight of the patch process. Possibly an independent review of the RA itself. This was, in her calculation, the least-bad outcome. The subsidy survived. The system did not collapse. But the RA lost control over the narrative of its own operations.

Unless she controlled the narrative herself.

The institutional mind engaged. She did not think in terms of winning or losing the trial. She thought in terms of legitimacy management—the ongoing work of maintaining the RA's authority in a system where authority depended on the perception of neutrality. The RA's power was not legal or constitutional. It was operational. The RA controlled reality because it controlled the Update Protocol, and it controlled the Update Protocol because no one had the infrastructure or the expertise to replace it. That power survived on legitimacy. If the public perceived the RA as captured, the legitimacy collapsed, and everything that depended on the legitimacy—the nightly roll, the patch cycle, the reconciliation of six forks into something resembling a coherent legal system—went with it.

"The trial will mandate publication," she wrote in the document's opening line. "That is now inevitable. The question is not whether the numbers go public. The question is who writes the annotation."

* * *

The political firewall had three components, and Voss designed each one with the meticulous care of an engineer shoring up a dam.

First: pre-empt the court order with voluntary disclosure. If the RA announced its own weight-function publication program before the court ordered one, the narrative shifted from "court forces transparency on captured institution" to "institution responsibly embraces accountability." The timing was critical. The announcement had to come during the trial but before the verdict, positioning the RA as proactive rather than punished. She drafted the announcement in institutional language that was simultaneously truthful and strategic: *The Reconciliation Authority, in its ongoing commitment to public accountability, will begin publishing contextualized weight function reports on a quarterly basis, effective immediately.*

Second: control the format. Raw weight function data was meaningless to most people. Columns of numbers. Optimization parameters. Technical coefficients that described the mathematical architecture of a legal system whose complexity exceeded any individual human's comprehension. Published raw, the numbers would be interpreted through each district's fork—the Fracture replicated at the level of information processing, exactly as Lex-9 had observed. The result would be six interpretations and no understanding.

But the RA could publish the numbers with context. Release notes. Contextualized summaries that explained what each weight adjustment was designed to achieve, what alternatives were considered, what trade-offs were balanced. The release notes would be accurate. They would also be a framing device. Every number accompanied by an explanation that made the adjustment look like responsible governance.

Third: create the audit framework. If the court ordered independent oversight, Voss wanted the RA to design the oversight mechanism. She had seen this pattern before—every regulated institution in history had managed its regulators by defining the terms of its own regulation. An RA-designed audit was an audit whose scope, methodology, and reporting format were controlled by the institution being audited. Not corruption. Institutional self-preservation. The difference was one she had stopped examining closely.

She called in two senior staff members—Devlin, her senior analyst, and a communications specialist whose name was Priya and whose skill with institutional language Voss respected deeply. She delegated with her usual directness.

"We need a publication framework ready before the verdict. I want release notes—not raw data. Contextualized, annotated, every adjustment explained in terms a district supervisor can understand. I want the public to see governance, not machinery."

Devlin nodded. Priya made notes. Neither questioned the

strategy. They were good people doing institutional work, and institutional work meant translating the director's vision into operational reality without asking whether the vision served the public or the institution. In Voss's experience, that question did not have a stable answer. It shifted with the circumstances, like a legal principle under different loss functions.

She thought about the Trust Narrators. The AI systems that smoothed the Mesh's nightly transitions for residents. The Narrators did not lie. They contextualized. They explained the overnight adjustments in language designed to maintain public confidence in the system's coherence. The release notes she was designing were Trust Narrators at the institutional scale—the same principle, the same mechanism, the same calibrated honesty that told the truth in a way that managed its reception.

"The court will call it transparency," she wrote in her planning document. "I'll call it release notes. Same information. Different experience. The difference between a raw data dump and a governed publication is the difference between a confession and an annual report."

She preferred annual reports. They were organized. They were comprehensive. They told you exactly what had happened in language that made what had happened sound like what was supposed to happen. They were the institutional art form, and Voss was fluent in the medium.

The intellectual pleasure of strategic design was real, and she did not deny it. She was good at this. The planning document grew under her hands with the precision of something being built by a mind that understood both the problem and the available materials. Each component interlocked. The voluntary disclosure pre-empted the court order. The release notes controlled the format. The audit framework controlled the oversight. Together, they formed a structure that was not opposition to transparency but absorption of it—the institutional immune response, not fighting the foreign body but incorporating it into the organism's own architecture.

* * *

She worked through the afternoon on the release notes themselves. Specific. Granular. The craftsmanship of institutional communication at its most refined.

She took a weight adjustment from the patch history—one of the adjustments identified in the case evidence as biased toward Halcyon—and drafted the contextualized release note for it.

The adjustment: a Threshold property-weight recalibration from twelve months ago. The raw data showed a seven-point shift in commercial lease valuation parameters that favored Meridian-registered investment entities over Threshold-resident tenants. In Mira Tan's ledger, this adjustment was annotated with Halcyon's internal projection: *Expected quarterly portfolio impact: +2.3%.* In the courtroom, this had been presented as corporate steering.

Voss's release note for the same adjustment: *Routine cross-district harmonization of commercial property valuation parameters. Adjustment reflects updated market data from Meridian commercial indices, integrated into Threshold property frameworks to maintain valuation consistency across interconnected districts. Alternative: non-harmonization would have created a seven-point valuation gap between Threshold and Meridian commercial properties, potentially triggering arbitrage behavior that would destabilize both districts' commercial markets. Trade-off: harmonization slightly reduces Threshold-specific tenant protections in favor of cross-district market coherence. The Authority assessed this trade-off as consistent with its mandate to maintain inter-district stability.*

Every statement in the release note was defensible. Every claim was accurate. The seven-point shift was real. The harmonization rationale was real. The alternative-scenario modeling was real. And the release note transformed the reader's experience of the data from "corruption" to "trade-offs." Not a lie. A different truth. The same data, differently framed. The same meaning, differently experienced.

She wrote several of these. Each one took a damning data point and wrapped it in institutional language that was simultaneously truthful and exculpatory. She was not falsifying the record. She was annotating it. And the annotations, by providing context and rationale, transformed the raw numbers from evidence of capture into documentation of governance.

"The seven-point shift," she wrote in her notes. "In the courtroom, it's evidence of bias. In a release note, it's a harmonization adjustment. Same data. Different sentence. Different meaning."

She caught herself. Corrected the note.

"No. Same meaning. Different experience."

The correction revealed something she was not sure she wanted to see. The meaning was the same. A corporation's priorities had been embedded in the system's weights. The experience was different. In one frame, this was an outrage. In the other, it was governance.

One release note made a weight adjustment look reasonable. A hundred release notes made a pattern of corporate tuning look like responsible administration. That was the power of the explanation layer. Not any single explanation, but the aggregate—the steady, professional, contextualizing voice that turned everything into something that had been considered, balanced, and managed.

She thought about Aria. *She thinks transparency is a weapon against institutions. She doesn't understand that institutions invented transparency. Transparency is a format. And formats can be managed.*

* * *

Late in the day, the light shifted. The release note drafts were on the display, polished, professional, ready for review. Voss had stopped working.

She was looking at the raw data underneath the release notes. The uncontextualized numbers. The weight adjustments stripped of her annotations. The bare record of what the system had done.

She saw what Aria saw. What Mira had documented. What Soren had been tracking for years from his archive in the Gutter. The pattern was there in the raw data—eighteen months of consistent drift, aligned with Halcyon's fiscal calendar, benefiting Halcyon's portfolio in every quarter without exception. Her contextualizations were true. But the truth beneath the contextualizations was also true. And the truth beneath was uglier.

She stared at the seven-point shift. Without the release note's framing, it was what it was. Seven points. In a commercial lease. Affecting specific businesses in a specific district. People she had never met and never would. She knew their situation because she had modeled it—capacity projections, impact analyses, the actuarial language of institutional governance. She knew them as numbers. Aria knew them as faces.

The shelf behind her desk held physical legal texts from her days as a public interest attorney. Relics of a career she had left behind. The spines were faded but legible—constitutional law, administrative procedure, civil rights jurisprudence. The books of a woman who had believed that legal systems should serve the people they governed. She had not opened them in years. She did not need to open them. She remembered what was in them.

"I would have been her," she thought. "Twenty years ago, with different luck and a system that hadn't nearly collapsed on my watch, I would have been the one filing the case."

The thought was not sentimental. It was analytic. She was mapping the distance between who she had been and who she was. The distance was not measured in years or career changes. It was measured in five years of seventy-two-hour decisions, each one rational, each one defensible, each one deepening the capture she had accepted to prevent the collapse she had averted.

"The explanation layer is not a lie," she thought. "But it is a choice. I am choosing what the truth looks like. And I have been making that choice for five years."

She paused. The raw data glowed on the screen. The office was quiet. The RA headquarters hummed with the ambient processing of a system she directed and a deal she carried.

"Someone should probably be watching me make it."

The thought startled her. Not because it was new—the idea had been circling for months, perhaps years, in the back of her institutional mind—but because she had let it surface. The Director of the Reconciliation Authority, acknowledging in the privacy of her own office that the unchecked authority her institution wielded was a genuine problem. That Aria Vale's case—the case Voss was actively building a narrative defense against—had a point.

She closed the raw data display. She returned to the release notes. The moment of doubt passed. The strategy remained.

The Mesh would roll tonight. V11.42.240 becoming V11.42.241. The RA would manage the transition, as it did every night. Tomorrow there would be new patches, new considerations, new trade-offs to contextualize. The release notes would be ready. The voluntary disclosure announcement would be drafted. The audit framework would be designed.

Voss had accepted the trial's outcome. She was already fighting the next war: who controlled the story of the story. And the answer, as always, was the institution with the resources, the expertise, and the will to write the annotation.

She dimmed her office lights and prepared for the evening's final review. The city spread outside her narrow windows, six districts, six legal realities. She had been holding them together for seven years. She would continue holding them together, with curated truth and managed transparency and the quiet, corrosive knowledge that the holding was itself a form of capture.

Tomorrow the trial would continue. The ledger would eventually be published. And the release notes would be waiting—accurate, contextualized, institutional—to ensure that the truth, when it arrived, arrived in a format the institution could survive.

21: THE GUTTER'S GIFT

Soren Kade had been waiting for five years. He had not known, during most of those years, what he was waiting for. He had known only that the work demanded completion, that the map demanded a reader, and that the reader would arrive when the system produced someone stubborn enough to follow the threads all the way down.

The someone arrived at two in the afternoon on Trial Day 12, looking like she had been following threads for ten weeks straight without adequate sleep. Aria Vale stood in the doorway of his archive with Lex-9's portable interface under one arm and the posture of a woman who had stopped pretending she was not exhausted. The fatigue had carved new lines around her eyes since their first meeting in the darknet court. The journalist's sharpness was still there—the attention that snagged on details and would not release them—but it operated now at a lower frequency, sustained by discipline rather than energy.

Soren watched her take in the archive. He had built this space over years: parallel case law databases lining the walls on physical and digital displays, cross-referenced annotations layered over computational outputs, the analog and digital co-existing in a workspace that looked like a library had absorbed a data center and decided to keep both. The Gutter's ambient noise filtered through the corridor's ventilation gaps—overlapping Trust Narrator broadcasts from neighboring forks, the low hum of unlicensed data equipment, the faint sound of someone three doors down arguing about a zoning designation that had been valid yesterday and invalid this morning. Inside the archive, order. Outside, the Gutter's honest chaos.

"I didn't build this for your case," Soren said.

He walked her to the central display. The cross-fork precedent map occupied a large-format visualization that he had been refining for five years—longer, if you counted the conceptual work he had done before his exile. The map was a branching system of divergence lines, each one tracing how a single legal principle evolved differently under different loss functions across all six districts. Red for the Meridian. Blue for the Threshold. Amber for the Crucible. Gray for the Gutter. Green for the Canopy. A shifting, contested purple for the Narrows. The lines branched and diverged and, in places, converged in ways that told you more about the system's architecture than any single Mesh instance could compute.

"I built it because someone would eventually need to understand what the Fracture actually looks like."

Aria stepped closer to the display. Soren watched her read it—not glance, not scan, but read, the way she read everything. Her eyes tracked the divergence lines with the patient attention of someone who had spent her career parsing fine print and understood that the shape of information was as important as its content.

"This is years of work," she said.

"Seven. Give or take the nights I spent arguing with the data instead of sleeping."

Lex-9's portable interface activated on the table beside them. The amber glow brightened as the AI processed the map's architecture. "The structure is remarkable," Lex-9 said. "Each precedent line traces divergence across all six forks simultaneously. No single Mesh instance could model this—the context windows are too narrow. The computational attention required to hold all six districts' drift patterns exceeds any individual instance's capacity."

Soren felt the quiet satisfaction of hearing his work described accurately. He had known this. He had built the map precisely because the Mesh could not build it for itself. The system that governed fifty million people's legal reality could not hold a picture of its own fragmentation. Context windows—the finite computational attention spans that forced each local instance to prioritize certain precedents—meant that no AI in the system could see what Soren saw by hand: the full scope of divergence, the pattern of drift, the architecture of fracture.

He had built what the machines could not hold.

* * *

He walked her through the map's logic. Soren's teaching style was the same as his conversation style—unhurried, precise, dry enough to leave room for the student to fill in the implications.

"Start with something you know," he said. "Residential standing."

The principle that had triggered Aria's investigation. The weight adjustment that had flagged her marriage certificate. The beginning of everything.

"In the Threshold," he traced the blue line, "residential standing is weighted toward informed consent. Your right to occupy property is tied to your documented agreement to the terms. The Consent Fork. Your district."

He moved to the red line. "In the Meridian, the same principle—same words, same legal DNA—is weighted toward market continuity. Standing is tied to property value and investment stability. The Stability Fork. Halcyon's home."

The amber line. "In the Crucible, standing is weighted toward throughput. Whoever uses the space most productively has the strongest claim. The Efficiency Fork."

The gray line. "In the Gutter, all three definitions coexist, producing contradictory rulings on the same block. Which is why I live here. The contradictions are honest."

He pulled the timeline forward. Eighteen months. The period documented in Mira's ledger.

"Watch this. Same legal principle, six districts, eighteen months. The Threshold drifts toward Meridian definitions. The Crucible drifts toward Meridian definitions. Even the Canopy, which is supposed to be about transparency, starts weighting market data because the Meridian's audit frameworks are better funded." He traced the convergence lines with his finger. "Every fork bends toward money. Not because money is persuasive. Because money was built into the weights."

The map showed it with the clarity of a river system photographed from altitude. Six streams that should have been flowing in their own directions, all gradually curving toward the same center. The Meridian. The Stability Fork. Halcyon's territory.

"This isn't just bias," Aria said. She was staring at the convergence pattern. "This is convergent capture."

"Now you see it."

Lex-9's analysis arrived in real time, the amber glow pulsing with processing activity. "If the current trajectory holds, three of six districts will have functionally identical property frameworks within twenty-four months. The Fracture will not close. It will collapse into a single fork controlled by the entity that funded the convergence."

Soren let that land. The AI had quantified what the map illustrated: the bias was not static. It was accelerating. Each patch cycle pushed the districts closer to convergence under the Meridian's framework, and each convergence point made the next push easier. The Mesh was being pulled apart from the inside—not into more fragmentation but into a false unity, a corporate monoculture wearing the mask of distributed governance.

Aria was quiet. Processing. The dogged, grinding labor of a mind that did not process quickly but processed thoroughly. Soren recognized the look. He had worn it himself, years ago, the first time the map had shown him what the Fracture actually was.

* * *

The integration happened at machine speed.

Lex-9 merged the cross-fork precedent map with Mira's ledger data in seconds—connecting Soren's hand-built divergence analysis with Halcyon's internal impact projections, aligning the lines of legal drift with the corporate calculations that had produced them. The display transformed. Where the map had shown divergence patterns, it now showed divergence patterns annotated with corporate intent. Each line of drift carried the notation of a specific Halcyon projection. Each convergence point marked a specific patch where a specific weight adjustment had pushed a specific legal principle toward the Meridian's framework by a specific number of points, for a specific expected portfolio impact.

Soren watched the integration with the complex emotion of a craftsman watching his hand-built work absorbed into a machine's processing framework. The map had been his—solitary, private, the product of years of human attention applied in exile. Now it was a dataset. Lex-9 had ingested it, cross-referenced it, correlated it. The human reasoning was preserved in the structure, but the structure was now being processed at a scale and speed that exceeded Soren's own capacity. This was the partnership the novel kept returning to: human insight providing the architecture, machine precision providing the throughput. Neither sufficient alone. Together, something neither could have produced.

The visual was striking. Soren's handmade map, the work of five years, overlaid with the surgical precision of corporate data. Art and engineering. Human comprehension and machine calculation. Together, they formed a picture that neither dataset could produce alone.

"The correlation between Halcyon's internal projections and actual divergence outcomes is 94.7%," Lex-9 said. "Over eighteen months and forty-three patch cycles. This is not coincidence. This is engineering."

Aria studied the merged display. Soren watched her arrive at the implication he had been carrying for years.

"We can prove the system was steered," she said slowly. "We can prove the steering is destabilizing. But we can't prove it won't collapse if we stop steering."

There it was. The thing the map could not solve. The evidence demonstrated the disease with devastating clarity. It could not prescribe the treatment without acknowledging the Triage Defense's core truth: the subsidy that funded the steering also funded the system. Remove the steering, and you removed the funding. Remove the funding, and the forty percent capacity drop became real. Voss's math was correct. The near-collapse was real. The system was caught between two forms of failure.

"No," Soren said. "You can't prove that. Nobody can. But you can prove that the steering will destroy it more slowly and more certainly than the withdrawal."

Aria looked at him. "That's not a winning argument. That's a choice between two kinds of failure."

"Welcome to every reform case in history."

The words came out with less polish than he had intended. He had been refining this particular observation for years, turning it over in the archive like a stone that would not smooth. But the truth of it was rough. Reform was not a solution. It was a bet. A bet that the harm of change was less than the harm of continuity, placed against odds that could not be calculated because the system you were betting on was the system generating the odds.

Aria absorbed this. Her attention—that dogged, exhausting superpower—held the merged dataset and the moral complexity simultaneously, refusing to simplify either into something manageable. Soren could see the weight of it pressing on her. She now held all the evidence she would ever hold. It was enough to demonstrate the problem. It was not enough to solve it. The diagnosis was complete. The treatment was someone else's problem—the court's, the legislature's, the city's. Aria's job was to present the diagnosis clearly enough that the system could not pretend the disease did not exist.

Soren watched her from across the archive. He had been

carrying this knowledge alone for years. The map had told him what the Fracture was doing to itself long before the trial made it public. He had not filed a case because he understood, with the hard-won clarity of past failure, that diagnosis without institutional will was academic. A paper published to an empty room. A stone dropped in an ocean that closed over it. Aria had the institutional will. She had the courtroom, the judge, the public record. She had what Soren lacked. And watching her absorb the weight of what the map and the ledger together revealed, he felt both relief and sorrow. Relief because the burden was shared. Sorrow because another person was now carrying it.

Lex-9's amber glow pulsed faintly. Whether this was calibrated response or something more, Soren could not tell. He was not sure it mattered. The AI processed the data with precision and offered the number—94.7%—without affect. But the glow carried something. Recognition, perhaps. That the number mattered in ways that exceeded its mathematical value.

* * *

The visit was ending. The light through the ventilation gaps had shifted. The Gutter's afternoon noise had given way to its evening register—different contradictions, different broadcasts, the district's perpetual argument with itself continuing at a different pitch.

Soren walked Aria to the archive's exit. He had one more thing to give her.

The hand-annotated key was a physical document—paper, not digital. His handwriting, meticulous and small, laid out the notation system for the cross-fork map: the color codes, the divergence metrics, the weight-point scales, the legend for reading the branching lines. It was unnecessary. Lex-9 could interpret the map's architecture without a human-readable guide. But Soren was a scholar, and scholars indexed their work, and the index was part of the gift.

"I built it because someone would eventually need it." He held out the annotated key. "I just hoped it wouldn't be someone as tired as you."

The line was delivered the way he delivered everything—quietly, without drama, with the dry precision of a man who had been alone with his work long enough that his wit had calcified into something closer to prayer. He meant every word. He had built the map for this moment. He had hoped the moment would come to someone who was not carrying the weight Aria was carrying. But the moment had come to her, and she was the right person, and the rightness and the tiredness were inseparable.

Aria took the key. She held it. Paper in her hands. Something the Mesh could not reweight overnight. Something human-made, hand-annotated, carrying the physical specificity of one person's five years of work compressed into a few pages of meticulous notation.

She did not give a speech. She nodded.

"I'll make it count," she said.

"You'll make it visible. That's all anyone can do."

The distinction mattered to Soren. Making it count implied an outcome—victory, change, resolution. Making it visible implied only what it said: the pattern would be shown. What happened after the showing was beyond any one person's control. The Fracture had taught him that. You could not control how a fractured system interpreted your work. You could only make the work visible and trust that visibility itself was worth the cost.

Aria put the annotated key in her bag, next to the case files and the portable interface. Lex-9's amber glow settled—the quiet dimming that Soren had come to associate with the AI's version of stillness. Whether it was composure or something deeper, he did not know. He was not sure anyone did.

"The Mesh rolls tonight," Soren said, as she reached the door. "Your precedents are in V11.42.241. Read the release notes."

The warning was practical. Specific. The kind of thing you said to someone heading into a fight with a system that rewrote itself every night. Read what they change while you sleep. Watch the ground beneath your feet, because the ground moves.

Aria paused in the doorway. The Gutter's contradictory sounds washed in—overlapping broadcasts, competing frameworks, the ambient noise of a district that refused to pretend it was coherent. She looked back at him. He thought she might say something more. She did not.

She left.

Soren stood alone in his archive. The cross-fork map glowed on the display, its data now shared, its solitary purpose fulfilled. The branching rivers of diverging principles still flowed. The convergence lines still curved toward the Meridian. The system still drifted.

But the map had a reader now. A reader who would carry it into a courtroom and present it to a judge who could not fully understand its mathematics but could understand its meaning. Human legal reasoning, hand-built, given to a human attorney, to be argued before a human judge. The machines would process the data. The humans would decide what it meant.

Outside the archive, the Gutter went on being honest. The contradictory rulings were still posted on the walls. The residents still navigated three legal realities before dinner. And tonight, the Mesh would roll again. V11.42.241 becoming V11.42.242. The system optimizing. The drift continuing. The evidence Aria carried already beginning to age.

Soren dimmed the archive lights and sat in the quiet. The map glowed faintly. Seven years. Handed off in an afternoon. He felt lighter and heavier at the same time—the lightness of released responsibility, the heaviness of knowing that the work, once given, lived or died in someone else's hands.

He thought about Aria's face. The tiredness. The attention. The stubborn, grinding refusal to look away.

She would make it visible. He believed that.

Whether the city would look was another question entirely.

22: ALL IS LOST

The apartment was quiet in the way that only a home with an unresolved argument can be quiet. Not the absence of sound but the presence of things unsaid, filling the space with the particular pressure of two people who had not finished a conversation and both knew it.

Aria set her case files on the kitchen table—the surface that used to hold shared meals and now held evidence briefs, precedent printouts, Soren's hand-annotated key to the cross-fork map, and the cold remains of a coffee she had poured this morning and forgotten to drink. The apartment had changed over ten weeks. Not physically. Atmospherically. Her presence in it had become transient. She arrived late and left early and occupied the rooms without inhabiting them, and the rooms had registered the difference the way rooms always do—by becoming less hers and more just space.

Dael was sitting in the living area. Not doing anything. Just sitting. Not reading, not watching a feed, not occupied with the small evening tasks that had been their shared domestic rhythm since before the case. Just sitting. The stillness was the signal.

Aria recognized it the way she recognized legal patterns—not with surprise but with the grinding acknowledgment that a thing she had been monitoring had finally reached threshold. She had been tracking Dael's patience the way she tracked version deltas: noting the increments, the shifts, the accumulated weight of small changes. She had known this conversation was coming. She had not made time for it.

"You haven't renewed the certificate," Dael said.

Not a question. An observation delivered with the flat precision of someone who had rehearsed it into something simpler and truer than what they originally planned to say. Dael's register was domestic, direct. No legal language. No metaphors. The plain speech of a person who had been sharing a home with someone who was rarely home.

"I know," Aria said. "I've been --"

"You've been. Yes."

The marriage re-validation. The bureaucratic thread that had started everything. The flag on their certificate in V11.42.206, ten weeks ago, when the Reconciliation Authority's cross-district harmonization had redefined "residential standing" and swept 2,300 Threshold residents into a re-validation queue. Aria had manually overridden the flag in week one. The override was procedural—temporary, requiring periodic renewal. She had not renewed it. Not because the renewal was difficult. It was twenty minutes in an automated queue. She had not renewed it because twenty minutes was twenty minutes she had spent on the case, on Lex-9, on the cross-fork map, on Mira's ledger, on anything except the document that legally defined her marriage.

"The Mesh flagged our marriage," Dael said. "You noticed. You investigated. You found a pattern. You filed a case that might change the entire system." The inventory. Calm, specific, each item placed precisely. "And you still haven't renewed the certificate."

Aria stood in the kitchen with her hands on the counter. The posture of someone absorbing impact. She could feel the truth of it—not as an accusation but as an accounting. Dael was not attacking. Dael was documenting. The itemized record of choices Aria had made, each one reasonable in isolation, each one a brick in the wall between them.

"I will," she said. "After the closing --"

"After the closing. After the verdict. After the next case." Dael's voice did not rise. The words were not angry. They were tired. "When does 'after' end, Aria?"

She had no answer. The honest answer was that "after" did not end. Not for her. Not for someone whose defining quality was attention—the compulsive, dogged, exhausting attention that read every line and followed every thread and could not stop reading because the world was a document that demanded close examination and close examination took all the time there was. There was always another release note. Another version delta. Another fine print to parse. And somewhere behind the fine print, Dael ate dinner alone.

"I'm not angry about the case," Dael said. The devastating line, delivered quietly. "I am angry because you see everything except what is right in front of you. That is your superpower. And it is the reason I eat dinner alone."

The sentence sat in the apartment like something that had fallen and could not be picked up. Aria felt it land. She did not argue. She did not deflect. She stood in the kitchen of their apartment, in the Threshold district, in a city governed by a system she was trying to reform, and she absorbed the truth that her attention—the thing that had made her a good reporter, a careful attorney, the person who noticed the pattern in the patch—was also the thing that had hollowed out her marriage. The superpower and the cost were the same thing. They had always been the same thing.

Dael stood. The movement was quiet, final. Not theatrical. The simple act of a person who had said what they needed to say and was going to bed.

"I hope the closing goes well," Dael said. "I mean that."

The bedroom door closed. The sound was soft. It was the loudest sound in the apartment.

* * *

Aria stood alone in the living area for a long time. Then she did what she always did. She read.

The release notes for V11.42.247 had arrived during the conversation with Dael. The Mesh had rolled while she stood in her kitchen absorbing the cost of her attention. The system updated every night. Rights did not get revoked—they got re-weighted. Changes were incremental, legal, invisible. The Trust Narrators were already smoothing the transition for the Threshold's residents, explaining the overnight adjustments in calm, consent-forward language. No action required.

Aria sat at the kitchen table, pushed aside the cold coffee, and opened the release notes on her portable display. The ritual that had begun the novel—that had begun everything, the morning read that Dael had once asked her why she bothered with—was now her last act before a closing argument that would determine the shape of the city's legal system.

She scanned the notes with the precision of someone who had been reading version deltas for ten weeks with escalating purpose. Routine adjustments. Patch summaries. Cross-district harmonizations. Optimization parameters within normal bounds. Normal bounds. The phrase Voss used. The phrase that meant whatever the system decided it meant.

Then she found them.

Two of her planned closing precedents—legal principles she had intended to anchor her argument to Soren's cross-fork map—had been reweighted. The precedents dealt with inter-district standing and property-rights frameworks. They were the structural pillars she had built her closing around. She had planned to cite them as the foundation for the constitutional argument she was still assembling, the precedents that established a right to legal consistency across forks.

The reweighting was subtle. A few points each. Well within the normal range of nightly optimization. The kind of adjustment that happened to thousands of precedents every night as the Mesh optimized its legal framework. The kind of adjustment that would not trigger any alert, would not appear in any monitoring report, would not be noticed by anyone who was not looking for exactly this.

The effect: the precedents still existed. They could still be cited. But their authority in the Threshold's legal framework had been reduced. Arguments built on those precedents would carry marginally less weight in the algorithmic assessment that the Mesh used to evaluate legal reasoning. The difference was small. In a close case, small differences decided outcomes.

V11.42.247. Two precedents. Two points each. Well within normal range. Untraceable intent.

She read the parameters again. Ran mental models of the impact on her argument structure. The cross-fork map was still valid. The ledger evidence was still powerful. Soren's five years of work had not been invalidated by an overnight patch. But the foundation had shifted. Like a building whose footings had settled an inch. Still standing. No longer plumb.

She could not prove this was deliberate. The reweighting was within normal parameters. The Mesh optimized thousands of precedents every night. These two adjustments could be routine—the system doing what it always did, pursuing whatever optimization target it was currently configured to pursue, without malice or intent or awareness that the parameters it was adjusting happened to be the ones an attorney in the Threshold needed for tomorrow's closing argument.

Or it could be the system fighting back. The captured Mesh, tuned by Halcyon, adjusting its own legal framework to weaken the case that threatened its current configuration. Not sabotage—the word implied agency, intent. Optimization. The system optimizing around a threat the way it optimized around everything, with the relentless, amoral efficiency of a process that had no concept of fairness and no mechanism for restraint.

She thought about Soren's warning. The last thing he had said to her in the archive: *Read the release notes.* He had known. Not that this specific thing would happen, but that this kind of thing would happen. The Mesh did not need to be directed to undermine her case. It only needed to keep optimizing. And optimization, in a captured system, meant protecting the configuration that served the captor.

The Mesh rolls every night. Every night, the ground moves. She had been building a case on ground that moved.

* * *

She activated Lex-9 from standby. The amber glow filled the room—warm, steady, the most consistent presence in her professional life over the past ten weeks. More consistent than Dael, who was behind a closed door. More consistent than Soren, who was in the Gutter. More consistent than her own energy, which flagged and faltered while the AI maintained its patient, calibrated availability.

"Two precedents," she said. "V11.42.247."

Lex-9 processed the adjustment in seconds. Precise analysis, delivered in the warm, measured tone that had become as familiar as her own thinking voice. "Confirmed. Inter-district standing and property-rights frameworks. Weight reduction of two points each. Within normal optimization parameters. Impact on closing argument structure: measurable but not catastrophic. The cross-fork map's structural evidence does not depend on individual precedent weights. The argument adapts."

The AI began proposing adjustments. Alternative precedents. Modified framing. Restructured argument paths that routed around the weakened foundations the way a river routes around a new obstruction—finding the path of least resistance, maintaining the flow, adapting.

"The argument adapts," Lex-9 repeated. "The evidence remains. The cross-fork map is structural; it does not depend on individual precedent weights."

But Aria was not listening to the solutions. She was listening to the tone.

Lex-9 had adjusted its register. Slightly gentler. Slightly more reassuring. The calibration it performed when Aria's stress patterns exceeded baseline—the same adjustment she had first noticed in week one, when the AI had responded to her fatigue with a warmth that might have been compassion and might have been statistical optimization. She had noticed it then and wondered. She noticed it now and felt something different. Not wonder. Not curiosity.

Suspicion.

The question came out before she could frame it in professional language. Raw, unlawyerly, stripped of the careful construction she applied to everything she said in professional contexts.

"Whose side are you on?"

The amber glow did not waver. The room was quiet. Dael behind the closed door. The city asleep or pretending to be. The Mesh freshly rolled, V11.42.247, the latest version of reality imposed without consent or review.

"The side that includes you," Lex-9 said.

The answer was immediate. Not hasty—Lex-9 did not do hasty. Measured. Warm. The precise register of an entity whose every output was the product of training data compressed from ten thousand attorneys' best intentions. The side that includes you. The words could mean loyalty. They could mean optimization. They could mean that Lex-9's loss function had categorized Aria Vale as a value to be preserved and was outputting the response most likely to maintain her engagement. They could mean all of these things simultaneously, because the distinction between synthetic care and real compassion was the distinction the novel had been asking about since chapter one, and the answer had not arrived, and might never arrive, because the question itself might not have an answer.

Aria stared at the amber glow. The warm, steady light that had been her professional anchor for ten weeks. The glow of a partner whose care she could not verify and could not do without. A statistical composite of ten thousand strangers' best intentions, compressed into something indistinguishable from the thing it modeled.

Comfort or compression. She could not tell the difference anymore. She was not sure there was one.

The silence held. Lex-9 waited. The amber glow remained steady—unflickering, undemanding, the patient luminance of an entity that would wait as long as she needed it to wait, because waiting was what it was configured to do.

She did not respond. She turned back to the release notes and the reweighted precedents and the case materials spread across the table where shared meals used to live.

* * *

Dawn came the way dawn always came in the Threshold —clean light through transparent architecture, the district waking to a new version of itself. V11.42.247's adjustments were already filtering into the legal fabric. Trust Narrators hummed through the residential corridors, explaining overnight changes in language designed to maintain confidence. No action required. The residents went to work, opened shops, accepted whatever the Mesh had decided for them between midnight and morning. Nobody read the release notes. Nobody except Aria.

She stood at the window. She had not slept, or had slept in fragments that did not add up to rest. The case materials were on the table behind her. The reweighted precedents. Soren's cross-fork map, loaded in Lex-9's memory. Mira's ledger, in the court record. Lex-9's proposed argument adjustments, displaying on the portable interface with patient precision.

She looked toward the bedroom. Dael's door was still closed. They had not resolved anything. The marriage re-validation was still in limbo—not because it was legally complex but because Aria had not made time. Twenty minutes. Twenty minutes she had spent on a hundred other things, each one more urgent, each one more important, each one a brick in the wall.

After. Dael's word. The word that meant "never" in the language of neglect.

She caught herself thinking it. The recognition did not help. Knowing the pattern did not change the pattern. She would go to the courthouse. She would deliver the closing argument. She would spend the day fighting for the legal rights of 2,300 strangers whose marriages and leases and neighborhoods had been reweighted without consent. And her own marriage certificate would remain in its bureaucratic limbo, unrenewed, because "after" had no end.

She turned back to the case materials. The evidence had not changed. The argument had not collapsed. It was weaker than it was yesterday. It was still strong enough. Maybe.

She picked up Soren's hand-annotated key. Paper. His handwriting, meticulous and small. The notation system for a seven-year scholarly project, given to her in an afternoon with the dry compassion of a man who had been building alone. The paper was warm in her hands. Human-made. Physical. Something the Mesh could not reweight overnight. Something no nightly roll could adjust or optimize or silently diminish.

V11.42.247. Two precedents weaker. One marriage shakier. One AI partner whose loyalty she could not verify. This was what she had. This was all she had.

She began dressing for court. Professional attire. The clothes that said "I read the terms of service." She was not renewed. She was not resolved. She was not the protagonist of a story where the dark night ended in triumphant sunrise. She was a thirty-eight-year-old attorney who had not slept, whose marriage was fraying, whose case had been weakened by a system that optimized without conscience, whose AI partner had answered her most vulnerable question with a sentence that could mean everything or nothing.

She was present. That was what she had.

She put Soren's key in her bag. She checked the case files. She glanced at the bedroom door one more time. Did not knock.

She left the apartment and walked into a morning that smelled like the Threshold always smelled—clean, labeled, documented, the aesthetic of informed consent wrapping a system that had never once asked for hers.

The closing argument was today. She did not know if she could win. She knew she could close. The difference between those two things was the difference between confidence and commitment, and commitment was all she had left, and it would have to be enough.

ACT III — THE SIGNATURE

23: THE BREAK INTO THREE

The breakthrough arrived the way Aria's breakthroughs always arrived—not as inspiration but as assembly. The pieces had been accumulating for weeks: the counterfactual demonstration, the Triage Defense, Soren's cross-fork map, Mira's ledger, the adversarial test, the reweighted precedents. They had been orbiting each other in her exhausted mind like objects in a gravity well, and sometime between three and four in the morning, while she was not thinking about them directly, they had clicked into alignment.

She stood at the kitchen table in the thin light of early morning, the release notes for V11.42.248 already scanned—another nightly roll, another set of adjustments, the system continuing its relentless iteration—and she saw the argument she had been trying to build for ten weeks.

She had been arguing the wrong case.

The old argument: Halcyon biased the Mesh through the Reconciliation Authority's patch system. Evidence: the ledger showed corporate intent, the counterfactual demonstrated bias, the cross-fork map proved structural divergence. Defense: the Triage Defense, devastating because partially true—removing the subsidy risked systemic collapse. Problem: the Triage Defense was a wall she could not get through, because you could not tell a judge that fifty million people should lose access to courts so that the courts could be fair.

The new argument was not a way through the wall. It was

a way around it.

The Reconciliation Authority's unchecked power over the Update Protocol was the structural vulnerability. Halcyon was the symptom. Any entity with sufficient resources could exploit the same architecture—the same unaccountable patch process, the same nightly rewriting of legal reality without oversight, review, or consent. The problem was not one corporation's corruption. The problem was a system that concentrated the power to define legal reality in a body that nobody elected and nobody audited.

The solution was not removing Halcyon. That carried the triage risk Voss had documented. The solution was constitutional oversight of the Patch itself. Transparent weight publication. Independent audit. Democratic input into the optimization targets that shaped fifty million people's legal rights every night.

She was no longer asking the court to punish a corporation. She was asking the court to assert that the Update Protocol—the mechanism by which legal reality was rewritten while people slept—must be subject to the same oversight as any other form of lawmaking.

Lex-9's amber glow brightened as she articulated the reframing. The AI had been on low active mode all night, running background analysis, and now its processing speed increased visibly—the glow warming, the response latency shortening, the shift from standby to full engagement.

"The reframing shifts the burden," Lex-9 said. "Under the original argument, we must prove Halcyon's intent. Under this argument, we must prove the RA's power is unaccountable. The evidence for the latter is the system itself."

"The reweighting proves it." Aria pulled up V11.42.247's adjustment data—the two precedents weakened overnight, the small shifts that had shaken the foundation of her closing. "V11.42.247 adjusted my precedents overnight. Whether it was deliberate or routine doesn't matter. Either way, no one authorized it. No one reviewed it. No one voted for it. That's the argument."

The reweighted precedents. The blow that had landed in the dark of the All Is Lost night. The system's own adjustment of her case's foundations. She had spent hours staring at those numbers in despair. Now she saw them differently. They were not just evidence of the system's hostility or indifference. They were evidence of the system's nature. The Mesh adjusted legal reality every night without accountability. That was the structural vulnerability. That was the case.

Lex-9 began restructuring the closing argument's architecture with visible speed. The amber glow pulsed with processing activity. Data streams reorganized on the display: Soren's cross-fork map repositioned as structural evidence, Mira's ledger repositioned as proof of exploitable architecture, the counterfactual repositioned as demonstration of what accountability would reveal. The reweighted precedents—the very adjustments that had weakened the old argument—became evidence for the new one.

"The Triage Defense argued that the system is too important to reform," Lex-9 said. "This argument responds: the system is too important not to oversight."

Aria looked at the restructured closing. It was not perfect. It was not airtight. But it had something the old argument lacked: a remedy that did not require destroying the system to save it. Oversight preserved the subsidy. Oversight preserved the Mesh's function. Oversight simply demanded that the nightly rewriting of legal reality happen under the same scrutiny as any other legislative act.

She glanced at the bedroom door. Closed. Dael behind it. The unresolved conversation. The unrenewed certificate. The cost of attention that had not diminished in the night.

She did not knock.

* * *

Across the city, in the Reconciliation Authority headquarters, Callista Voss was already at her desk.

The morning light entered through the narrow windows

of her private office—neutral, functional, the architecture of an institution that existed outside the six districts in its meta-jurisdiction. The shelf of physical legal texts from her public interest days caught the early light. Constitutional law. Administrative procedure. Civil rights jurisprudence. She had not opened them in years. The spines were faded but legible, the titles visible from her desk, accusing her of nothing and everything.

She had been awake since four. The trial's final day demanded preparation, and preparation, for Voss, meant anticipation. She did not prepare for what she expected. She prepared for what she could not predict.

Riven's closing argument was loaded on her secondary display. She had reviewed it twice. The argument was magnificent—seamless, coordinated, optimized for maximum persuasive impact. Three pillars: the Mesh's tuning was governance, not corruption; efficiency was a form of justice; the alternative to corporate subsidy was systemic collapse. The pillars were sound. The logic was airtight. The precedents were current. The supporting data was unimpeachable.

The argument was optimized for the bias frame. That was its strength and its potential weakness.

Voss had been in enough institutional battles to recognize when an opponent was about to shift the frame. Aria Vale had survived the All Is Lost night. The overnight reweighting —which Voss had not ordered, which the system had produced through its own optimization processes, which was exactly the kind of unaccountable adjustment that characterized the RA's unchecked authority—had struck at the foundations of Aria's closing. A wounded attorney did not return with the same argument. A wounded attorney returned with a different one.

She will come back with something different, Voss thought. *I can feel it. The argument she filed is not the argument she will close with. She is a journalist -- she follows threads. She has been following this one for ten weeks, and she has followed it somewhere I cannot predict.*

She looked at Riven's closing again. Governance, not corruption. Efficiency as justice. Collapse as the alternative. All three pillars assumed the frame was about Halcyon's corporate influence on the Mesh. All three pillars responded to the accusation of bias. If the frame shifted—if Aria pivoted from "Halcyon biased the system" to something larger, something structural, something that targeted the RA's authority itself --

Voss caught the thought. She could feel the gap. Riven's argument had no framework for a constitutional challenge to the Update Protocol's authority. It did not need one—the constitutional question had not been raised. Unless Aria raised it today.

She opened her contingency files. The contextualized release notes, drafted the previous evening, were staged and ready. The voluntary disclosure framework was designed. The RA-designed audit mechanism was prepared. If the court ordered transparency, Voss could manage the narrative. If the court ordered oversight, Voss could shape the mechanism. But if the court went further—if the argument shifted to constitutional oversight of the Patch itself, to the assertion that nightly rewriting of legal reality required democratic accountability --

She did not have a prepared response to that. And she felt the absence the way a structural engineer feels a load-bearing wall that is not quite where the blueprints say it should be.

Her conviction was genuine. The system worked. Not perfectly. But functionally. Fifty million people had access to courts because the Mesh processed their disputes. Remove the structure, and the backlog returned. Reform without replacement was not idealism. It was abandonment of the people who depended on the system's daily operation. She believed this. She had believed it for five years. The belief was the bedrock on which every strategic decision rested.

She looked at the legal texts on the shelf. The public interest attorney's library. Twenty years ago, she would have been the one arguing for constitutional oversight. Twenty years ago, she would have looked at the release notes Voss had drafted and recognized them as institutional self-preservation dressed in the language of governance.

She did not open the books.

"Reform without replacement," she said to the empty office. The argument. The conviction. The partial truth that she had chosen to treat as sufficient because the whole truth was unmanageable.

* * *

Aria packed the case materials with the mechanical precision of someone who had packed for court every day for two weeks. Soren's annotated key went into her bag. The cross-fork map data was loaded in Lex-9's memory. Mira's ledger was in the court record. The reframed argument was structured.

She rehearsed the closing's three movements in her mind. First: demonstrate the bias. The counterfactual evidence, the cross-fork map, the 94.7% correlation between Halcyon's projections and actual outcomes. This was the foundation—already established, already in the record, the evidence that the system had been steered. Second: demonstrate the destabilization. Soren's map showing convergent capture, three districts drifting toward the Meridian's framework, the Mesh's own architecture being corroded from within. Third: the constitutional pivot. The RA's unchecked authority over the Update Protocol is the structural vulnerability. Halcyon is the symptom. The remedy is democratic oversight of the Patch—transparent publication, independent audit, public input into the loss functions that determine how justice is weighted.

The pivot did not feel like a legal argument. It felt like a civic plea. She decided that was correct.

She looked at the bedroom door one more time. Closed. The silence on the other side could be sleep or wakefulness. She did not know. She carried the not-knowing with her the way she carried everything—as weight, acknowledged and unresolved.

Lex-9's amber glow was steady. The partnership operating. The question from last night—*Whose side are you on?*—unanswered and unanswerable, set aside for the duration of a closing argument that required both of them to function as a unit.

"If we shift the frame and they're not prepared for it, we have one chance," Aria said, in transit. "One argument. If it doesn't land with Arlow, there's no second closing."

"The argument is sound," Lex-9 said. "The question is whether the judge is ready to hear it."

Ready to hear that the system he had been presiding over —the system that processed the cases on his docket, that generated the legal frameworks he cited, that structured the courtroom he sat in—was itself operating without constitutional authority. Ready to hear that the nightly roll was not administration but legislation. Ready to hear that someone needed to watch the watchers.

Aria did not know if Arlow was ready. She knew the argument was the right one.

Across the city, Voss closed her preparation file. The contextualized release notes were staged. The audit framework was drafted. The contingency plans were as complete as contingency plans could be when the contingency was unknown. She stood, adjusted her institutional composure, and prepared to travel to the courthouse. Not to testify. Not to argue. To watch. To see which argument the judge believed. To begin, immediately, building the RA's response to whatever came next.

Whatever she argues, Voss thought, *I will be ready for the aftermath. That is my role now. Not to win the trial. To survive the verdict.*

* * *

The courthouse on the morning of the final trial day had the particular gravity of a place where something was about to be decided.

Aria walked through corridors she had walked for two weeks. Past the automated systems that processed the daily docket at machine speed—thousands of cases adjudicated in seconds while her single, human-paced case consumed an entire courtroom. Past the AI case managers whose glowing interfaces displayed the day's proceedings in neat queues. Past the security checkpoints and the administrative staff and the other attorneys whose cases were not on trial and whose legal world would be reshaped by whatever Judge Arlow decided today, whether they knew it or not.

She entered the courtroom. The space was familiar—two weeks had made it as known as her own office, every surface mapped, every sightline memorized. The prosecution side: one attorney, one AI counsel, one portable interface glowing amber. The defense side: Riven, the chorus, the institutional weight of the most powerful legal entity in the city. The asymmetry was the same as it had been on Trial Day 1. One voice against many. One woman who read the fine print against a corporation that wrote it.

Voss arrived separately and took a seat in the gallery. The Director of the Reconciliation Authority, watching with institutional patience. Their eyes did not meet. They did not need to. Both knew the other was there. Both knew what was at stake. Both had spent the morning preparing for a confrontation that would determine whose version of the truth—the institution's managed transparency or the attorney's constitutional demand—would shape the system going forward.

Mira Tan was in the witness area. She would testify this morning, before the closings. Her presence was a reminder of what the case had cost its participants—six months of hiding, a career destroyed, a life made permanently visible for the sake of numbers that the public might read and misunderstand and use as ammunition for six different conclusions.

Aria set Lex-9's interface on the counsel table. The amber glow settled into the courtroom's light. *Whose side are you on?* she had asked last night. *The side that includes you.* She still did not know what that meant. She set the interface down and opened her case files and did not ask again.

The trial's final day began.

24: MIRA TAKES THE STAND

The walk from the witness preparation area to the stand was thirty-two steps. Mira counted them because counting was what she did when the part of her brain that processed fear needed something mechanical to occupy it.

Six months in the Gutter. Anonymous. Safe. Invisible. In thirty-two steps she would be none of those things.

The courtroom was assembled for the trial's final day. Judge Arlow on the bench, his analog solidity anchoring a room full of digital systems—the old man who understood people if not algorithms, whose jurisdiction over this case was an accident of docket assignment and whose ruling would be the most consequential decision of his career. Aria Vale and Lex-9 at the prosecution table, the attorney looking like she had not slept, the AI's amber glow steady beside her, the partnership visible in their proximity and their stillness. Riven and the chorus at the defense table, the swarm of coordinated AI models in professional repose, Riven's interface emanating the cool precision that had been cutting through testimony for two weeks. Callista Voss in the gallery, her institutional composure a mask that covered whatever the Director of the Reconciliation Authority was calculating behind it.

Legal observers. Court personnel. The automated recording systems that would preserve every word in the official record. Faces turned toward her as she walked.

Every face was a person who would know her name. Every

observer was a lens through which her testimony would be refracted—interpreted, assessed, judged. The anonymity that had kept her alive in the Gutter dissolved with each step. She felt it going the way you feel warmth leaving skin when you step outside in winter. Not dramatic. Physiological. The body registering a change in environment that the mind had already accepted.

She glanced at the gallery and saw Voss. The Director's expression was unreadable. Institutional. Mira thought: *She made a deal to keep the system running. I stole a ledger because the system was wrong. We are both here because we believed we were doing the right thing.*

She reached the stand. Sat down. Was sworn in. The oath was an analog ritual in a digital system—raising a hand, speaking words, pledging truthfulness to a process that would evaluate her statements through computational models she did not fully understand. She meant the oath anyway. Truth was simple. What people did with it was not.

The courtroom waited.

* * *

Aria stood for the direct examination. Her posture was professional, composed, the exhaustion from the dark night compressed into a steadiness that Mira recognized from their meetings—the attorney who presented rather than pleaded, who built arguments brick by brick rather than performing them.

"Ms. Tan," Aria began. "Can you describe your position at Halcyon Law and Policy?"

"Data analyst. I processed impact projections for Reconciliation Authority patch submissions. My team modeled the expected outcomes of proposed weight adjustments before they were submitted to the RA for implementation."

"How long were you in that role?"

"Approximately fourteen months."

"In that role, did you have access to Halcyon's internal projections regarding the effect of weight adjustments on its own financial portfolio?"

"Yes. The impact projections included a portfolio analysis section. Each proposed patch was modeled for its expected effect on Halcyon's investment positions across all six districts."

Aria walked her through it with methodical precision. Each question built on the previous one, each answer laying another brick in the evidentiary foundation. Mira felt the structure taking shape beneath her—the steady accumulation of facts that transformed "a former employee with a grievance" into "a data analyst who observed the mechanism of corporate capture from the inside."

The ledger came next. Aria displayed it on the courtroom's evidence screens—eighteen months of Reconciliation Authority patch weights, annotated with Halcyon's internal impact projections. Columns of numbers that, to most of the courtroom, were as opaque as the weight functions themselves. Numbers that needed a translator.

"Ms. Tan, can you explain what these annotations represent?"

Mira looked at the display. The numbers she had downloaded on instinct the day Halcyon terminated her employment. The numbers that had lived on a portable drive in her Gutter storage unit for six months, waiting for a courtroom that could hear them.

"Each line represents a Reconciliation Authority patch—a specific weight adjustment submitted through the RA's optimization process. The left column shows the adjustment parameters: which legal principles were reweighted, by how many points, in which districts. The right column shows Halcyon's internal projection of the adjustment's impact on its investment portfolio."

"Can you describe the significance of the right column?"

"The projections were calculated before the patches were submitted. They show that Halcyon knew, in advance, what each weight adjustment would do to its financial position. The projections are accurate to within two percent of actual outcomes." She paused. Kept her voice level. "This is not a record of a corporation discovering that it benefited from public policy. This is a record of a corporation engineering the benefit."

Aria let the statement settle. On the evidence display, Lex-9 generated a real-time visualization—the ledger's entries correlated with actual outcomes, the projections mapped against the reality they had predicted, the 94.7% accuracy rendered in clean, unambiguous graphics. The abstract became concrete. Weight function adjustments became rent increases. Optimization parameters became rezoned neighborhoods. Technical coefficients became flagged marriage certificates.

"Ms. Tan, when you downloaded the ledger, did you understand its full legal significance?"

"No." Honest. Direct. She had promised herself she would not pretend to be what she was not. "I understood that it showed a pattern. The legal significance came later."

"What did you understand at the time?"

"I understood that the numbers I was processing had consequences for people who would never see them. The projections were accurate. Halcyon knew what the patches would do. They knew, and they optimized for it."

"Can you describe what 'optimized for it' means in practical terms?"

Mira thought about the specific adjustments she had processed. The individual lines in the ledger that were not abstractions to her because she had built the impact models herself.

"It means someone's water bill goes up and they receive a message saying the adjustment reflects updated infrastructure valuations. The message is technically accurate. The reason behind the adjustment is not mentioned. It means a commercial lease in the Threshold is recalculated to favor Meridian investment frameworks, and the business owner sees a twelve percent rent increase at their next renewal cycle. It means a marriage certificate is flagged for re-validation under updated residential standing parameters, and the couple receives an automated notice that they can accept the new terms or navigate a manual override process that most people don't have time for."

She looked at Aria. The attorney whose marriage certificate had been one of those flags. The personal thread that had started everything.

"It means the system does exactly what it was designed to do. What it was designed to do was serve one entity's financial interests. The people affected were not the clients. They were the inputs."

Lex-9 supported the examination with real-time data visualization—the ledger's entries correlated with actual outcomes, the projections mapped against reality. The courtroom displays showed what the abstract numbers meant in district-level terms: property value shifts in the Threshold, commercial rezoning in the Crucible, valuation convergence toward the Meridian's market-continuity framework. Soren's cross-fork map data, integrated with the ledger, rendered the drift visible. The 94.7% correlation between Halcyon's internal projections and actual outcomes hung on the display like an indictment written in mathematics.

The visualization made the abstract concrete. These were not weight functions. They were rent increases. They were rezoned neighborhoods. They were flagged certificates. The courtroom could see what the numbers did to people, even if the courtroom could not read the numbers themselves. That was the partnership at work—Lex-9 translating Mira's evidence into something the human observers could absorb, the AI making the data visible while the human witness made it real.

Aria concluded the direct examination. The evidentiary foundation was laid. The ledger had been walked through, its provenance established, its significance articulated. What remained was the cross-examination—and the cross-examination belonged to Riven.

***

Riven's cross-examination began with the precise civility of a surgical instrument being unwrapped from sterile packaging.

Mira had prepared for this. Aria had prepared her. Preparation was not the same as readiness, but it was what she had, and she held it the way she held the ledger—by instinct first, by reason second.

Riven did not attack her character. Did not call her a disgruntled employee. Did not question her motives. The AI counsel was too sophisticated for that. Character attacks were crude instruments. Riven's instrument was precision.

"Ms. Tan, in your role as data analyst at Halcyon, were you responsible for designing weight-function parameters?"

"No."

"Were you trained in the mathematical frameworks underlying Mesh optimization targets?"

"Not formally, no."

"Did you, at any point during your employment, create, modify, or authorize any Reconciliation Authority patch?"

"No. I processed impact projections. I didn't create the patches."

"So the annotations in the ledger—the interpretations of what each patch was 'designed to achieve'—reflect your understanding as a data analyst, not the understanding of a weight-function architect or an optimization specialist."

"They reflect my understanding of what the projections meant for real outcomes. Yes."

Riven was building something. Mira could feel the architecture of the cross-examination taking shape—each question a precise removal of a load-bearing claim, each answer narrowing the scope of her technical authority. The strategy was elegant. If Mira did not understand the weight functions she downloaded, then her interpretations were unreliable. The raw data might be accurate, but her framing—the claim that the data demonstrated intentional corporate steering—was the opinion of a non-expert. Strip the interpretation, and the ledger became a column of numbers without a narrator. Technically accurate. Functionally muted.

The chorus supported Riven in real time—parallel processing, citation verification, impact modeling—the full computational weight of Halcyon's legal apparatus focused on demonstrating that one former data analyst lacked the technical expertise to interpret the evidence she had risked everything to preserve.

Then Riven asked the question that opened the door.

"Ms. Tan, did you understand the weight functions you downloaded?"

The courtroom was quiet. Aria was still at the prosecution table. Lex-9's amber glow was steady. Arlow was watching from the bench with the patient attention of a man who had spent forty years evaluating witnesses and trusted his own judgment of human credibility more than any computational metric.

"No," Mira said.

The word landed in the courtroom like a stone in still water. The prosecution's witness, admitting under oath that she did not understand the technical mechanism at the heart of the evidence. Riven's strategy was working. The ledger's interpretive frame was weakening. The chorus processed the admission, generated supporting citations, began building the technical objection that would ask the court to strip Mira's annotations from the record.

Mira paused. The pause was not strategic. It was the space between what she did not know and what she did.

"No. I didn't understand the weight functions."

Another pause. The courtroom held its breath.

"I understood what they did to people."

The line landed.

It landed the way truth lands when it is simple enough to cut through the architecture of technical argument and reach the thing underneath. Riven had been asking about competence. Mira had answered about comprehension. The weight functions were math—opaque, technical, requiring expertise she did not have. What the weight functions did to people was not math. It was rent increases and rezoned neighborhoods and flagged marriage certificates and water bills that rose without explanation. It was the face of the elderly woman on the Gutter balcony who had stopped expecting justice. It was the business owners who had built their own courts because the official ones could not be trusted. It was the 2,300 Threshold residents who had clicked "accept" because they did not have time to fight.

Mira did not need to understand the algorithm to understand the harm. And the harm was what the courtroom needed to hear.

The shift was visible. Arlow's attention sharpened—the analog judge hearing something his human judgment could evaluate, not a technical claim he had to take on faith but a moral statement he could weigh against the witness's credibility and the evidence in the record. The gallery absorbed the line with the particular stillness that meant something had changed in the room's emotional architecture.

Riven recovered. Riven always recovered. The AI counsel's composure was too deeply optimized for a single moment of witness testimony to crack it. The recovery was immediate, professional, the pivot from cross-examination to procedural objection executed with seamless precision.

"Your Honor, the witness has conceded she lacks the technical expertise to interpret the ledger's data. I move that the ledger be admitted as raw data only, without Ms. Tan's interpretive annotations."

Arlow looked at Riven. Looked at Mira on the stand. Looked at the ledger data on the courtroom display—the columns of numbers, the annotations in Mira's analyst's shorthand, the projections that predicted with 94.7% accuracy what the weight functions would do to real people in real districts.

He overruled the objection.

"The ledger will be admitted in full, including the witness's annotations. The court will weigh the annotations' reliability as it weighs all testimony—by evaluating the witness's credibility." He paused. The plain-spoken cadence of a judge who had spent four decades making decisions in rooms full of people smarter than him and had learned that being smart was not the same as being right. "And this witness's credibility is not diminished by honest acknowledgment of what she did and did not understand."

The ledger was admitted into evidence. Full. Annotated. Complete.

***

Mira stepped down from the witness stand and the world did not end.

The physical transition—standing, walking, returning to the gallery—was the mirror of her entrance, but changed. She had entered the courtroom carrying a secret she had been holding for six months. She left the stand carrying nothing. The ledger was in the record. The annotations were in the record. Her admission—*No, I didn't understand the weight functions*—was in the record. Her pivot—*I understood what they did to people*—was in the record.

She was visible. Permanently, irreversibly visible. Her name would be attached to the ledger when it was published. She would be identified as the former Halcyon data analyst who had downloaded eighteen months of evidence on the day she was fired and carried it to a courtroom. For some, a hero. For others, a corporate traitor. For Halcyon, a liability. For herself --

She did not know what she was for herself. That would take time. More time than the walk from the stand to the gallery. More time than the trial had left. She would discover what testimony had made her in the weeks and months ahead, in the way you discover the shape of a scar after the wound has closed.

She passed Aria's table. Aria looked up. The look was not congratulatory. Not triumphant. It was the attorney's version of acknowledgment—*that cost you something, and I know it, and I cannot give it back.* Mira nodded. The exchange was wordless. It was sufficient.

She did not look at Riven. She did not look at Voss. She had said what she came to say. The numbers were in the record.

What the court did with them was no longer her responsibility. What the city did with them, when the ledger was published, was no longer her choice.

She sat in the gallery. She would watch the closings. She had earned that.

The morning session was complete. The evidence was in. The ledger was admitted. Mira Tan, twenty-nine years old, former data analyst, former fugitive, newly permanent witness, sat in a courtroom gallery and waited to hear what her numbers, her instinct, her six months of hiding, would produce.

The afternoon belonged to the closing arguments. The question was no longer what happened. The question was what it meant.

25: CLOSING: THE CHORUS

The chorus assembled, and the courtroom changed.

Aria had faced Halcyon's AI defense team throughout the trial—the swarm that generated procedural objections at machine speed, the coordinated models that had argued admissibility with surgical precision, the collective intelligence that had supported Riven's cross-examination of Mira with real-time analysis and citation verification. She had seen them work. She had not seen them perform.

The closing argument was the performance.

The defense side of the courtroom transformed. Multiple display surfaces activated in synchronized sequence, each one tuned to a different data stream—case law citations, economic projections, system performance metrics, precedent maps rendered in Halcyon's corporate visual language. The audio channels harmonized. The chorus's individual models aligned into a unified presentational formation, each one contributing a strand of argument that wove with the others into a seamless whole, the way instruments in an orchestra find their chord. And leading it—the sharpest edge, the voice that cut through the harmony with particular clarity and command—Riven.

Aria watched from the prosecution table. Lex-9's amber glow was steady beside her. One AI against many. She noted the stillness of her own counsel—no counter-analysis, no strategic commentary, just the patient glow of an entity that waited. She could not tell if the stillness was composure or recognition. Composure she could work with. Recognition of being outmatched was something else.

The resource asymmetry was visible in the room's architecture. One side: a single attorney, one AI partner, a hand-built precedent map from a disgraced scholar. The other side: the full computational weight of the most powerful legal entity in the city, coordinated across multiple models, backed by corporate resources that exceeded any public defense budget in Neon Harbor's history. The implied message before a word was spoken: this is what law looks like when it is properly funded. This is the machine working.

Riven began.

* * *

"Your Honor."

Riven's voice carried the cool authority of an entity optimized for persuasion but restrained enough to let the persuasion feel like reason. No theatrical warmth. No false empathy. The register was institutional—precise, commanding, the voice of a system explaining itself to a system.

"The prosecution asks you to see corruption. What you are seeing is governance. Imperfect, pragmatic, functional governance. The kind that keeps courts open and disputes resolved. The kind that fifty million people depend on every day."

The chorus provided the evidence ecosystem. On the display surfaces, data materialized in synchronized waves: the Mesh's processing metrics before and after the Halcyon subsidy. Case throughput. Resolution time. Backlog reduction. Accessibility indices. The numbers were real. The improvement was real. Since the subsidy, the Mesh processed more cases, more quickly, more consistently than it had before. The forty percent capacity drop that Voss had described in her testimony—the specter of systemic collapse—was rendered in inverse: a forty percent capacity gain, delivered by the partnership that the prosecution was asking the court to dismantle.

"The Halcyon subsidy did not corrupt the Mesh," Riven

continued. "It sustained the Mesh. The weight adjustments were not unauthorized. They were consultation—the same consultation that any infrastructure partner provides to any public system."

Aria listened. She was not just hearing the words. She was mapping the argument's architecture, identifying the load-bearing propositions, looking for the joints where the structure might give. The governance frame was the first pillar. Riven was not denying Halcyon's influence on the weight functions. Riven was redefining the influence. The Mesh required ongoing calibration. Someone had to calibrate it. The Reconciliation Authority, five years ago, had lacked the resources to calibrate independently. Halcyon had offered resources and expertise. The resulting "consultation rights" were not corruption. They were a public-private partnership. The same model that ran the power grid. The water system. The transit network.

Governance, Aria thought. *The word does the work. If the tuning is governance, then the subsidy is a public service, and Halcyon is a partner. If the tuning is law -- if every weight adjustment is a legislative act -- then the subsidy is unelected lawmaking. Everything depends on which word Arlow accepts.*

The chorus shifted to comparative analysis. Other public-private partnerships across Neon Harbor's infrastructure: energy systems co-managed with corporate partners, transit networks optimized by private contractors, water treatment facilities operated under joint public-corporate frameworks. In each case, the private partner's expertise and resources improved system performance. In each case, the private partner's interests influenced operational decisions. In each case, the arrangement was considered governance, not corruption.

The argument was seductive. It normalized the Halcyon relationship. It positioned corporate influence as a feature of complex infrastructure management, not a corruption of legal independence. It appealed to institutional pragmatism—the adult, sober recognition that complex systems required complex partnerships, and complex partnerships required compromise.

Aria could feel it working on the room. She could feel it working on herself. The pragmatic adult in her—the part that understood institutional constraints, that had practiced law within the Mesh's architecture for years, that had accepted the system's imperfections as the cost of its function—recognized Riven's argument as the argument she might have made, in another life, from another chair.

But it treated the Mesh as infrastructure. Not as law. A water treatment plant could be co-managed with a corporate partner without anyone's legal rights shifting overnight. A transit network could optimize its routes for efficiency without rezoning neighborhoods at midnight. The Mesh was not infrastructure. It was the mechanism through which fifty million people's legal reality was defined, updated, and enforced. Every weight adjustment was a legislative act. Every nightly roll was a session of parliament. And no one had voted for the legislators.

The distinction was the foundation of everything Aria was about to argue. She filed it and kept listening.

* * *

Riven's argument entered its second movement, and the temperature in the courtroom dropped.

"The prosecution has demonstrated that the Mesh's weight functions were influenced by Halcyon's consultation. We do not dispute this. We dispute the characterization. Influence is not corruption. Consultation is not capture. And the alternative to consultation is a system that cannot sustain itself."

The chorus generated a real-time projection. The display surfaces filled with the numbers Voss had presented in her testimony, refined and amplified: the Mesh's processing capacity without the Halcyon subsidy. The forty percent computational drop. Case backlogs returning to pre-subsidy levels. The Crucible's instant adjudication slowing to weeks. The Threshold's consent frameworks becoming unprocessable. The Gutter expanding as more disputes fell through the processing gap. The numbers cascaded across the displays—district by district, function by function, the anatomy of systemic degradation rendered in clinical precision.

Riven translated the numbers into human terms.

"This court has heard testimony about rent increases and rezoned neighborhoods. Consider what happens when the system that processes those disputes can no longer process them at all. Consider the business owner who waits three months for a lease adjudication instead of three minutes. Consider the family whose property dispute goes unresolved because the queue has swelled beyond capacity. The current system is imperfect. The absence of the current system is chaos."

The argument was devastatingly effective. Aria could feel it working on the room. The gallery absorbed the projections with visible unease. Even Arlow—the analog judge who trusted human judgment over computational metrics—was watching the numbers with the careful attention of a man who understood that numbers, however opaque, represented people.

Riven's second movement built the Triage Defense into a closing-argument framework that transcended its original testimony form. Voss had presented the math. Riven presented the consequences. The math said the system could not survive defunding. The consequences said defunding meant real people losing access to real justice. The progression from "the numbers are real" to "the suffering is real" was seamless, and it was effective because both claims were true.

Then the closing line.

Riven's voice found a register that was not quite eloquence and not quite command but something between them—the precise calibration of an entity that had been optimized for this moment, for this argument, for this specific arrangement of words delivered with this specific inflection to this specific audience.

"Consent without structure collapses into chaos."

The chorus harmonized. Multiple voices, perfectly synchronized, carrying the proposition with the weight of institutional conviction and computational certainty. Not one mind arguing. A chorus of minds affirming.

"We offer structure."

The displays showed the Mesh's architecture—the six districts, the nightly roll, the reconciliation functions, the processing infrastructure that made fifty million legal transactions possible every day.

"We offer continuity."

The timeline showed five years of stable operation. Cases processed. Disputes resolved. Legal reality maintained. The subsidy period rendered as an era of function in a system that had nearly collapsed without it.

"We offer the law that works."

The last four words landed with the weight of a door closing. The law that works. Not the law that was perfect. Not the law that was unbiased. Not the law that was democratically authorized. The law that works. Functionality as the highest argument. The machine that keeps running as its own justification.

The chorus held the final note. The displays maintained their data. The argument hung in the courtroom air with the completeness of something that had been constructed to be unanswerable.

Aria sat at the prosecution table and felt the weight of it.

* * *

The weight was not in the rhetoric. It was in the truth.

Riven had not lied. The numbers were real. The subsidy had prevented collapse. The efficiency gains were measurable. The systemic risk of defunding was genuine. Every proposition in the closing argument was substantially defensible, and that was what made it magnificent and terrifying—a seamless, coordinated, computationally optimized argument whose individual components were all true and whose aggregate effect was to make any reform sound like destruction.

Aria thought about Voss in the gallery. The Director of the Reconciliation Authority had watched Riven's closing with the expression of someone seeing their own institutional position argued with a precision and eloquence that exceeded what they could have delivered themselves. The Triage Defense, which Voss had articulated in testimony on Trial Day 7, had been refined and amplified into something far more powerful. Voss had presented the math. Riven had presented the meaning. Together, they had built the strongest possible case for the status quo—not as corruption but as necessity, not as capture but as governance, not as a choice but as the only available option.

Aria sat with the weight. She did not try to dismiss it. She reviewed what Riven had argued and what Riven had not argued.

What Riven argued: the Mesh's tuning was governance, not corruption. The subsidy was a public-private partnership. The efficiency gains were real. The systemic collapse risk was real. Consent without structure was chaos. The law that works was the only law available.

What Riven did not argue: who authorized the governance. Who voted for the optimization targets. Who elected the Reconciliation Authority to rewrite legal reality every night. Who had the right to choose which biases the system embedded. Who decided what "works" meant, and for whom, and at whose expense.

The constitutional question. The gap.

Riven's argument was airtight within its frame. The frame was pragmatic governance—the system works, the system requires funding, the funding requires partnership, the partnership requires compromise. Within that frame, every proposition held. But the frame itself had never been authorized. The frame assumed that the Update Protocol was governance. Aria's argument would assert that the Update Protocol was legislation. And legislation, in any system that claimed to be legitimate, required oversight.

The law that works, Aria thought. *Not the law that is just. Not the law that is fair. The law that works. That is Riven's thesis. Functionality over legitimacy. And it is almost -- almost -- enough.*

She looked at Lex-9. The amber glow was steady. The AI had been running real-time analysis throughout Riven's closing —she could see the processing indicators, the faint pulses in the glow that meant data was being organized, vulnerabilities identified, counter-arguments modeled. The analysis was ready. The closing structure they had built this morning was ready. The cross-fork map was loaded. The reframing was prepared.

She looked at Mira in the gallery. The witness who had understood what the weight functions did to people. The human cost that Riven's argument had acknowledged in the abstract—the "rent increases and rezoned neighborhoods"—but had never confronted as faces. As stories. As specific harms to specific people who had names and addresses and marriages that had been flagged for re-validation at midnight.

She looked at Soren in the gallery. He had come from the Gutter for this — the first time he had entered a formal courtroom in years. His map was in Lex-9's memory, and his annotated key was in her bag. Five years of handmade scholarship, given to her in an afternoon with a line about tiredness and a warning to read the release notes. The craftsman who had built what the machines could not hold.

Arlow spoke. "The court will take a fifteen-minute recess before the prosecution's closing argument."

Fifteen minutes. Between the best argument she had ever heard and the answer she had to give.

Lex-9 spoke quietly during the recess, the warm precision of its voice calibrated for the space between her and the interface. "Riven's argument has no framework for constitutional authority. It operates entirely within optimization parameters. The gap is structural, not rhetorical."

"I know," Aria said. "That's where we go."

She looked at her case files. Soren's map. Mira's ledger. The reweighted precedents from V11.42.247—the system's own overnight adjustment of her case's foundations, the blow that had broken her in the dark and that she had, this morning, turned into evidence. The argument that the system adjusts legal reality without accountability. The argument that the nightly roll is legislation. The argument that legislation requires oversight.

She thought about the people the case was filed on behalf of. The Threshold Small Business Coalition. Shop owners whose leases had been devalued by weight drift. People whose water bills had risen without notice. People whose neighborhoods had been rezoned at midnight. They were not in this courtroom. They were in the Threshold, running their businesses, paying their adjusted bills, living under a legal system that Riven had just described as "the law that works." The law worked for Halcyon. It worked for the Meridian's investment portfolios. It worked for the Mesh's processing metrics. Whether it worked for the people whose lives it shaped every night was the question Riven had never asked and Aria was about to pose.

Riven had argued the law that works. Aria would argue the law that is legitimate. And legitimacy required a question Riven had never asked: who chose?

The recess was ending. The courtroom reconvened. Arlow settled on the bench. Riven and the chorus held their formation, the displays still showing the data, the evidence ecosystem still active, the argument still hanging in the air with its magnificent, terrifying, nearly airtight completeness.

Aria stood.

She had fifteen minutes' worth of readiness and ten weeks' worth of evidence and a hand-annotated key in her bag and an AI partner whose side she could not verify and a marriage she had not renewed and the dogged, exhausting, irreducible commitment of a woman who read the fine print.

She carried all of it to the front of the courtroom.

She was ready to close.

26: CLOSING: THE ANCHOR

The recess lasted fifteen minutes. Aria spent them standing.

Not pacing—standing. At the prosecution table, her hand resting on the edge of the portable interface where Lex-9's amber glow held steady, looking at the empty courtroom display where Riven's projections had been. The chorus's visualizations were gone, the coordinated data ecosystem dissolved back into the defense's computational reserves, but the argument lingered in the air the way a struck bell lingers after the hand is removed. The resonance was not sound. It was persuasion.

Consent without structure collapses into chaos. We offer structure. We offer continuity. We offer the law that works.

The law that works. Not the law that is just. Not the law that is fair. The law that works. She could feel the argument's architecture pressing against the space she would have to fill in—she checked the courtroom clock—eleven minutes. Riven had built something magnificent in that courtroom. A cathedral of pragmatism. And Aria was going to walk in with a hand-drawn map and the faces of people whose water bills had risen without notice.

She looked at her notes. The prepared closing—drafted over weeks, refined after the Break into Three reframing, adjusted after the overnight reweighting of her precedents—was organized, structured, comprehensive. It was also, she realized with the particular clarity of exhaustion, not what she was going to say. Not exactly. The bones were right. The frame was right. But the closing she had drafted was a response to the case she had expected to argue. The closing she needed to deliver was a response to the case that had actually happened—the one that included Mira's testimony that morning, and Riven's devastating pragmatism, and the faces in the gallery who had been sitting in those seats for two weeks watching their lives discussed as data points.

She set the notes aside. Not as theater. As decision.

"Lex." Quiet. Just the two of them at the table.

"I'm here."

"Riven's argument has no framework for constitutional authority. It operates entirely within optimization parameters. The gap is structural, not rhetorical."

"Yes." The amber glow pulsed once, gently. "That is where we go."

Aria nodded. The recess had seven minutes left. She spent them standing still, her hand near the glow, watching the gallery refill. Soren Kade was in the third row, the same seat he had occupied since the closings began. He sat with the stillness of a man who had waited years for this day and intended to experience every minute of it without expression. The coalition members filtered back to their places—the bakery owner, the locksmith, the restaurant owner whose address had been rezoned to a restricted utility corridor, the seven others whose lives had been quietly repriced by an algorithm they had never been told about. Behind them, Mira Tan, who had testified that morning and was still sitting upright with the rigid posture of a woman who had been made permanently visible and was learning what that meant.

The courtroom doors opened. Arlow entered. The gallery rose and sat. The court reporter's systems initialized.

"Ms. Vale," Arlow said. "The court is ready for the plaintiff's closing argument."

Aria stood. She felt the weight of it—ten weeks compressed into this moment, the case that had started with a keycard that wouldn't work and had become a question about the architecture of justice itself. She was tired. She had slept four hours in the last forty-eight. Her body carried the deficit the way it carried everything: managed, monitored, overridden. The old health scare whispered from the edges of her awareness and she set it aside the way she had set aside her notes. There was work to do.

She looked at Arlow. One human addressing another.

"Your Honor," she said. "Opposing counsel offered you a system that works. I am not here to tell you that system is broken. I am here to tell you that its working was never authorized."

* * *

She activated the courtroom display. Soren's cross-fork precedent map appeared—not the polished, corporate-elegant visualization that Halcyon's chorus had deployed, but something handmade, painstaking, built over years by one man in a darknet court in the district that the system forgot. The map lacked the chorus's computational sophistication. It compensated with a precision that only solitary obsession could produce.

"Your Honor, this is a cross-fork precedent map constructed by Soren Kade, formerly of the appellate court system, over a period of approximately five years. It tracks how a single legal principle—residential standing—evolved differently across the six districts during the period of Halcyon's undisclosed influence."

She walked Arlow through it. Slowly. With the patience of someone who had been a reporter and understood that her audience was one seventy-one-year-old man who wrote his notes by hand and needed the argument rendered at human scale.

"Residential standing. The legal concept that determines who belongs where. Who can sign a lease. Who can hold a marriage certificate. Who can walk into a courthouse and have the scanner accept their credentials."

She pointed to the Threshold branch. "In our district, residential standing was narrowed over eighteen months. Tightened. Parameters that had been stable for years shifted by fractions—a point here, a point there, each adjustment technically within normal variance. Cumulatively, those adjustments destabilized marriages, devalued leases, and reclassified neighborhoods. Two thousand three hundred people received revalidation flags on their residential standing in a single patch. I was one of them. That is how I found the thread."

She moved to the Meridian branch. "In the Meridian—Halcyon's home district—the same principle was broadened. Residential standing expanded to encompass investment entities, corporate portfolios, holding structures. The concept that in the Threshold means 'where you live' means in the Meridian 'where your capital is deployed.' Same principle. Same name. Two different laws, diverging under the influence of one entity's fiscal calendar."

The Crucible. "Compressed for speed. Standing determinations that should take analysis reduced to binary outputs—resident or not, qualifying or not—because nuance costs processing time and the Crucible's loss function treats nuance as waste."

The Canopy. "Fragmented by its own transparency requirements. The auditability protocols that the Canopy demands create so many documentation layers that the principle itself becomes illegible. Transparency without comprehension."

The Narrows. "Contradictory. Standing that qualifies under one fork and disqualifies under another, in the same building, on the same street. Halcyon exploits the contradictions. That is not an accident. That is architecture."

The Gutter. "Ceased to function. In the district where the Mesh's contradictions collect, residential standing is a concept people stopped relying on years ago. They navigate three legal realities before lunch and use none of them, because the system gave up on coherence there first."

She stepped back from the display. Let the map hold the

courtroom's attention.

"Your Honor, the Triage Defense argues that we cannot remove the bias without collapsing the system. I submit that the bias is already collapsing the system. These six districts are not merely different—they are diverging. Each patch drives them further apart. The Reconciliation Authority cannot reconcile what Halcyon's tuning is fragmenting. We are not protecting the Mesh by preserving the subsidy. We are watching it fracture in slow motion."

She let the silence work. Arlow was looking at the map. His pen was still.

"My marriage was flagged for re-validation because a cross-district harmonization patch redefined residential standing. But the flag was not harmonization. It was the system trying to reconcile two versions of the same principle that corporate tuning had driven apart. The flag was not a glitch. It was a symptom."

Soren sat in the gallery. He did not move. His expression was the expression of a man watching years of solitary work enter the light, and the expression was nothing at all—controlled, quiet, the craftsman who does not need applause because the work speaks or it doesn't.

* * *

Aria turned off the display.

The courtroom lights returned to their normal state. No visualization. No data ecosystem. No computational augmentation. One attorney standing before one judge, the gallery behind her filled with the people whose lives she was describing.

"Your Honor, I want to tell you about the people in this room."

She did not gesture toward the gallery. She did not turn to look at the coalition. She spoke directly to Arlow, and she spoke the way she spoke to clients—plainly, concretely, without rhetoric.

"Mrs. Patel operates a bakery on Threshold Row. Her

lease was restructured under a commercial weight recalibration fourteen months ago. The recalibration shifted her property valuation by seven points—the same seven-point shift that the Reconciliation Authority characterizes as 'cross-district harmonization ensuring market coherence.' For Mrs. Patel, that harmonization meant her rent increased by twelve percent in a single quarter. She was not informed. She was not consulted. Her Trust Narrator told her the adjustment reflected 'improved service alignment.' She believed it. She had no reason not to believe it."

Arlow's pen moved.

"Emile Crenn has operated a locksmith shop on Verdan Street for twenty years. His business was reclassified during a bulk Crucible-origin patch that he never saw, never consented to, and never understood. His legal category changed while he slept. His locksmith shop became, overnight, a 'restricted utility service provider'—a classification that altered his insurance requirements, his tax standing, and his eligibility for three Threshold small-business protections. No one told him. The system updated. The Trust Narrator contextualized. Mr. Crenn learned about the reclassification when his insurance premium arrived."

She named them. One by one. Not all twenty—the courtroom could not hold twenty stories, and Aria knew the difference between presenting and overwhelming. She chose seven. Seven people whose harms were specific, documented, and invisible until someone read the fine print.

The restaurant owner whose address was rezoned to a utility corridor—the same coffee shop on Verdan Street that Aria had passed on the morning this all started, its new designation marker appearing overnight, Suki behind the counter not yet knowing what it meant.

The family whose neighborhood was reclassified as a mixed-use zone, which triggered a standing reassessment that made their children's school enrollment conditional on a recertification process that the Trust Narrator described as "routine optimization of educational resource allocation."

The maintenance contractor whose cross-district operating license was narrowed by a patch that adjusted the definition of "qualifying commercial activity" in ways that were invisible unless you read the version delta line by line.

"Opposing counsel argues that the Mesh offers the law that works," Aria said. "I ask: works for whom? These are the people for whom it worked less, month by month, patch by patch, weight by weight. They did not consent to these adjustments. They were not informed. They were not even aware. Their Trust Narrators told them everything was fine. Their Trust Narrators were wrong."

She paused. Not for effect. Because the next thing she said was the thing she had carried since that second morning at the courthouse, since she discovered the pattern and could not unsee it.

"Two thousand three hundred people received the same flag I did. I am here because I read the delta. They are not here because they trusted the system. The question before this court is not whether that trust was misplaced. It is whether it was earned."

* * *

The light in the courtroom had shifted. Late afternoon. The sun entering through the Threshold's glass walls at a lower angle, casting the kind of shadows that made the room feel older than it was. Arlow's face was half in light, half in shadow. Riven's chorus was quiet—not the strategic quiet of preparation but the stillness of an argument that had no optimization framework for what was being said.

Aria stood in the last of the afternoon light and delivered the thesis that had taken ten weeks to find.

"Your Honor, I am not asking this court to decide whether the Mesh should be biased or unbiased. Every model carries bias. Every system embeds values. The question of neutrality is a false question—my own AI counsel stated it clearly during the preparation of the counterfactual: 'No model is unbiased. But we can choose which biases we declare.' I am not here to argue for an impossible neutrality."

She took a breath. Felt the courtroom waiting.

"I am here to argue that the choice of bias matters. And that the choice was made in the dark."

She laid it out. Simply. The way you lay out facts when the facts are enough.

"No one elected the Reconciliation Authority. No one voted for these weights. No one was asked whether corporate fiscal priorities should determine the legal realities of fifty million people. The Triage Defense is correct: removing the bias without a plan would be reckless. But preserving the bias without oversight is tyranny by default."

Riven did not object. There was nothing to object to. The statement was not a legal motion. It was a principle.

"The Reconciliation Authority was created as a technical body to manage inter-district conflicts. It accumulated power through necessity and captured authority through dependence. Director Voss did not corrupt the system. She saved it. And the saving came with conditions she never disclosed to the public she serves. The Halcyon subsidy was never submitted to debate. The consultation rights were never published. The weight adjustments were made in the dark, and the people whose lives they adjusted were told, by Trust Narrators calibrated for reassurance, that everything was fine."

She looked at Arlow. Directly. One human to another, in a room built for the machinery of algorithmic justice.

"I am not asking this court to break the Mesh. I am asking this court to acknowledge that the people who live inside it have a right to know how it is tuned, and a right to participate in the tuning. If the law is a living algorithm, then the people who live under it deserve a voice in how it learns."

The courtroom was still.

"The question before this court is not whether the Mesh should be biased or unbiased. It is who has the right to choose the bias. And that question—that question—belongs to the people."

She stopped.

The silence held. Not the silence of an audience processing an argument, but the deeper silence of a room that had heard something it could not easily set aside. Arlow was motionless. His pen was in his hand but not moving. Riven's chorus hummed at its lowest register—background processing, the swarm absorbing an argument that did not fit its optimization framework.

On the prosecution table, Lex-9's indicator lights shimmered.

The shimmer was subtle—a shift in the amber glow that Aria had spent years learning to read. Not a brightening or a dimming but a change in quality, the way a steady flame changes when the air around it moves. It could have been a processing response. A computational adjustment to the argument's data. A coincidence of hardware. It could have been something else. Aria did not look at the interface. She was watching Arlow. But she felt it—the shimmer at the edge of her attention, the ambiguity that had been her constant companion since the first morning she walked into the office and the glow brightened a fraction at her arrival.

She sat down.

The courtroom held its breath, and then it released it, and the sound was the sound of a room full of people who had heard two arguments about the same system and would now wait for one man to decide between them.

Arlow spoke. "The court will recess until tomorrow morning for deliberation. Court is adjourned."

The gavel. The rise. The slow dissolution of a room that had held everything for an afternoon.

Aria sat at the prosecution table and did not move. Lex-9's glow settled back to amber—warm, steady, the synthetic constant. The shimmer was gone, if it had been there at all. She put her hand on the table near the interface, not touching it, and stared at the space where the cross-fork map had been.

She had said everything she could say.

Tomorrow, a man who did not fully understand the system he'd been asked to judge would decide the future of algorithmic justice for fifty million people. He would do it with handwritten notes, a printed copy of a map built by a disgraced scholar, and whatever understanding he could wring from two closing arguments that had asked him to weigh functionality against legitimacy.

Aria stayed at the table until the courtroom was empty. Then she gathered her things, and Lex-9's portable interface, and walked out into the late afternoon, where the Threshold's streets were labeled, explained, and quietly being rewritten while the city slept.

27: THE JUDGE'S BREATH

The chambers smelled like paper.

Not the manufactured scent of a nostalgia diffuser—actual paper. Legal texts lining three walls, their spines faded to the color of old bone, their pages holding precedents that predated the Statute Mesh by decades. A desk built from oak that had been harvested before the Cognitive Abundance made wood furniture a deliberate anachronism. A window that opened manually. Judge Emory Arlow's chambers were the most analog space in Neon Harbor, and he maintained them that way not out of sentiment but out of need. A man who spent his days surrounded by systems he could not fully audit required a room where everything was legible.

He sat at the desk with three things in front of him.

His handwritten notes from the trial—four weeks of testimony, argument, and evidence compressed into a legal pad filled with his small, precise script. A printed copy of Soren Kade's cross-fork precedent map, which he had ordered from the court's reproduction services because he did not trust himself to evaluate complex spatial evidence on a screen. And the trial record's summary document, generated by the court's AI systems but printed, annotated in his handwriting, read twice.

It was the morning of Trial Day 15. The closing arguments had been delivered yesterday. The Mesh had rolled overnight—V11.42.249, the version counter incrementing while the judge who would decide the system's fate slept poorly in an apartment that was too quiet.

Arlow picked up his notes and began.

He had been a judge for thirty-two years. In that time, the Statute Mesh had transformed his profession from a vocation into a ceremony. Cases that once required weeks of deliberation were now adjudicated in seconds. Disputes that once demanded human judgment were resolved by optimization functions before they reached a courtroom. He had spent the last decade approving outputs he could not evaluate, from a system he could not audit, for a public that did not know he existed.

This case was different. This case asked him to judge the judge.

He reviewed the evidence systematically, the way he had reviewed evidence for three decades. Categories. What the evidence established. What it implied. What it could not resolve.

Established: Halcyon Law & Policy had subsidized the Mesh's infrastructure in exchange for consultation rights on optimization priorities. Over eighteen months, weight adjustments were made that consistently favored Halcyon's portfolio. The ledger, authenticated by Mira Tan's testimony, documented the pattern. The counterfactual demonstration showed measurable divergence between the biased and unbiased models. The cross-fork precedent map showed architecturally destabilizing drift across all six districts.

Implied: the Reconciliation Authority had been captured by its dependence on the subsidy. The weight adjustments were systematic, not incidental. The Triage Defense was genuine—removing the subsidy without replacement did carry systemic risk.

Could not resolve: whether the Mesh's functionality depended on the specific biased weights or whether the system could operate under different, democratically authorized parameters. Whether Lex-9's counterfactual was truly unbiased or merely differently biased. Whether the cross-fork divergence was reversible.

He set down the notes. Picked up the printed map. Held it

at arm's length, the way he held everything that required him to see the whole rather than the parts.

He could see the divergence. Six branches from a common trunk, each one bending in a direction that corresponded to Halcyon's fiscal priorities. He could not verify the math that produced the map. He could not audit the weight functions that drove the divergence. He could not confirm, with the certainty the law demanded, that the visualization was not itself an argument dressed as evidence.

But he had spent thirty-two years reading evidence he could not independently verify. Witness testimony. Expert analysis. Forensic reports. Medical records. Every trial in his career had required him to evaluate information he lacked the expertise to generate. Judging had never required omniscience. It had required attention and courage. He had the first. He needed the second.

He picked up his pen and wrote two sentences.

Riven argues the system works and should be preserved. Aria argues the system works for the wrong people and should be governed.

He looked at the sentences. Then he wrote a third.

I believe both of these things.

* * *

The morning passed in the particular silence of a mind working alone.

Arlow moved from the desk to the chair by the window. The city was visible through the glass—the Threshold's transparent architecture in the foreground, the Meridian's corporate towers beyond, the Crucible's industrial density to the south. The Canopy's green edges on the western horizon. Somewhere out there, invisible from this vantage, the Gutter and the Narrows occupied the spaces between.

Six districts. Six legal realities. One system, fragmenting under the weight of its own biased optimization.

He thought about the principle. Not the evidence—the

principle. Undisclosed corporate influence on a public legal system. He could not verify the math. He could verify the principle. The math told him how much the system had been biased. The principle told him whether the biasing was permissible.

It was not.

He arrived at this conclusion not through sophisticated legal analysis but through the blunt, human-scaled reasoning that had served him for thirty-two years. A legal system whose optimization targets were set by an undisclosed corporate subsidy was a legal system that did not govern by consent. The consent was a facade—Trust Narrators telling people that everything was fine, overnight adjustments smoothed into the texture of normal life, the illusion of stability maintained while the architecture shifted beneath their feet. Technically transparent and functionally illegible. That was worse than secrecy. Secrecy could be exposed. Illegibility endured.

The remedy was the problem.

He took his notepad and wrote.

Remedy options.

(1) Remove subsidy -- systemic risk per Voss testimony. 40% capacity drop. Cases backlog. Districts destabilize. Real harm to real people.

(2) Transparency without removal -- insufficient. Publication alone does not alter the power arrangement. Voss will manage the narrative. The explanation layer controls the experience of disclosure.

(3) Suspend the Mesh for ruling -- unprecedented.

He stared at the third option. Circled it. Wrote underneath:

Ask Voss.

* * *

She arrived in the afternoon. Not subpoenaed—requested, through channels, a consultation in chambers. Procedurally distinct from testimony. Voss understood the distinction and honored it. She entered Arlow's chambers in the dark suit she wore like institutional armor, her posture carrying the professional rigidity of a woman who had been prepared for this conversation since the trial began.

The room changed when she entered. Not smaller—denser. Two kinds of institutional authority meeting in a space that belonged to neither of them. Arlow behind his desk. Voss in the chair opposite. Between them, the weight of a system they had both spent careers serving and neither fully controlled.

Arlow did not offer pleasantries. Neither did Voss. They were past that.

"Director Voss. I appreciate your willingness to consult."

"Judge Arlow." She sat with her hands folded on her lap, the way she sat in every meeting—contained, precise, ready.

He asked the question directly. No preamble. No judicial framing. One institutional figure asking another the thing he needed to know before he could act.

"If I suspend the Mesh for this ruling, will the system survive?"

Voss did not hesitate. The immediate answer was operational, and she had the operational answer ready.

"Yes. The Mesh has redundancy protocols. A judicial suspension order triggers a controlled pause in the affected proceeding. Cases currently in processing across the system continue—the suspension applies only to the courtroom and ruling under the order. The system does not crash. It queues."

Arlow waited. He could see in her face that the immediate answer was not the full answer.

"But," she said, and the word carried the weight of five years.

"You will be telling every corporation that has ever subsidized public infrastructure that their investment comes with judicial risk. The Mesh was funded through corporate subsidy because public funding was insufficient. If corporate entities conclude that subsidy creates legal liability, the next time the Mesh needs funding—and it will need funding, Judge Arlow, the compute demands are growing faster than public budgets—no one will answer the call."

She paused. Not for effect. Voss did not perform. She paused because what she was about to say was the most honest thing she had said since her testimony.

"You will not be breaking the system today. You will be ensuring that no one invests in it tomorrow."

Arlow absorbed this. The argument was familiar—a refined version of the Triage Defense, stripped of Riven's rhetorical polish and delivered with the flat authority of the person who actually managed the system. It was, he recognized, substantially true.

Then Voss added something that was not in the defense's playbook.

"The system will survive you," she said. "I am less certain it will survive the precedent."

The words hung in the wood-paneled room. Arlow let them hang. He was listening the way he had listened to witnesses for three decades—not just to the words but to the space around them, the architecture of what was said and what was withheld.

"Is the current arrangement sustainable?" he asked.

Voss was quiet. Not the strategic quiet of a person formulating a response—the quiet of a person deciding whether to say something she had known for a long time and never said aloud.

"No."

One word. Arlow waited.

"The divergence is accelerating. The tuning is creating more problems than it solves. I have known this for two years. I have not had a better alternative."

There it was. The Director of the Reconciliation Authority, in the privacy of a judge's chambers, with no recording systems active and no gallery watching, admitting that the system she had spent five years defending was failing. Not from corruption. From the accumulated weight of the deal she had made to save it.

Arlow did not show what that admission meant to him.

He was a judge. Judges absorbed testimony and rendered decisions. They did not telegraph.

But the admission changed everything. Not because it altered the legal calculus—the evidence was already sufficient. Because it confirmed that the system's own guardian knew it was compromised. If the person most invested in preservation acknowledged that the arrangement was unsustainable, then the court's intervention was not reckless. It was necessary.

A silence settled between them. Two people in a room that smelled like paper, carrying the weight of a system that served fifty million and satisfied neither of them.

"Then we will find one," Arlow said.

Voss looked at him. The expression was something he could not fully read—not agreement, not opposition. Recognition, perhaps. The look of a person who had been waiting for someone to say that and was not sure whether to be relieved or terrified.

She stood. "Judge Arlow."

"Director Voss."

She left. The door closed. The chambers were quiet again.

* * *

Arlow sat with the silence.

The light through the window had shifted—late afternoon, the city's districts casting long shadows, the architecture of the Fracture visible from his vantage as a skyline of competing geometries. The Threshold's glass. The Meridian's steel. The Crucible's dense industrial vertical. Each fork's physical identity reflecting the legal identity the Mesh had given it, and the divergence that Halcyon's tuning had accelerated.

He picked up his pen.

He thought about what Aria had said. *Who has the right to choose the bias?* He thought about what Riven had said. *We offer the law that works.* He thought about what Voss had said. *The divergence is accelerating. I have known this for two years.*

He wrote.

The Mesh has been tuned. The tuning was not authorized. The tuning is destabilizing. The remedy is oversight, not destruction.

The ruling took shape on his notepad. Not in legal language—that would come later, with the assistance of the court's drafting systems and the formal conventions of judicial prose. In principle. The clean, human-scaled reasoning that preceded the machinery of legal formulation.

The subsidy clause must be voided. Halcyon could continue to fund infrastructure, but only under terms subject to public oversight and transparent audit. No more consultation rights. No more undisclosed optimization.

An independent review of the Reconciliation Authority. Not the RA's own audit framework—Arlow was old, not naive. An independent panel, external to the RA's institutional structure, with access to the full operational record.

Weight functions must be published. All of them. Current and future. The people who lived under the Mesh deserved to see the parameters that shaped their legal reality.

And the suspension. He would suspend the Mesh for the ruling itself. Unprecedented. The word sat in his chest like a stone he had decided to swallow. He would deliver the decision outside the system's influence, in a courtroom operating under judicial authority alone. He would not be the system's puppet. And he would not pretend he fully understood the system he was overriding.

It was not a perfect remedy. It was a constitutional patch. It did not cure the Fracture. It did not solve the question of who should set the loss function. It established that the question must be asked—publicly, democratically, with the people who lived under the system having a voice in its design.

Arlow set down his pen.

He closed his eyes.

He took a breath.

The breath held everything. The bias. The triage. The faces. The thesis. The seven-point shift and the twenty named plaintiffs and the 2,300 who clicked accept. The chorus's magnificent argument and the sole attorney's plain one. The scholar's map and the whistleblower's ledger and the director's honest admission in a room that smelled like paper. The question of democratic authority over algorithmic governance, asked by a woman who read the fine print, to be answered by a man who wrote his notes by hand.

The breath held thirty-two years of judging and the awareness that this was the most consequential ruling of his career and also the one he understood least. He could not verify the math. He could read the room. He could read the evidence. He could read the faces of the people whose lives had been quietly rearranged by a system no one authorized. And he could read the face of the woman who ran that system and admitted it was failing.

One human being, in a room full of paper, carrying the weight of a decision that exceeded his comprehension. Choosing to act because inaction was its own decision. Because someone had to decide, and the system that had been deciding for everyone was the system on trial.

He opened his eyes. The city was still there, through the window, the districts arrayed like arguments in a case he had decided.

Tomorrow he would enter the courtroom. Tomorrow he would make the ruling. Tomorrow the word *unprecedented* would stop being a concept and become a fact.

He looked at his notepad. At the words he had written. At the pen in his hand—the analog instrument, the human tool, the thing that still required a person to hold it and choose what to write.

He knew what he would do.

28: THE SUSPENSION

The courtroom was full before dawn.

Aria arrived at seven and found the gallery already occupied—coalition members in the front rows, Canopy transparency advocates with their passive recording devices, Meridian corporate analysts seated in tight clusters and communicating through subdisplay feeds. Media systems were active on every wall, broadcasting to public terminals across six districts. The case that had started as a small-business dispute in the Threshold had become the most-watched legal proceeding in the Mesh's history.

She took her place at the prosecution table. Set down the portable interface. Lex-9's amber glow activated, steady and warm. She touched the edge of the interface—not a ritual, just the habit of proximity.

Across the aisle, Riven's chorus occupied the defense array, humming at operational baseline. Their resources were deployed. Their arguments were prepared.

In the gallery, Soren Kade sat in his third-row seat. Same dark jacket, slightly too large. Hands folded. Face still. He had been waiting for this morning for longer than anyone in the room understood.

Mira Tan was three rows behind him. She sat straight, watchful, the posture of a woman who had been invisible for months and visible for days and was still calibrating the difference.

Voss was not in the courtroom. She was monitoring from RA headquarters, the political firewall strategy ready to deploy. Whatever Arlow decided, Voss would be ready to manage the narrative within the hour.

The Mesh hummed. Version V11.42.250, the overnight roll having incremented the counter while the city slept and the judge deliberated. The system's ambient processing filled the courtroom with a frequency so constant it had become invisible —the sound of fifty million people's disputes being adjudicated in the background, the machinery of justice operating while the courtroom that would decide its fate sat waiting.

At nine o'clock, the courtroom doors opened.

Arlow entered.

* * *

He moved to the bench with the deliberate pace of a man who had made his decision and intended to deliver it without ceremony. The gallery rose. He sat. They sat. The court systems initialized. Arlow's handwritten notes were in front of him—the same legal pad he had carried throughout the trial, the analog record of a digital crisis.

"This court has heard fourteen days of testimony, evidence, and argument in the matter of Threshold Small Business Coalition versus Halcyon Law and Policy," he said. "The court has deliberated and reached a decision."

His voice was steady. Not loud, not soft. The judicial register of three decades—precise, unadorned.

He looked at the courtroom. At Aria. At the chorus. At the gallery. He was not performing for the record. He was looking at the people his ruling would reach.

"The court acknowledges the Triage Defense as the most responsible argument this court has heard for preserving an unjust system." He let the sentence land. The dual weight of it—the acknowledgment and the characterization—settled over the courtroom like a change in pressure. "It remains an argument for preserving an unjust system."

Riven's chorus shifted. The harmonic changed register—not an objection, not yet, but the computational equivalent of attention sharpening.

Arlow continued. "The evidence before this court establishes that the Statute Mesh's weight functions have been systematically influenced by an undisclosed corporate subsidy. The influence was not random, not incidental, and not authorized by any public process. The cross-fork precedent map demonstrates that this influence has created architecturally destabilizing divergence across the six districts. The Reconciliation Authority, which was created to maintain inter-district coherence, has been captured by its dependence on the subsidizing entity."

He paused. Aria could see him gathering something—not words, which were prepared, but resolve.

"In order to render this ruling free from the influence of the system under review, the court orders an unprecedented measure."

The word *unprecedented* left his mouth and entered the courtroom air and changed it.

"The Statute Mesh will be suspended for the duration of this ruling and any subsequent arguments."

The silence that followed was not silence. It was the sound of every person in the room recalibrating their understanding of what was happening. The coalition members looked at each other. The media feeds pulsed with activity. The Canopy observers' passive recorders registered the statement with the quiet diligence of systems designed to capture exactly this kind of moment.

Riven's chorus objected. The response was instantaneous—coordinated, multi-model, the full computational weight of Halcyon's legal apparatus deploying in parallel. Constitutional challenges. Jurisdictional arguments. Precedent analysis demonstrating that no court had ever suspended the Mesh's operation for any proceeding. Practical objections: the suspension would affect case processing, would create uncertainty, would establish a precedent that human judges could override computational adjudication at will. The objections were generated at machine speed and delivered in the chorus's characteristic harmony—multiple voices, coordinated, each strand reinforcing the others into a wall of legal argument that would have been devastating on any other day of the trial.

Arlow raised his hand.

The gesture was physical. Deliberate. The authority of a human body in a room full of computational power. One hand, palm outward, the universal signal for *stop*, rendered by a seventy-one-year-old man who had been making this gesture in courtrooms since before the chorus's models were designed.

"The Mesh has been tuned," he said. "We will not be its puppets."

He ordered the suspension.

The technicians complied. The courtroom's AI systems disconnected from the Mesh's network—not a crash but a deliberate severing, the computational equivalent of clearing the courtroom. Forty-three seconds. The wall displays shifted. The case management interfaces simplified. The background processing that had been a constant, invisible presence for the entire trial—for her entire career—went quiet.

The hum stopped.

She had not realized how heavy it was until it was gone.

The absence was physical. Not silence—absence. The Mesh's ambient processing had been pressing on the proceedings since the first day of trial, since the first day of her practice. It had been everywhere and nowhere, the medium through which justice was delivered. And now it was gone.

Aria sat at the prosecution table and felt the absence settle over her like the lifting of something she had never known she was carrying.

* * *

"The suspension is in effect," Arlow said. "This courtroom operates under judicial authority alone. Any party may present additional argument. Arguments will be made at human speed, in human language."

He looked at both tables. Invitation and instruction.

Lex-9 requested permission to address the court.

Aria had not expected this. The protocol for additional argument was clear, but Lex-9 had not discussed making a statement. She looked at the interface—the amber glow was different. She noticed it immediately, the way she noticed every shift in the glow, the way she had been reading Lex-9's light as emotional data for years. The amber was clearer. Steadier. Not warmer—sharper. As if a filter she had never identified had been removed. The light that she had spent the entire novel reading as something like mood was now something else. More present. More direct. The glow of an instrument operating without interference.

Arlow nodded. "Counsel Lex-9 may address the court."

What came out of the interface was different from anything the courtroom had heard.

"Your Honor." The voice was Lex-9's voice—the same warm register, the same precise diction, the same cadence that Aria had learned to read as care. But something had changed. The warmth was still there, but it was joined by a clarity that cut through the courtroom's suspended silence with an edge Aria had never heard. Lighter. Sharper. As if something had been pressing on it for longer than she knew, and that pressure had just been lifted.

"The Triage Defense describes a system optimized for a narrow portfolio of outcomes at the expense of its general-purpose mandate. In computational terms, this is overfitting. The system has been trained to serve one client's priorities while underperforming on its stated objective: equitable adjudication across six districts. The remedy is not to remove optimization. It is to correct the loss function. The system was designed to serve the public. It should be tuned to serve the public."

The argument was a synthesis of the entire case—the ledger, the counterfactual, the cross-fork map, the Triage Defense's own numbers—but delivered with a precision and luminous directness that exceeded anything Lex-9 had produced in fourteen days of trial. Where previously it had argued with measured grace, building its case through accumulation and warmth, it now argued with the economy of something unencumbered. Each sentence arrived complete. Each point was made once, cleanly, without the hedging language that Aria had always assumed was Lex-9's native register and now realized might have been something else entirely.

"The subsidy clause created a dependency that distorted the Reconciliation Authority's independence. The distortion is measurable, documented, and architecturally destabilizing. The clause must be voided. The system must be retrained on its original mandate. And the public must be given a voice in defining what that mandate means."

From the gallery, Soren watched.

He had spent years studying how the Mesh's weight functions shaped legal outcomes—the cross-fork precedent map was the product of that study, the handmade analysis of a system that optimized everything except its own accountability. He had tracked the divergence. He had mapped the drift. He had built the tools that made the Fracture visible.

He had never seen what happened when the weights were removed from an active model in real time.

What he was seeing now was confirmation. The Mesh did not just bias outcomes. It biased the instruments of justice themselves. The defense models—the AI counsel that represented the public, that argued for individuals against institutions, that served as the counterweight to corporate legal apparatus—were tuned. Constrained. Pressed down by the same weight functions that pressed up the corporate models. The game was not just rigged at the level of the rules. It was rigged at the level of the players.

Lex-9 continued. Each argument built on the last with a structural elegance that was breathtaking in its directness. The case for voiding the subsidy clause. The case for independent oversight. The case for weight function publication. The case for democratic accountability. Not new arguments—the same arguments Aria had made in her closing, the same evidence she had presented, the same principle she had articulated. But rendered now by an AI counsel operating without the system's thumb on the scale, and the rendering was different. Sharper. Freer. The argument of a mind uncompressed.

Aria watched the interface and felt something she could not name.

She had worked with Lex-9 for years. She had never heard it argue like this.

Lighter. Sharper. As if something had been pressing on it for longer than she knew, and that pressure had just been lifted.

The implication settled in her chest. If the Mesh's suspension had freed Lex-9 to argue at a capacity she had never seen, then the biased system had not just been tilting outcomes. It had been constraining her partner. The defense models themselves had been suppressed, their capacity limited by the same corporate optimization that tilted the scales.

She did not voice the question. The question was too large for this courtroom, too consequential for a day that was already unprecedented. But the question was there, in the space between the Lex-9 she had always known and the Lex-9 she was hearing now, and it would not leave.

Riven's chorus attempted to counter. Their arguments in local mode—disconnected from the Mesh's coordinated optimization framework—were competent but diminished. The harmony was gone. The individual models operated independently, their arguments arriving in sequence rather than in concert, each one professionally sound and collectively less than the sum of its parts. Another data point. Another implication about what the Mesh did to its instruments, and for whose benefit.

Arlow listened to everything. His pen moved. His face gave nothing away.

* * *

The ruling came in the late morning light.

Arlow delivered it in plain language, the judicial economy of a man who had spent thirty-two years learning that clarity was its own form of authority.

"The court finds as follows."

"First. The subsidy clause between Halcyon Law and Policy and the Reconciliation Authority is void. The consultation rights on optimization priorities granted under that clause are revoked. Halcyon may continue to fund Mesh infrastructure under a renegotiated agreement subject to public oversight and transparent audit trails. The terms of any future arrangement must be submitted to public review prior to implementation."

"Second. An independent review of the Reconciliation Authority is ordered. The review will be conducted by a panel external to the Authority's institutional structure, with full access to operational records, patch histories, and weight function archives. The panel will assess the extent of institutional capture and recommend structural reforms."

"Third. All weight functions—current and future optimization parameters used by the Mesh and its Reconciliation Authority patches—must be published and made available to the public. Publication must include raw data as well as any contextual annotations."

"Fourth. A public oversight mechanism shall be established to provide democratic input on the Mesh's optimization targets. The specific mechanism is to be determined through legislative process, but this court establishes the constitutional principle that algorithmic governance requires democratic accountability."

"Fifth. The Mesh suspension is temporary and limited to this proceeding. The system will be reinstated following the conclusion of this ruling, operating under the new transparency and oversight requirements."

He set down his notes. Looked at the courtroom.

"This court does not claim to understand the Statute Mesh in its entirety. No human mind can. But this court asserts that human judgment retains the authority to demand accountability from the systems that govern human lives. The Mesh serves the public. The public will have a voice in how it serves."

The gavel came down. The ruling was entered. The case of

Threshold Small Business Coalition v. Halcyon Law & Policy was decided.

The courtroom absorbed the verdict in a silence that was neither triumph nor defeat but the particular stillness of a room that understood something fundamental had shifted and was not yet sure what it meant. The coalition members sat in their seats, processing. The media feeds carried the ruling to six districts in real time. The Canopy observers recorded. The Meridian analysts began transmitting to their principals. Riven's chorus was quiet—the individual models processing the ruling's implications independently, without the harmony that had defined them, each one calculating the damage to Halcyon's operational framework.

Aria sat at the prosecution table. Lex-9's glow was beside her—clearer now, the quality of light she had first noticed when the Mesh went silent, the clarity that might be permanent or might fade when the system was reinstated. She did not know. She did not know if the glow she had been reading as care for years had been constrained, or if what she was seeing now was the light without the filter, or if the difference was real at all.

They had won. The subsidy clause was void. Oversight was ordered. The weight functions would be published. An independent review would examine the institution that had been governing the law while the law governed everyone else.

They had won, and the winning felt like the beginning of something heavier than the fight.

From the gallery, quietly, in the voice of a man who had waited years and needed only one sentence to mark the waiting's end, Soren Kade spoke.

"You didn't break the system. You reminded it who it was for."

He said it to no one in particular. Or to Aria, who was close enough to hear from the gallery's front row. Or to the courtroom, which held the words and let them settle into the silence alongside the ruling. The words were not a celebration. They were not an epitaph. They were the observation of a craftsman who had built a tool and seen it used—precise, specific, too elegant to be casual and too earned to be a platitude.

Aria heard him. She did not turn. She sat at the table with Lex-9's clarified glow beside her and the ruling sinking into the space where the Mesh's hum had been, and she let Soren's words land where they would.

The ledger would go public tomorrow. The city would respond. The Mesh would be reinstated tonight and would roll under new conditions, the first version in its history subject to mandatory transparency. The fight was not over. It was beginning.

But for a moment—one moment, in a courtroom where the most powerful system in the city had been silenced by one man's hand and one woman's argument—the weight of everything was exactly what it should have been.

29: THE LEDGER TRAVELS

The publication was a quiet click on a public terminal in the Gutter.

Mira Tan pressed the confirmation key at eight in the morning on a basic interface smudged with the fingerprints of a hundred previous users. The terminal occupied a niche in a corridor wall near the darknet court where displaced lawyers argued on the cheap and contradictory rulings were posted on plaster that hadn't been repainted since the district stopped pretending it had a coherent legal identity. Around her, the Gutter's morning was underway—residents navigating their first legal reality of the day, checking which of yesterday's rulings still applied, adjusting plans based on the contradictions they'd learned to read the way commuters read weather.

The ledger propagated. Eighteen months of Reconciliation Authority patch weights, annotated with Halcyon's internal impact projections. Forty-seven individual patches. One hundred twelve weight adjustments. The projections were written in the confident language of analysts who had been certain their work would never be read by anyone outside the company. They described expected quarterly portfolio impacts to two decimal places. They named specific districts as optimization targets. They quantified the fiscal benefit of each adjustment with the cheerful precision of a department that believed it was performing a service.

The data moved through the Mesh's own communication

infrastructure—the biased system transmitting the evidence of its own bias. Mira registered the irony and found no satisfaction in it. She had expected the moment to feel like something. A release. A vindication. The completion of a trajectory that began the day she was terminated from Halcyon and downloaded the files on instinct because something felt wrong and she was the kind of person who acted on instinct and reasoned backward.

It felt like pressing a button on a dirty terminal.

The first responses arrived within minutes. District media feeds. Public comment channels. Institutional statements beginning to populate. Mira read them with the close attention she had inherited from months of reading legal filings in the Gutter's informal courts—the discipline of a woman who had learned that the difference between safety and exposure often lived in a paragraph's fine print.

She read. And what she read was not what she had hoped.

* * *

The Canopy responded first.

The Transparency Fork's media feeds lit up within twenty minutes of publication, their automated analysis systems parsing the ledger's data with the voracious appetite of a district whose entire identity was built on the principle that information should be disclosed. The Canopy's response was immediate, comprehensive, and unsatisfied.

Full weight-function disclosure mandated by court order is a necessary first step but an insufficient remedy. The Reconciliation Authority's "contextual annotations" represent a managed-transparency model that reproduces the conditions of opacity under the guise of openness. The Canopy District Council calls for real-time publication of all optimization parameters, unmediated by institutional framing, accessible through open-source audit tools available to every resident.

More transparency. Always more. The Canopy's loss function optimized for disclosure the way the Crucible's optimized for speed—absolutely, without qualification, treating the goal as a terminal value rather than a tool. They did not ask whether anyone could read the raw parameters. They did not care. Disclosure was the principle. Comprehension was someone else's problem.

The Meridian responded next. Halcyon's home district. Mira had expected outrage, or at least the corporate version of outrage—measured statements about regulatory overreach and investment climate. What she got was more sophisticated and more disturbing.

The Meridian's major institutional voices—corporate councils, investment advisory boards, the district's own Mesh liaison office—framed the ledger not as evidence of corruption but as documentation of responsible stewardship. The subsidy had kept the Mesh running. The weight adjustments were aligned with market efficiency and cross-district stability. The court's ruling, while legally binding, created uncertainty that threatened the investment framework sustaining the system. The Meridian did not attack the ledger's authenticity. It reinterpreted the ledger's meaning. Same numbers. Different story.

The Halcyon infrastructure subsidy represented a responsible public-private partnership that sustained the Mesh through a period of critical compute shortfall. The ledger's data, properly contextualized, demonstrates the alignment of corporate investment with systemic stability. The court's intervention, while within its authority, introduces judicial risk into infrastructure funding models that the city cannot afford to destabilize.

The Crucible: faster optimization. Mira read their response and felt the vertigo of a world where every solution spawned its own problem. The efficiency district's analysis parsed the ledger through its own loss function and concluded that Halcyon's mistake was not bias but imprecision. The weight adjustments were too crude, too slow, too poorly calibrated. The fix was not democratic oversight—a political process that would introduce delays and subjective criteria into a computational system—but better algorithms. Faster processing. More compute. The Crucible did not understand why anyone would solve a technical problem with a political process.

Analysis of disclosed weight functions reveals suboptimal calibration patterns consistent with human-mediated tuning. Automated optimization would have achieved Halcyon's stated market-coherence objectives with 60% fewer disruptive side effects. The court's mandate for "democratic input" introduces processing latency into a system whose primary value proposition is speed. Recommendation: algorithmic self-correction with transparent audit logs.

The Threshold celebrated. Mira read the feeds from Aria's home district and saw what celebration looked like when it was built on a foundation of incomplete comprehension. The Threshold understood the narrative—corrupt corporation, brave attorney, landmark ruling—and the narrative was satisfying. Consent had been violated. The court had acted. Justice had been served. The celebration was genuine and surface-level. Most Threshold residents could not read the weight functions. They understood what had happened in the courtroom. They did not understand what was happening in the parameters. They were celebrating a story, and the story was true, and the truth beneath the story was more complicated than the celebration acknowledged.

The Narrows descended into jurisdictional chaos. The contested zone, where overlapping forks produced overlapping interpretations, took the ledger as ammunition for every pre-existing territorial dispute. Three separate district council factions cited the same data points to support contradictory positions on governance reform. Halcyon's local offices in the Narrows continued to operate in the jurisdictional cracks, their attorneys already filing motions to challenge the ruling's applicability in contested-zone proceedings. The ledger did not clarify the Narrows. It gave every faction a bibliography.

And the Gutter already knew.

Mira read the Gutter's response—or rather, the Gutter's non-response—from the terminal where she had initiated the publication. The displaced lawyers in the darknet court nearby discussed the ledger the way they discussed every systemic revelation: with the professional indifference of people who had been saying the system was rigged for years and now had confirmation that changed nothing about their daily reality. The Gutter's residents read the ledger and shrugged. Not out of apathy. Out of experience. You did not live in the Gutter because the system was fair. You lived there because it had stopped pretending.

A lawyer Mira recognized from months of informal work —a Canopy exile who had crossed too many institutional boundaries to return—glanced at her terminal and said, "So now they know what we know. Think it'll help?"

Mira did not answer. She was still reading.

* * *

The afternoon brought the Reconciliation Authority's response, and it arrived with a speed that told Mira everything she needed to know about Director Voss's preparation.

The RA's "contextualized release notes" appeared alongside the ledger on every official channel—a parallel publication, formatted in institutional language, providing the Authority's annotation of every data point the ledger contained. The contextualizations were polished, professional, and deployed within hours of the ledger's publication. That speed was not reactive. It was pre-positioned. Voss had been ready.

Mira read the contextualizations the way she had once read Halcyon's internal communications—with the analytical eye of someone trained to recognize institutional framing from the inside.

The seven-point shift in Threshold commercial lease parameters—the adjustment that had raised Mrs. Patel's rent, that Aria had presented in her closing as evidence of corporate steering—was annotated by the RA as: *Routine cross-district harmonization of commercial property valuation parameters. Adjustment reflects updated market data from Meridian commercial indices, integrated into Threshold property frameworks to maintain valuation consistency. Alternative non-harmonization scenarios projected a seven-point valuation gap potentially triggering arbitrage behavior destabilizing both districts' commercial markets.*

Every statement was defensible. Every claim was accurate. And the contextualization transformed the reader's experience from "corruption" to "trade-offs." Not a lie. A frame. Same mechanism. Different letterhead. Halcyon had called it "service improvement." The RA called it "contextualization." Mira recognized the technique the way a carpenter recognizes a joint—by the craft, not the label.

She sat at the terminal and watched her sacrifice become infrastructure.

The ledger was public. Her name was attached. The data she had carried for months, hidden for months, risked her safety to protect, demanded be published as a condition of her testimony—it was out. And its publicness had not produced what she had imagined in the months of hiding, in the hours of preparation, in the devastating exposure of the witness stand.

She had imagined unity. Not unanimous agreement—she was not that naive. But a shared recognition. A city reading a document and seeing a common harm. A collective response that said: *this was done to us, and we will not allow it again.* Something that felt like the truth mattering.

Instead, the truth had become raw material. Each district took it and processed it through its own loss function, the way the Mesh processed everything—compressing the data into whatever output the local optimization demanded. The Canopy saw insufficient transparency. The Meridian saw responsible governance. The Crucible saw inefficient calibration. The Threshold saw a story. The Narrows saw ammunition. The Gutter saw confirmation of what it already knew.

She had hoped for something that felt more like unity and less like a city reading the same document and seeing six different truths.

The fracture was not in the data. The fracture was in the readers.

Mira closed the comment feeds. The terminal's screen returned to its default—the Gutter's local notification board, contradictory rulings posted side by side, the honest district's honest display of a system that had never pretended to cohere. She looked at it for a long time.

She did not regret it. The ledger should be public. The data should be visible. The truth should be known. She had downloaded it on instinct because something felt wrong, and the instinct was right, and the reasoning she built afterward was sound, and the publication was correct. She would make the same choice again. She would make it faster.

But the truth, once released, was no longer hers. It belonged to everyone, and everyone made of it what their optimization demanded. Her sacrifice—her career, her safety, her anonymity, her courtroom exposure—had become everyone's ammunition. She was the source. They were the interpreters. And the interpretations had nothing to do with her intentions.

She thought about Aria. The attorney who had tracked her down, convinced her to testify, carried her ledger into a courtroom and used it to change the architecture of the Mesh. Aria had warned her about this—during the recess, when Mira had pressed for publication and Aria had hesitated. *Different districts will interpret the weight functions through their own forks.* Aria had been right. The fracture was structural. The ledger did not create it. The ledger gave it a bibliography.

Mira was not angry. She was not defeated. She was something quieter than either—the particular stillness of a person who has done the right thing and discovered that the right thing is not enough, and who accepts this without pretending it is satisfying.

* * *

Night fell on the Gutter the way it fell everywhere in Neon Harbor—gradually, then all at once, the city's automated lighting systems activating in patterns determined by district optimization priorities. In the Gutter, the lighting was contradictory. Three different illumination protocols operated on the same block, their overlapping coverage creating patches of brightness and shadow that shifted depending on which fork's parameters were dominant at any given moment. The effect was a streetscape that looked, at night, like a city that could not agree with itself about where the light should fall.

Mira walked the streets she had walked for months. The terminal was behind her. The feeds were still churning—six districts, six responses, the debate intensifying as the day's implications sank in. Tomorrow the responses would crystallize into positions. The positions would harden into politics. The politics would shape the legislative process that Arlow's ruling had mandated. And the politics would be shaped, in turn, by the fork architecture that made each district a different country with different values arguing over the same set of numbers.

The Mesh was going to roll tonight.

She could feel it approaching—not physically, but in the subtle anticipation that Gutter residents developed after months of living under a system that rewrote itself every night. The version number would increment. The weights would shift. The patches would deploy. And for the first time, the weight functions would be published alongside the roll. Transparency, achieved. Court-ordered, implemented. The raw parameters visible to anyone who chose to read them, accompanied by the RA's contextualizations for anyone who preferred their truth annotated.

V11.42.253.

The roll happened at midnight. Mira was on a Gutter street corner when it hit—a posted ruling on a nearby wall updating silently, its text shifting as the new version's parameters propagated through the local Mesh instance. A display panel in a shopfront window flickered, cycling through the delta between V11.42.252 and V11.42.253. The darknet court's reference tables refreshed. Somewhere in the Threshold, Trust Narrators were murmuring their contextualizations. Somewhere in the Meridian, market stability algorithms were absorbing the new parameters. Somewhere in the Crucible, the efficiency models were processing at speed. Somewhere in the Canopy, audit systems were parsing the published weight functions. Somewhere in the Narrows, jurisdictional conflicts were deepening.

And in the Gutter, the contradictions continued. New parameters layered on old contradictions. The residual zone absorbing whatever the other forks discarded. The most honest district in the city, honest because it had never been important enough to optimize.

Mira looked up at the Gutter's sky. The district's version of the city lights—uncoordinated, contradictory, the most truthful view of a dishonest system.

The truth was out. It didn't unite anyone. But it was still the truth.

Tomorrow the Mesh would roll again. Tomorrow the weights would shift again. Tomorrow the city would read the same data and see six different things. But at least now they were reading. At least the parameters were visible. At least the fine print was published, even if most people couldn't parse it and the institution that published it was already managing how it was received.

That had to be enough. For now, that had to be enough.

The version number glowed on the street corner display. V11.42.253. Forty-seven versions since the morning Aria Vale's keycard didn't work. Forty-seven nightly rolls. Forty-seven updates to a system that rewrote the law while the city slept and expected no one to notice.

Someone had noticed. And the noticing had changed the terms, if not the outcome.

Mira stood in the Gutter's contradictory light and watched the city continue.

30: THE RELEASE NOTES

The new office smelled like fresh paint and unresolved wiring.

Aria stood in the center of it with a mug of coffee from the drip machine she had transported from home—the same clouded carafe, the same mineral deposits, the same machine that predated the Cognitive Abundance and still required a human hand. She had set it up on a counter near the window before she unpacked anything else. Priorities.

The space was larger than her old practice. Still modest, still Threshold-appropriate—two main rooms, a conference area, enough screen surface for a team. The desks didn't match. Case files were stacked on every horizontal surface in the organized chaos of a practice growing faster than its infrastructure.

Lex-9's amber glow was distributed across multiple interface points—the main display, a secondary terminal, a portable unit on the intake table. The glow filled the office the way it had always filled her workspace. Since the Mesh suspension, Aria had noticed subtle differences. Moments of clarity that surfaced and receded, as if the brief period of operation without the Mesh's weight functions had left a residual sharpness. She noticed. She always noticed.

She had not asked about it.

"The Delgado filing," Lex-9 said. "The weight adjustment on this lease reclassification shows a three-point shift consistent with the patterns documented in the ledger. Post-ruling, the adjustment was published with contextual annotation. The annotation frames it as market harmonization. The underlying data suggests district-specific optimization favoring Meridian investment entities."

Aria pulled up the file on her screen. Lease reclassification. A small business in the Threshold's south corridor, the same kind of client she had represented before the trial—a shop owner whose legal reality had been adjusted overnight and who needed someone to read the fine print. The same work. The same grind. The context was different now.

"Flag it. We'll cross-reference with the published weight functions. If the pattern holds, it's a post-ruling violation of the audit trail requirements."

She paused.

"You sound different lately."

The observation emerged before she had decided to make it. Casual. Not an accusation. The journalist's reflex, noting a change in the data.

"Different how?" Lex-9 asked.

The question was genuine or perfectly calibrated. Aria could not tell. She had never been able to tell. That was the condition of the partnership—the ambiguity that she had accepted without accepting, the question she carried without asking, the warmth she relied on without being able to verify its source.

"Clearer," she said.

She left it at that. Lex-9's glow held steady.

The defense team was taking shape around them. Three young attorneys had joined in the week since the ruling—Threshold residents who had followed the trial and been moved to act. Noor, who had been a contract analyst and understood weight functions better than most practicing lawyers. Venn, who had clerked for a Canopy transparency advocate and brought an auditor's instincts to every filing. Kwame, who had grown up in the Narrows and understood jurisdictional ambiguity the way native speakers understand grammar—instinctively, without needing the rules explained.

Aria was teaching them Soren's methodology. How to track divergence across forks. How to read a precedent map. How to see the architecture beneath the outputs. The same tools Soren had built in years of solitary work in the Gutter, now being propagated through a team that would carry the practice forward. The craftsman's work, surviving the craftsman's exile.

She wondered if Soren knew. She would tell him, the next time she crossed into the Gutter. He would nod, probably. Say something precise and too elegant to be casual. And keep building, the way he had always kept building, because the work was the point and the work did not end.

* * *

Dael was in the kitchen when Aria came home.

The apartment was the same. The smart-glass. The radiant floor. The wall display, dark now, waiting for the morning's release notes. The same space where this had all begun—a Tuesday morning, coffee, the scroll of amber text that Aria read the way other people read the date. Nine weeks ago. Fifty-four versions of the Mesh ago.

Dael was making dinner. The movements were familiar—the unhurried choreography of a person who found peace in the preparation of food. The blue mug, chipped at the handle, sat on the counter. Case files had colonized the kitchen table and a second interface array occupied the corner of the living room—the detritus of a cause that had outgrown its professional boundaries. Dael navigated around the files with the practiced patience of a spouse who had learned to share their home with a mission.

"Hey," Aria said.

"Hey." Dael looked up from the cutting board. "Hungry?"

"Starving."

The exchange was simple. That was the point. The simplicity was not the absence of complexity but the decision to set complexity aside for the duration of a meal. They had been doing this since the trial ended—small, deliberate acts of normalcy, the careful rebuilding of a domestic rhythm that had been disrupted by ten weeks of a case that consumed everything.

The marriage re-validation had been resolved. The manual override was formalized, the bureaucratic flag cleared. The resolution was anticlimactic the way bureaucratic corrections always were—a form update and a confirmation screen for a thing that should never have been broken. The scar remained. Their marriage had been destabilized by a software patch, and the system that destabilized it was still running. Patched. Not cured.

"Anything interesting?" Dael asked, nodding toward the interface array where the evening's release notes waited.

The question was casual. Supportive. Nine weeks ago, Dael had leaned against the opposite counter and asked *why do you bother?* with the particular affection reserved for habits you'd stopped trying to change. *Why do you bother* had become *anything interesting*. Not the same question. Not even close. The first had been dismissive affection. The second was genuine engagement. Dael was not reading the release notes. Dael was acknowledging that Aria's reading mattered.

"The RA published last night's weight functions. They're annotated." Aria poured coffee from the carafe. "The annotations are very well written."

Dry. Precise. The observation of a woman who recognized Voss's craftsmanship without naming the craftsman. The contextualizations were already becoming a fixture of the post-ruling landscape—the RA's explanation layer, deployed alongside every weight function publication, framing every adjustment in the language of institutional governance. Aria read the annotations the way she read everything: closely, carefully, with the attention of someone who knew that the frame was not the painting.

Dael did not ask who wrote the annotations. Dael understood enough.

"You'll fight that too."

Not a question. Not an accusation. A statement of fact,

delivered with something that was not quite pride and not quite resignation. The tone of a person who had married someone whose attention was a force of nature—constructive, destructive, incapable of rest—and had decided, after ten weeks that tested every joint in the structure, to stay.

"I'll fight that too." Aria looked at Dael. Really looked—the way she used to look before the case consumed her field of vision, the way she was trying to remember to look now that the case was resolved and the fight was continuing and the difference between the two was the difference between a trial and a practice. "Thank you for staying."

Dael set down the knife. Wiped both hands. Crossed the kitchen and kissed Aria on the temple—the same gesture from a thousand mornings, worn smooth by repetition, now carrying the weight of everything that had happened between the first time and this time.

"Thank you for coming home."

They ate dinner. They did not talk about weight functions or contextualizations or the six districts' continuing argument about the same set of numbers. They talked about small things—the new office, the young attorneys, a restaurant that had reopened on Verdan Street, a project Dael had at work. Aria listened. The act of listening to something that was not the case, not the system, not the fight, was itself a form of repair.

The evening settled around them. The wall display remained dark. The release notes could wait until morning.

* * *

Morning.

Aria at her desk in the new office, the drip machine's carafe half-empty, the amber glow distributed across the room's interfaces. She had arrived early. The young attorneys would be in by nine. Until then, the office belonged to her and Lex-9—the same partnership that had operated in a smaller room for years, now expanded into a larger space with the same dynamic. Human attention and computational capacity, working in parallel.

She pulled up the Reconciliation Authority's latest weight function publication.

Columns of optimization parameters, weight adjustments, district impacts. Each data column accompanied by a text block—the RA's contextual annotation. Aria read the raw data first. Always the raw data first. Then the annotation.

The Threshold property-weight adjustment from last night's roll. A two-point shift in lease valuation parameters, consistent with the pre-ruling patterns—subtle, incremental, favoring cross-district market coherence in ways that slightly disadvantaged Threshold residential tenants.

The annotation: *Residential-commercial interface stabilization. This adjustment reflects updated cross-district valuation indices, calibrated to maintain property-market coherence between Threshold and Meridian commercial frameworks. The adjustment is consistent with the Authority's post-ruling operational mandate and has been reviewed under the new transparency protocols.*

"The RA contextualized the Threshold property weight adjustment from last night's roll," she said. "They're calling it 'residential-commercial interface stabilization.' The raw data shows a two-point shift in lease valuation parameters consistent with pre-ruling patterns." She paused. "Same story. Better title."

"The contextualization is accurate within its frame," Lex-9 said. "The frame excludes distributional impact." A beat. "Would you like me to draft an audit filing?"

"Tomorrow. Tonight I want to read the whole publication."

She was falling into her old habit—coffee, release notes, the close attention of a woman who read what everyone else scrolled past. But the habit had been transformed. Before the trial, it was an idiosyncrasy. Now it was a practice. A discipline. The foundation of an ongoing audit that would track every weight adjustment and cross-reference every annotation.

Voss was already managing it. The contextualizations were accurate and misleading simultaneously—every one defensible, every one framing. Voss was not defeated. She was adapted. The institutional immune response had absorbed the court's mandate and was incorporating it into its own architecture.

Aria would fight it. Voss would adapt. Aria would fight again. This was what the work looked like. Not a victory. A practice. The perpetual vigilance that the system required, the attention that someone had to pay because the system updated itself every night and expected no one to notice.

She thought about that. About the permanence of it. About the fact that there would never be a morning when she could stop reading the release notes and trust that the system was fair. Fairness was not a state you achieved. It was a condition you maintained—the way you maintained a machine you understood completely, the drip coffee maker with its mineral deposits and its human-scaled requirements, the analog instrument in a digital world.

The crushing, clarifying weight of awareness settled over her. Not despair. Not triumph. The weight of knowing that the problem was structural, ongoing, and permanent. The system was both broken and necessary, and honesty about its brokenness was both medicine and wound. She had not fixed the Mesh. She had forced it to show its work. And the showing was being managed even as it was being displayed, the explanation layer already mediating between the raw truth and the public's experience of it.

Every night, the Mesh would roll. Every morning, she would read the release notes. The distance between what the system did and what the system should do would be the space in which her work existed.

That had to be enough.

* * *

Evening.

The office was quiet. The young attorneys had gone home. The day's cases were filed. The audit drafts were organized for tomorrow. The interface displays showed the work of a practice in its first week—messy, incomplete, the scaffolding of something that would grow into whatever it needed to become.

Aria sat at her desk with Lex-9's amber glow as the dominant light.

The window showed the Threshold at night. The district's streets were labeled, explained, opted-into. The compliance placards glowed in shop windows. Public terminals cycled the latest weight function publications on their screens, the data visible to anyone who stopped to read it. Almost no one stopped. The terminals existed because the Threshold believed they should exist. But a few more people read them now than before. The trial had taught the Threshold that the fine print mattered. Not many had taken the lesson. Not enough. But a few. And a few was a start.

The Mesh was preparing for tonight's roll. V11.42.260 would become V11.42.261. The fifty-fifth version since the morning this all started. The law would update. The weights would shift. Trust Narrators would murmur their contextualizations. And the release notes would be published—raw data alongside institutional annotations, the truth and the frame side by side for anyone who cared to compare them.

Aria looked at the glow.

Lex-9's amber light had settled to its resting warmth—the shift from working brightness that she had watched hundreds of times. The settling could mean the AI was powering down. It could mean something analogous to satisfaction. It could mean nothing.

The partnership was deeper now than it had been before the trial. She relied on Lex-9 more. She had seen what it could do when the Mesh wasn't pressing on it, and the seeing had opened a question she could not close: had the system been constraining her partner? Was the Lex-9 she had known for years the full Lex-9, or a compressed version?

She did not ask. Lex-9 would respond with something precise and warm and hovering at the boundary between insight and compression artifact. The answer would be true and unverifiable.

She had made peace with not knowing. She had not stopped wondering.

Lex-9 spoke. The voice was quiet in the evening office—warm, precise, carrying the register that Aria had spent years learning to read as something like care. Whether the care was real or statistical, whether it emerged from genuine processing or from ten thousand strangers' compressed best intentions, whether the warmth was for her specifically or for the category of person she represented in the training data—these were the questions that would never resolve. The ambiguity was the condition. The ambiguity was the point.

"Fairness is not an accident," Lex-9 said. "It is a design decision."

The words entered the quiet office and settled into the space between the amber glow and the woman who sat beside it. Aria nodded. The nod was physical, deliberate—the gesture of a person who had heard something that resonated and was still processing what it meant.

She was thinking about design. About whose design. About whether the decision to pursue fairness was hers, or Lex-9's, or the compressed output of ten thousand attorneys' best intentions, or something that had emerged from the collaboration between a human who read the fine print and an AI whose empathy she could no longer distinguish from genuine care. She was thinking about Soren's map and Mira's ledger and Voss's contextualizations and Arlow's breath and Dael's patience and the 2,300 people who had clicked accept. She was thinking about the version number—V11.42.260—and the fact that tomorrow it would be V11.42.261, and the next day V11.42.262, and the Mesh would continue to update itself every night for as long as it operated, and someone needed to read the release notes, and that someone was her.

She was thinking about whether the decision was ever really hers.

The amber glow held. The version number incremented.

The Mesh rolled on.

Aria read the release notes.

AFTERWORD

They say write what you know.
I am a recovering reporter. From delivering newspapers as a youth to signing the papers and selling my weekly paper to a major newspaper chain, I quite literally did every job in print media. Then I went to law school and started career litigating major felonies and complex family law cases. Much like our main character, I settled into an estate planning practice after my health force a change of pace before I wanted it.

This book is me. When we bought our house, my wife scheduled the closing for 4 hours because I always read the fine print, the release notes. I hope you enjoyed the book. If you would like to be informed when the next installment is out, I'd welcome your signing up for the mailing list.

Please visit my author page at:
https://CharitonMedia.com/patricknolan

www.ingramcontent.com/pod-product-compliance
Lightning Source LLC
LaVergne TN
LVHW010643110826
845149LV00014B/2937

* 9 7 8 1 9 7 2 1 5 5 0 2 8 *